| *Death in Danzig* |

Stefan Chwin

| *Death in Danzig* |

Translated from the Polish
by Philip Boehm

Harcourt, Inc.

Orlando   Austin   New York   San Diego   Toronto   London

This is a translation of *Hanemann*.

The translator gratefully acknowledges the generous support of the
Ledig House International Writers' Colony.

www.HarcourtBooks.com

Library of Congress Cataloging-in-Publication Data
Chwin, Stefan, 1949–
[Hanemann. English]
Death in Danzig/Stefan Chwin;
translated from the Polish by Philip Boehm.—1st U.S. ed.
p. cm.
ISBN 0-15-100805-1
1. Gdańsk (Poland)—Fiction.   I. Boehm, Philip.   II. Title.
PG7162.H84H3613 2004
891.8'538—dc22   2004002099

Text set in Dante MT
Designed by Linda Lockowitz

Printed in the United States of America

First U.S. edition
K J I H G F E D C B A

| *Death in Danzig* |

| *August Fourteenth* |

IT WAS A LONG TIME before I found out about August fourteenth, and not even Mama was convinced everything happened the way they told the story at the Steins'. Mr. Kohl, who'd worked in Anatomy ever since the Institute was founded, was reluctant to talk about it; he had too much respect for the men who wore white uniforms draped over fine English woolens, who used monogrammed silk handkerchiefs to wipe their gold-rimmed spectacles—too much respect to . . .

Zeiss lenses, wiped calmly and deliberately as the men stood in the vestibule, next to the porter's window. . . . On summer days the grass would be dusted with yellow pollen from the flowering linden trees on Delbrück-Allee, next to the Anatomy Building, where the cool, shaded air from the Evangelical cemetery mixed with the dry piny breezes that drifted off the morainal hills. Every morning at eight o'clock, a black Daimler-Benz would pull up to the entrance of the Institute, just before a crowd of somberly dressed young women spilled out of the streetcar coming from Langfuhr. They would march along the wall of the cemetery and a few minutes later pass by the porter's cubby on their way to Block E, where they would don white bonnets and pale blue aprons with the ties crossed in back . . .

So even Mr. Kohl had his doubts concerning what he'd heard from Alfred Rotke, the swarthy orderly who glided up and down the underground corridors of Anatomy like an Elysian shadow clad in a rubber apron, forever searching for something among the copper vats used for soaking the white sheets needed to cover the long, rectangular marble slab table, the table that was cold to the touch and always felt a little damp, the table on wheels that was rolled under the large round lamp with its five milk white bulbs, in room 9 on the ground floor of the building at Delbrück-Allee 12.

And although Mrs. Stein was ready to swear that everything had happened exactly as people said, Mr. Kohl merely tilted his head back, his eyes flickering with tiny sparks of irony, and squinted at her condescendingly. He didn't mean to offend her, of course, but what could he do about the fact that he, as one of the initiated, knew more about the matter than she did? In any case, she had made up her mind and wasn't about to let anyone or anything change it. Stepping off the pier at Glettkau onto the boardwalk by the hotel, Mrs. Stein tapped the tip of her white parasol on the wooden planking as she said to Mr. Kohl:

"But it couldn't have happened any other way. He had no choice. This was something stronger than he was—the man was powerless. He has to be forgiven . . ." "Powerless?" Mr. Kohl arched his eyebrows. Because even if what they were talking about *had* occurred, the sheer ambience of the Anatomy Building—the rows of windowed doors with their rattling panes of iridescent crystal; the enameled plaques, as solemn as gothic sarcophagi, engraved with the names of the rooms; the somber stillness, accentuated by the soft squish of the orderlies' rubber soles moving across the green linoleum and the occasional clamor of nickel-plated kettles and tin trays that filtered up from the basement like music from some gigantic kitchen—all that created enough tension without Mr. Kohl's wanting to make matters worse with dubious speculations concerning things impossible to understand. And even if what Alfred had told him when they ran into each other at Kaufmann's on the Lange Brücke was true, Mr. Kohl believed that the wisest thing to do was keep quiet, because there was something about the event in question that he didn't fully grasp, though he'd seen quite a few things in his time; for instance on the retreat from Metz, and later during the counteroffensive at Strassburg, where people he thought he knew well, people of whom he would never have said an ill word, were suddenly transformed, as if the skin had peeled off their faces, baring their wet, shiny teeth. No, Mr. Kohl knew all too well that people change, but not to that degree, and not here, not at Delbrück-Allee 12!

If it had happened to one of the students, or for example to someone like Hanemann's assistant, the prosector, Martin Retz—exactly, if something like that had happened to Retz—Mr. Kohl would have just nodded knowingly at the fragility of human nature and the frailty of human nerves—but Hanemann? Doubtless there were secrets lurking in him as well, invisible even to the keenest eye among all the doctors so caught up in the teachings of Bleuler (not to mention the eye of the porter behind the milk-glass pane, who saw only light-colored hair, a dark silhouette, and then a hand returning the key to room 9), but after all, there was a limit to how much a human psyche could be altered. And what could conceivably happen to one of the young men from Thorn, Elbing, or even Allenstein who had come here following their passion for delving into the secrets of anatomy couldn't possibly happen to someone who had been here for years and who had supposedly studied with

Ansen in the hospital near Moabit, where he had apparently seen quite a few things himself.

In any event, nothing on the fourteenth augured anything unusual. The students sauntered down the stairs and settled on the oak benches outside the door marked with a Gothic *A*. Ernst Mehl (son of the iron wholesaler in Marienwerder) arrived a few minutes after two, sporting an impeccably tailored smooth corduroy jacket and yellow leather shoes and carrying a pince-nez; he was accompanied by Günther Henecke, whose father owned a cotton warehouse and wholesale grocery on the Speicherinsel. They were soon joined by others whose names, unfortunately, Alfred Rotke couldn't remember. The students spoke in hushed tones, and it was clear that their muted, nervous laughter, which faded whenever they glanced at the door to Hanemann's office—for the moment still empty—was meant to stifle the uneasiness they felt despite the fact that none of them was there for the first time.

In fact, they were speaking so quietly—mostly in whispers and muffled exclamations—that all Prosector Retz could make out was the odd Latin word mixed in with some vulgar German and a few snippets from assorted operettas (inspired, no doubt, by pleasant memories of Heinrich Mollers's Hamburg troupe, which had come to town the previous week) that caught his ear as he passed through the middle of the corridor, carrying the implements that would be needed in room 9. More and more students gathered outside the door with the enameled plaque and its row of black Gothic letters. Canes with knobs of brass and ivory gleamed from an umbrella stand garlanded with a wrought-iron lily, set in the dark corner behind the oak railing, while coats steamed on the black rack mounted over the pale green, faux-marble wainscoting, their collars still dewy with fog. The loudest laughs echoed nervously off the vaulted ceiling until they were lost in the din rising from below—the clatter of copper kettles, the clanging of slick sheets of tin, and the clinking of nickel-plated instruments.

Hanemann—according to Mrs. Stein—appeared on the stairs a few minutes before three. The students rose respectfully and returned his greeting. A moment later Martin Retz entered the corridor, wearing his bone-buttoned jacket, a little too large, and smelling of Riedlitz cologne, and even though he walked with the same solemnity as Hanemann, there was nothing in him that inclined one to nod one's head.

Martin Retz. . . . How many times had Mrs. Stein seen him standing by the railing on the end of the Zoppot pier, turned to the sea, seemingly oblivious to anyone and everyone, though on summer and even autumn afternoons so many people flocked to the piers and landings to take the air or to stroll along the promenade by the Casino. No doubt his melancholy came from lingering thoughts about his mother, who had lain dying for weeks at the hospital on Weidengasse, her eyes fixed on the ceiling, unable to hear what her son was asking when he came every few days to visit, always with a bouquet of flowers, but, really, men shouldn't simply give in like that! Mrs. Stein, who took her daughters for a dose of sea air at four in the afternoon even in cold weather, interrupted her discourse on the life-giving properties of iodine as soon as they set foot on the landing, when she saw how perplexed the girls were at the sight of the slender gentleman standing on the end of the pier, dressed in his dark jacket with the bone buttons, staring off into the distance oblivious to the wind that was tousling his hair. "My dear girls," pronounced Mrs. Stein, her voice marked with admonition and warning, "Mr. Retz is a Melancholic."

So Martin Retz was a Melancholic, and whatever he said about Hanemann was bound to be permeated with Melancholy, which—Mrs. Stein knew for a fact—discolors everything that crosses our mind. A Melancholic—and Hilda Wirth, Retz's landlady on Johannisberg Strasse, who woke him every morning with a cautious knocking, would undoubtedly confirm the diagnosis. After all, who else would lug around that small plaster-cast face wrapped in a scrap of rabbit fur and tucked inside a black leather bag, that nacreous mask of an unknown girl, which Mrs. Wirth had seen in his room one afternoon resting on the shelf of the mahogany dresser? Why would someone so steadfast and even-keeled, who went to such pains to make sure his tie clasp and cuff links always matched—why did a man like Retz keep that little plaster face on his dresser? After all, what was so special about it? Just a plaster cast of some nameless girl's face—a girl who might have been his younger sister, but clearly wasn't. (Then again, could Mrs. Wirth—wise though she was in the ways of the world—really be faulted for not knowing that thousands of identical masks graced bedrooms and salons throughout Alsace, Lorraine, and Lower Saxony, not to mention central France?)

On August fourteenth, at a few minutes past three o'clock, when the sheet was pulled back to reveal the features of the girl whose body had been delivered to Anatomy just an hour before, Martin Retz couldn't help but sigh: this face looked so similar ... And if Retz saw what he saw, is it possible that Hanemann hadn't seen the same thing? Yes, Martin Retz was ready to swear that Hanemann's eyes lost their sparkle the moment the linen was pulled back. Besides, could it have happened any other way? Could anyone who had ever seen that slumbering face of snow white plaster possibly remain indifferent? Anyone who had even once laid eyes on La Belle Inconnue de la Seine?

"That Retz has gone completely mad." Mrs. Stein couldn't hide her impatience when Maria, her cousin from Thorn, repeated word for word what Retz had told her concerning August fourteenth. Because hadn't she learned from Alfred Rotke where things really stood? If Hanemann's hands had recoiled the instant the cover was pulled off the blanched face of the girl laid out on the marble slab table, it wasn't because she reminded him of some alabaster cast that sent Retz into a melancholy fit!

Although he remembered that day very well—and it's hard to forget something that comes hurtling out of the blue and shatters all our previous conceptions about the flimsy web that links the possible to the real—Alfred Rotke nevertheless could not recall Hanemann's face at that particular moment. Lost in his own amazement, the orderly just stared at the figure that had materialized on the marble slab table minutes after the green ambulance pulled up and the police carried it in on a stretcher wrapped in a rubber cover fastened with leather straps. The same vehicle had pulled up to the Anatomy receiving dock several times. Slamming doors, rapid footsteps, shouts. The orderlies were summoned from Building E, and soon the entire Academy knew that at around nine in the morning, the *Star*, a small excursion boat that ran between Neufahrwasser and Zoppot, had sunk off the pier at Glettkau. With the help of the Himmel Brothers' floating crane they had been able to raise the hull, where they found a body in the dining room identified as a man whose name figured in police records. This in turn had attracted the attention of Commissioner Wittberg from the Zoppot precinct headquarters. The unfortunate accident was, in fact, not the first along that route: on August 12, 1921, the *Urania*, belonging to the Danzig Crew Association, had collided with a tugboat from Neufahrwasser right off the Glettkau pier.

In such cases, whenever there was even a shadow of doubt, they would send for Hanemann. The black Daimler-Benz would drive to Lessingstrasse 17. At the sound of the car stopping outside his gate, Hanemann would reach for his dark overcoat, quickly leave the house, and walk down to the street, where his assistant Retz was already waiting, all freshened up, with a white handkerchief in his breast pocket. The chauffeur would open the door, and a moment later they would drive onto Kronprinzenallee and pass the railway viaduct, then turn and head in the direction of Langfuhr. Having answered a number of similar summons in the past, Hanemann reacted to this one with little surprise; although the incident was considered sensational (that very evening a special supplement of the *Volksstimme* provided the shocking details), from the perspective of the Anatomical Institute it was all in a day's work. Even Retz (whose sensitivity had been severely tested on more than one occasion), though undoubtedly deeply moved by the catastrophe, did not seem particularly anxious as they sped through the homes of Langfuhr and crossed over the railroad tracks at Magdeburger Strasse, passing by the riding school on their way into town; he merely reported the case they had been entrusted to unravel.

Evidently—said Retz—there were indications that one of the victims found aboard the *Star* had died some time before the boat went under. (That speculation, which originated with some witnesses who were present when the bodies were recovered from the flooded hull, had led a few journalists to the overly hasty conclusion that the sinking of the *Star* was no accident but an attempt to cover up a far more serious crime—and that the perpetrator had miscalculated and perished along with the other victims.) This case, then, was not different from the ones typically referred to Hanemann, so that Commissioner Wittberg from Zoppot and the commissioners from the city of Danzig, with whom Hanemann usually worked, could rest assured that everything would be clarified, and that any doubts—

if they should arise—would not be disguised by the feigned confidence of a glib diagnosis.

So as the Daimler-Benz sped toward the Anatomy Building,
as the tall linden trees that shaded the Evangelical Cemetery
flashed by on the left and dropped from sight, Orderly Alfred
Rotke moved the marble slab table, now bearing a figure
shrouded in rubberized canvas, slowly wheeling it from the ice
chamber into room 9, careful to avoid any bumps as he crossed
the brass threshold. When the table rolled into place beneath the
circular lamp with five milk white bulbs, the white rubber aprons
with their metal clasps were already waiting on the coat tree beside the door, the nickel-plated instruments resting in the tin
trays beside the window, and by the time Orderly Rotke had
switched on the light (which always made him squint), from outside the room he could hear footsteps coming down the granite
stairs. First came Martin Retz, followed by Hanemann, who had
taken off his dark overcoat on his way down. Retz handed him an
apron; Hanemann closed the metal clasp, smoothing the white
rubber against his chest, and murmured a greeting to Orderly
Rotke; then, when everyone had gathered around the table, he
asked that the lamp be lowered so that the concentrated light of
five bulbs would illumine the figure lying on the marble slab.

After that—Mr. Rotke remembered the moment well—
Hanemann deftly unknotted the leather thongs securing the
canvas and drew back the cover ... but all Rotke really remembered were Hanemann's hands, their calm, patient, nimble movements as the thongs came undone and the cloth was pulled back,
he didn't remember what Hanemann's face looked like at that
moment, just the hands caught in the strong milky spotlight of
the five bulbs, the hands that recoiled when the rubberized canvas was drawn back and revealed the face of Louisa Berger. On

her neck, just below the chin, was a thin, darkening line, shot through with reddish violet. Her hair was wet.

So that's what happened on August fourteenth—Mrs. Stein couldn't hide her indignation—and nobody should get the wrong idea no matter what melancholy concoction Martin Retz (whose slender figure posed a danger to every family blessed with daughters) might come up with, because here was the real reason, the clear and wrenchingly painful explanation. And while some people would discount the words of a mere orderly (and why are we always so quick to shrug off the words of simple men, just the way we dismiss those who openly profess their belief in a world of pure and undiminished feeling?)— Rotke saw what there was to see.

Silently grouped around the marble slab table, the students were puzzled when Hanemann broke off the examination, and exchanged glances among themselves, but Prosector Retz's face showed nothing to support even the most guarded supposition. So they stood in silence, wearing their canvas-lined rubber aprons, waiting for some gesture to dispel the tension, which seemed about to pass as Hanemann motioned for Retz to begin, and the prosector reached with his rubber-gloved hands into the tray filled with shiny instruments, picked up a cotton ball that had been soaked in some pink liquid, rubbed the abdomen of the supine woman from her sternum to her navel (which still contained a glassy bead of water), and taking a blade to the skin, slowly began the incision. At that point, Hanemann turned around and—without removing his apron—left the room. As Retz carefully guided the instrument, exposing the dark red rises netted with violet veins inside the opening body, Alfred Rotke turned to the door and listened to Hanemann's footsteps dying away on the stairs, but it wasn't until after the hemostats were in place and it was time for Hanemann's postprep lecture, during which he typically used a glass rod to point out the exposed organs, that were pictured in the large-scale illustrations hanging in room 9, and Retz had interrupted his work for a moment to say to Rotke, "Please tell Professor Hanemann the clamps are in place," it wasn't until then that they realized Hanemann was no longer in the building.

Not even the sight of the dark overcoat hanging by the door could dispel their certainty that he had gone.

| *The Window* |

BACK HOME ON Lessingstrasse, Hanemann stacked the photos in the bronze epergne and tossed in a lit match. Little yellow flames darted from picture to picture, swaying gently whenever the breeze blew in from the window. Soon the bottom of the tray was covered with blackened flakes. He watched the shiny paper crinkle up in the fire.

The next moment, however, he smothered the fire with his bare hand and quickly started picking the charred bits and pieces out of the ashes. The tip of a shoe flashing by on one smoke-smudged corner. The hem of a lace dress. A white hand clutching the crook of a parasol. The brim of a dark hat wreathed with roses of gauze. As he realized what he had done, he closed his eyes. Then he hurriedly began putting the burned pieces back together, but it was too late; nothing could be reassembled from the sooty scraps. Ashes. Black fingertips. The odor of burnt emulsified paper. He opened the drawer. On the bottom: a passport photo tinged with green. A feather. A dull gray coin. A pen nib. Nothing else.

The face in the photograph seemed unfamiliar.

Is that her? He hadn't been able to collect his thoughts. Now everything started coming together. All the lines pointed to one place: the murky waters beside the dock. How could he have failed to see it? The pictures coalesced like magnetic filings into an icily transparent pattern.

After all, it had been only three days since they'd met at the hotel in Glettkau. Their second-story room had a window overlooking the pier, where that boat always docked at three in the afternoon.

Three days...

She had been standing by the window. Pinning up her hair, whose luster always amazed him. She reached for the hairpins with the delicate bone heads that were scattered on the windowsill, fetched up a lock of hair, and deftly threaded her fingers through the strands. She had taken more time than usual, hadn't she? Now he was sure of it—the way her hands had moved, how could he have missed that? Standing by the window, her profile mirrored in the windowpane, against the azure shimmer of the sea. Her profile so close he could have reached over and touched it, but hadn't he sensed that something had come between them, some barely perceptible screen, which made her face a little lighter than usual, a shade cooler, perhaps, or paler? Her complexion...cool? Moonlit white? He should have noticed it back then, when she was standing by the window, squinting in the sunlight. It was early morning; splotches of warm yellow light came splashing against the wall beside the window frame. Outside, the white excursion steamer *Ariel* from Neufahrwasser was moored along the pier. A few boys were traipsing down the beach toward the landing. A red ball. The sky. Bright sand. The squawking of gulls lazily shooed away by the fisherman as he plucked the living fish from his net, pink flashes of gills. The sea was calm, and nearly waveless...

She was standing by the window, lost in thought, perhaps a little annoyed—but she didn't show the same kind of faraway musing he sometimes saw in the faces at Kaufmann's café or in the restaurant on the hotel's first floor, like that beautiful woman with her hair tied up in a Roman knot who stared absently off into space while she poked at her Viennese torte with a silver spoon, perhaps lost in recollections after a night of love, saying nothing even though her companion, a meticulously groomed officer from the Hochstriess barracks, was telling her something in spirited tones as he went about picking crabs off a shiny platter with a pair of metal tongs.

No, back then, when she was standing by the window, it was something different, a sense of dread, though he had dismissed this as the reflex of a startled heart.

Or had he noticed it even earlier? When she was standing in the bathtub with the door ajar, her skin so bright against the dark green bathroom wall, her hair piled high, lit by the lamp over the fogged-up mirror.... He saw her profile, the white line of her breasts. The Grecian sponge sliding down her arm, the residue of foam clinging to her gold-tinged skin, the wet hem of hair around the back of her neck, the slow movements of her hands, as if she didn't feel a thing beneath her fingers...

While he watched her then, as she glided the Grecian sponge along her arm, he had felt a jolt of fear, sudden and short-lived as sunlight caught in a shattering mirror.... No, it wasn't fear; it was a revelation: as her fingers skimmed across her skin, he saw the utter solitude of that body, and in a flash he realized that she was destined for herself alone, that he would never reach her.

Now there was nothing left but self-reproach. They could easily have left for Königsberg the day before yesterday. Everything was ready. Two train tickets with a change in Marienburg. But she had insisted on putting it off to Sunday, because her mother wasn't doing well, why don't we wait, just a couple more days. . . . And one firm word would have been enough.

Now the time spent inside the Anatomy Building seemed dark and hollow. He had wanted to unlock secrets, had opened the bodies that ended up on the marble slab table in order to discover what separates us from death. But what good were all those hours spent in the basement at Delbrück-Allee, if he hadn't managed to hear what her living body was saying, if he hadn't seen what was clear—as he now knew—in her every movement? Because now he was certain that then, standing by the window in their second-story room, she had felt it coming. And he had simply gone on gaping at her shoulder, her neck, her hair—as if he were blind and deaf. Back then he could have stopped her with a single word, when she was standing by the window, against the azure shimmer of the sea, but all he did was ask: "What's the matter?" Still holding on to the green comb, she had stopped untangling her hair for a moment and said, "I don't know."

He remembered everything. Every gesture. With painful clarity. The images torn from those moments. And one word would have been enough.

And that trace of exasperation when she turned from the window. Her nimble fingers pulling a light strand of hair out of the hairbrush. The seashell on the windowsill. Rings. The pink cameo medallion. The brooch pinned beneath her collar. Then her hand arranging the hair on the back of her neck. Fingers buttoning her dress. A yellow lace-up shoe on the rug. Hurried footsteps. Water splashing in the sink. The soft thud of soap being put down. The warm traces of bare feet on the tiles. She passed him on her way to the mirror. A barely perceptible stiffening of the shoulders when he tried to hug her. She had gently wriggled out of his embrace and laughed, but her laughter was shallow and faded on the spot. She reached for her hat and smoothed the ribbons. Straightened the roses pinned around the brim. The swish of silk. Pale pink fingernails. Sliding the ring on her fourth finger. Holding out her hand to look: a malachite eye set in silver. The black-handled parasol tossed on the couch. The creaking of the wardrobe being opened. The flash of a mirror inside the door. A light-colored coat, fuzzy fabric, pearl buttons. The warmth of her dress vanishing beneath the coat.

He brushed her cheek with his fingers. She pressed her face against his hand but was looking somewhere off to the side. Lowered eyelids. "So, Sunday at four in Langfuhr. You won't forget?" A stupid, silly question—hadn't he bought the tickets himself? "Just don't be late. And no luggage. I'll take everything we need." They had planned to travel in separate cars; it was more fun. Just like strangers from Stettin or Köslin, they would meet in the dining car once they were under way, somewhere between Dirschau and Marienburg, on the long bridge that spanned the Vistula and that seemed to go on forever, with the water down below, the water dark with swirling.

But while she was standing there by the window, against the azure shimmer of the sea, the white boat from Neufahrwasser was already waiting for her—the white summer dress, the parasol, the small white handbag. . . . Was she on her way to her sister's in Zoppot? But why didn't she take the train, why did she have to board that little boat with its slanted funnel, like a severed Greek marble column, emblazoned with the Westermann *W*? Her sister? That girl with dark reddish hair and eyes like ripe grapes? In a red dress? Had she been waiting on the pier at Glettkau? Did she see the whole thing?

He jumped up from the armchair and reached for the coat he'd tossed on the bed. There's no time to lose, he had to go to Frauengasse right away, to tell her everything that had happened!

Her?

Suddenly he realized that the person he wanted to tell about what happened in Glettkau was no longer there. He'd always told her about anything interesting or important going on in Danzig, Dirschau, Zoppot, or even Marienwerder, and now he wanted to tell her this news too . . .

He recovered his senses. My God . . .

How did Retz put it? "In our suffering we can feel the hand of God"—was that it? Poor Retz . . . that melancholy young man with fingers so deft he could readily be entrusted with even the most difficult operation. What kind of philosophical drivel was that? The hand of God? All Hanemann felt at that moment was raw pain; she wasn't at Frauengasse now, and never . . .

No tears. Only cheeks tense with pain and a choking in the throat. He couldn't understand. Why this punishment? Even if it had to be him—why her? Hanging on the wall—a dark patch next to the bronze-framed mirror—was Caspar David Friedrich's *Cross in the Mountains,* but the lacy silhouette of the spruce trees that crowned the figure of the Lord suddenly went blurry. Hanemann closed his eyes. He felt himself convulsed by sobs.

| *Dismissed* |

THE WAY MRS. STEIN told the story, Hanemann's niece Anna showed up at Lessingstrasse 17 a few days later—tall, beautiful, wearing a white and yellow floral print dress, mesh gloves, and a broad-brimmed hat. She called up to him the minute she set foot on the flagstones: "The things they're saying about you, it's simply unbelievable. Those girls are always thinking up things that take a whole year to undo!" Hanemann smiled as he headed for the wide-open French doors on the veranda, took Anna by the arm, and led her into the dark sitting room, where patches of sunlight were chasing one another around the floor, which was mottled with shadows from the leaves of the large birch tree in that corner of the garden.

Beautiful Anna! He offered her the wicker armchair that faced the window—he enjoyed watching her squint as he asked about news from the city. Afterward, when the sun in the garden had taken on the warm glow of late afternoon and the conversation was dying down, Anna peered at him a long time. "Can't you put her out of your mind?" Hanemann turned away, as if a flame had singed his cheek, but Anna kept peering: "Besides, that man they found with her might have been a complete stranger.... Stop thinking about it.... And even if there was something between them, it's not important...she isn't here anymore..." He stroked her hand through her glove with a quick, cautious movement, as if he were trying to calm her down and not vice versa: "Enough." For a moment she was quiet, but as soon as the silence in the sitting room yielded to the rustle of leaves from the garden, her eyes began to flicker with little needles of flame: "You have to go back to the Institute, it doesn't make sense..."

But why should he go back there? His house on Lessingstrasse brought in enough income—so why was she insisting? According to Mrs. Stein, the only way to dispel the bad aura beginning to cling to the family was for Hanemann to return to Delbrück-Allee. "Come on, Hanemann"—Anna shook her head—"It's time for you to let it go.... Why don't you come over Sunday, you can talk with Mother.... You can't go on living like this..." No doubt she was right, but despite her repeated invitations, he no longer went to Falkweg, to that beautiful white house with its black Prussian timbers, slowly surrendering its facade to the encroaching dark-leaved ivy; he no longer climbed the steep stairs to the grassy terrace where they used to sit in cast-iron chairs around the circular table, in the shade of the blue spruce on the other side of the little stream that ran down from the Gutenberg Grove.

"Ach, those ladies from Lower Saxony..." Franz Zimmermann sighed ironically when I visited him many years later in his small apartment in Stockholm at Vita Liljansväg 65 and told him what Mama had heard from Mrs. Stein. "All that gloomy Lower Saxon sadness, no matter how pretty the weather, even on the sunniest summer day. Everything always has to be infused with the color of tangled Bremen ivy; it all has to glisten with yearning like fresh dew on the trees at Worpswede, all has to be submerged in weltschmerz, which—concealed though it always is—weighs on every Low German heart. Before you get any wild ideas you should remember that that's where Mrs. Stein came from!

"Because Hanemann didn't leave the Institute at all! Sure there was something between him and that Louisa Berger, but let's not exaggerate. No, he didn't resign—he was dismissed, after somebody heard him in the restaurant out by Karlsberg saying more than he should about things best kept quiet. Are you familiar with the Wichmann case? Well, a number of dignitaries from the Senate, various city bureaus, and the Polytechnic were out there in Karlsberg celebrating the birthday of Professor Hans Unger, the rector of the Medical Academy. Hanemann made some remarks about mass meetings with songs and marching around with torches, remarks that were deemed out of place right there in Oliva, just a few streets away from where various 'unknown perpetrators' had forced Hans Wichmann into a car the week before: his body was recovered three or four days later from the port channel in Elbing and wound up on the marble slab table in room 9. Anyway, from what I heard"—Zimmermann went on—"one of the guests that night out by Karlsberg was a young man with the nice Aryan name of Forster. I'm sure that name means something to you."

Sitting across from me on the leather armchair, stirring his Colombian coffee in its light-blue demitasse, Franz Zimmermann shook his head at the Low German lyricism of Mrs. Stein. Franz Zimmerman—a gray-haired man with tawny skin and clear hazel eyes, who had been active in the Catholic Center Party, and had managed to make it to Sweden by way of Königsberg and Memel, back in 1937. "The things she told your mother..." he repeated, leisurely, though Mrs. Stein as well as the Free City of Danzig were both long since gone. Gone was the soft darkness of the streets that sloped down toward the Mottlau River, gone were the glistening cobblestones on Frauengasse and the milky light of the streetlamps along Breitgasse, lit every evening by Hans Lempke, Mr. Zimmermann's neighbor from Osseck, who rode from lamp to lamp on his old Urania bike, stepping on a ladder to hold his flame to each one—all gone, save for the dark photos mounted above the little glass table where we sat drinking our coffee, original prints from the Ballerstaedt studio itself.

"Because, you know, even back in those days Hanemann kept some pretty dubious company!" Mr. Zimmermann had set down his blue coffee cup inside his apartment in Stockholm and picked up a photo album. "You know he went more than once to that infamous building on Lange Brücke where the Social Democrats from the *Danziger Volksstimme* used to meet, not far from the Old Crane, just a few doors down from Hermann Kagan's business. Valentina Reimann kept a shop next door and"—Mr. Zimmermann thought for a moment—"just past Kagan's, Robert Süss sold guns, I think. What number was it? Probably nine, since Kagan's was at number ten. Right above Süss's shop, Jost Hirschfeld had a palm tree in a wooden pot— the pigeons glazed it white the minute he set it out. But what was over Valentina Reimann's place?" Franz Zimmermann remembered the iron balustrade clearly, but what was behind that? Something white and round, leaning against the wall? Cohn at number eleven always kept his wooden venetian blinds half-shuttered in the large arched window; there were some yellow letters painted on the reddish stucco, but what did they say? And what was on the little signs Cohn used to hang outside? Things for sale? Was that all he had? That had to be at Lange Brücke 11:

Franz Zimmermann, who passed by there frequently, nearly always tripping over a slab that jutted out of the sidewalk, even remembered the smell coming from the small basement windows of the spice shop. Past Emil Białkowski's—his son hung out a canvas banner in 1935 over the door to their shop saying "Beloved Leader, Take Care of Us. We Know the Duty of Every Pole. Let's All Vote Slate 7"—at Number 22, I think, another Cohn had his store: Franz Zimmermann could still see the gold lettering of the word *Cigarren* painted on the narrow facade, which kept disappearing behind the heavy blue-and-white-striped awning that fluttered in the wind.

So Hanemann had been seen there a few times—Franz Zimmermann wasn't sure how many, but he was certain he could place Hanemann in that room on the second floor, that room with the green lampshade and the paintings by Emil Nolde and drawings by Oskar Kokoschka displayed on the walls. Who else used to show up there? Heinsdorff? Erich Brost? Richard Tetzlaff? Or maybe Ernst Loops, whom they later beat so badly he was crippled for life? Nobody from the *Danziger Vorposten,* of course . . . But the faces of the people who frequented that address on Lange Brücke, the faces were buried in the fog, emerging from forgetfulness only for a moment, pale ovals peering like specters from a glass photographic plate.

Franz Zimmermann flipped through the leaves of his album.

Gustav Petsch? That giant man in his dark overcoat, with his wing collar and patterned tie, secured in a big long knot, clean-shaven and always meticulously combed with a part on the left, and his heavy black mustache curled up at the tips, a veteran of the Great War, who growled at the packs of boys marching down from the Hotel du Nord to the Langer Markt, where they were greeted by women with hands raised in a Roman salute. Hadn't he been seen with Hanemann at Schneider's restaurant?

Albert Posack? Hadn't someone seen him with Hanemann back in 1935 on the pier at Zoppot?

"And besides," Franz Zimmermann rubbed the back of his head, which was covered with silver fuzz, "besides, he kept company with Rauschning, you know. Well maybe 'kept company with' is too much, but Hanemann did visit the man at his estate out in Warnow (where they probably talked about music, or the concerts in the Marienkirche), and of course you know Rauschning visited Hitler in Obersalzberg in thirty-two. Not just visited, either! Hitler supported him in the elections for the Danzig Senate, and even though he changed later on, they never had much good to say about him in Schwarzschild's *Neues Tagebuch*. The only reason Rauschning dumped Greiser and Forster is because they wanted to shunt him off to the side. And if he had made it in the party, he never would have written his *Revolution of Nihilism*, not to mention *Conversations with Hitler*! If he had made it, he would have stuck with them!"

Nevertheless, even if Mrs. Stein could have heard Franz Zimmermann's words and his ironic sighs in that small Stockholm apartment, even if she'd been able to get her hands on the yellowed photos Greiser's people had taken (using a Leica reflex camera) of everyone they observed poking about the building at Number 21 near the Old Crane, and even if she had seen Hanemann in those photos, dressed in a light-colored suit, walking beside Albert Posack, she still would have done nothing more than shrug her shoulders with forbearing compassion.

Because she'd seen it with her own eyes, that afternoon in June, when she and her friends had stopped at the hotel in Glettkau and taken a table on the terrace bordered with white rails and potted orange trees. As she looked around at the other tables, whom had she seen but Hanemann, sitting with Louisa Berger, next to a lamp with a tea-colored shade? Mrs. Stein saw him kiss

Louisa's hands and saw how devotedly Louisa had returned the gesture. And anyone who'd seen them then, on the terrace of the hotel restaurant there in Glettkau, when the evening sea was gleaming in the windowpanes of the dining room, and the surf was rolling behind the dunes overgrown with buckthorn, anyone who had seen them wouldn't have had the slightest doubt why on August fourteenth things happened the way they did.

Mrs. Stein would half close her eyes to summon the dark silhouettes—the black profile of a man and the black profile of a woman, framed against the silver background of the glittering sea—the exact same picture that she could swear she witnessed that June evening in Glettkau, a scene of such sweet power it would cause anyone's heart to melt, including hers. And whenever Mrs. Stein's thoughts drifted back to that evening, the long-gone city's past became like a shy young fiancée at twilight, undressing with a blush of shame before her lover's longing gaze, between bedsheets smelling of roses.

| *Things* |

ALL UP AND DOWN the Langer Markt, inside the offices at Hersen's, by the granaries on the Speicherinsel, at Kaufmann's café on the Lange Brücke, Hanemann became the subject of conversation, but really the city had too much else on its mind to want to hear about him—too much watching and waiting. For in drawers, cupboards, and chests, on the bottom of tins, crates, and trunks, in attics and cubbyholes, on racks and shelves, in basements and pantries, on tables and windowsills, things were lying in wait—some tender, some mocking—rarely used implements for specialized tasks and everyday tools used with fierce persistence for sewing, hammering, slicing, cutting, peeling, polishing, and writing, all adrift in the unmoving ark of the city along with Mrs. Stein, Hanemann, Mrs. Walmann, Anna, Mr. Kohl, Alfred Rotke, Stella, Albert Forster, Franz Zimmermann, Albert Posack, Hans Wichmann, Greiser, Mrs. Bierenstein, Emil Białkowski, the Schultzes, Professor Unger, Martin Retz, Hermann Rauschning, Mr. Lempke, Hilda Wirth. . . . And all these things were readying themselves for the road.

At that precise moment, in the quiet that was filling the city, a last judgment was already taking place—a repositioning, a gentle movement to be always in view and within reach so they could make it on time. Things that were indispensable separated themselves from things slated for destruction.

White tureens, shaped like swans and pelicans, tender silver sugar bowls fashioned like wild ducks with turquoise eyes, and dainty little boats for pear preserves were frightened by their own fanciful, impractical forms; they envied the ordinary flatness of baking trays, so easily slid under floors or stashed among the rafters of barns and abandoned mills. Although for the moment they continued to flaunt their polished elegance on Sunday tablecloths in homes on Breitgasse, Frauengasse, and Jäschkentaler Weg, where they welcomed the silver teaspoons with a playful jingle, deep inside they felt their doubts growing like a dark layer of tarnish—their fear that they were nothing more than small sarcophagi. Using an old felt rag, Liselotte Peltz buffed the top of a coffeepot that had nightmares of being a vessel of death. The sconces and reflectors mounted high on the walls inside the Artushof went on showing off their candle spires, feigning delight in their burnished gleam, but under their ruby-tinged gilding they were already convinced that, when the time came, they would dissolve in the flames into thick icicles of cooling copper. Nine-branched menorahs that trembled with flame during the Festival of Lights, bulbous Sabbath candlesticks, the Torah crown from the synagogue off Karrenwall that gleamed whenever the ark was opened—all bending their silver sheen toward Erfurt, where the noble metal would go to embellish the parade saber of Sturmbannführer Greutze. On such a sunny summer afternoon, full of crying gulls and chirping swallows, who among us could have imagined that the gold teeth belonging to Anna Janowska of Brösener Weg 63 would be melted down together with wedding rings from women in Theresien-stadt and the coins of Salonika Jews, into a kilogram brick of gold?

The wardrobes full of linens safely arranged on their shelves like Miocene strata at the Mitzners', the Jabłonowskis', the Hasenvellers'; the oak bed frames with carved headboards at the Greutzes', the Schultzes', the Rostkowskis'; the tables nap-ping under their star-patterned crochet throws at the Kleins', the Goldsteins', the Rosenkranzes'; the brick walls by the old ramparts along the Stadtgraben, the stuccowork adorning the porches on Hundegasse, the iron gratings on Jopengasse, the gilded portals of Langer Markt, the granite balls guarding thresholds on the Frauengasse, the copper gutters, window frames, doorjambs, statues, roof tiles—all of this was drifting toward the flames like so much dandelion fluff.

In the room on the ground floor at Ahornweg 14, Mrs. Stein's niece carefully unfolded the new dress of Westphalian linen she had received as a birthday present from her aunt and laid it across the ironing board, then reached for the cup with the hand-painted rowan leaves, took a sip of water without swal-lowing, puckered her lips, and blew a fine spray over the white linen. She licked her finger to test the iron, and after making sure it would leave no trace of brown, began smoothly gliding it over the steaming white surface, but even as she did so, every thread of the fine hemstitching was already advancing toward the flames and the smothering gray ashes that would ultimately wilt the crispness of the pleats and lace.

Mrs. Kohl's beautiful Japanese rush fan, which resembled a white leaf edged with purple, was already glowing in her fingers as she leaned against the window frame at Breitgasse 8, cooling her shoulders with undulating breezes as she absentmindedly stared at the Reimitz house across the street, while Mr. Kohl's souvenir fountain pen, with "Dresden" engraved on the gold cap in tiny letters, lay glistening and still on the table in the middle of the sitting room, seemingly calm—though it, too, was already being drawn into the whirlpool of fire, along with the gilt mirror, the mahogany wardrobe, and the wine-colored door curtains. And the things it had yet to say! Whole oceans of words swelled inside the yellow jasper inkwell when Mr. Kohl sat down in the evenings to his pale blue stationery with the anchor watermark to write to his beloved daughter Heidi, who waited impatiently in the Weimar Gymnasium for every letter bearing a stamp marked "Freie Stadt Danzig," its crimson color like fire against the purple of the envelope.

Günther Schultz ran to school over the cobblestones laid in a fish-scale pattern; the Bierensteins tripped over the streetcar tracks on Langer Markt on their way to the theater; Mrs. Peltz's son used a fine brush to paint the word "Kaffee" on the window of the coffeehouse at Breitgasse 13, but the glass scoffed at his efforts, glaring with reflected sunlight that mocked the gold lettering, because it already knew that when the time came the transparent pane would shatter into a thousand sparks like a fragile sheet of ice.

Only small objects, ones easily grabbed in an escape, flaunted their smug self-assurance—a shaving brush, a razor in a leather sheath, alum, a round bar of soap, a tin box of Vera tooth powder, a tiny flask of Amiels cologne. The more luxurious, fluffy towels shrank in bathroom corners, ashamed at their unwieldy bulk, and ceded their place to the cool charm of linen canvas, so easily torn into long strips good for staunching wounds.

The thick green woolen coat lying folded and forgotten on the bottom of the armoire in the main room at Hundegasse 12, unfashionable, discarded, and disdained, the coat that Anneliese Leimann fought wearing so many times because it made her look older, was already stirring in its storage place, promising deliverance at the moment when men in uniforms dark with dust and soot would force open the door and stand on the threshold. But none of us was yet saying, "Anneliese, don't complain, a dirty old coat like that is a good thing to have, all stained with kerosene and too long and too wide in the shoulders; it makes you look awful, ten years older at least. Keep your chin up, Anneliese, don't complain, that coat is looking after you, watching out for you, and you act as though you'd gladly see it thrown away, heaped on the rag cart with the rest of the disgraced old clothes Johann Lietz picks up now and then for the paper mill in Marienwerder. How can you be so ungrateful, Anneliese!"

Only the solid gold coins kept truly calm, the wedding bands, rings, necklaces, crosses, gold dollars, gold rubles, Polish silver zlotys, the Danzig guldens and special medallions minted to commemorate royal visits. They knew they would survive, thanks to the collar they'd be sewn into; knew they would sleep through hundreds of kilometers inside a hollowed heel, carefully swaddled in cotton wool to keep from jingling when death lurked nearby. Meanwhile, Mr. Rotke's bamboo cane dozed peacefully in the stand next to the door at Jopengasse 4, assured that, when the time came, it would swallow whole rolls of coins before being plugged up with oakum.

Kitchen knives, indifferent to everything, chopped away on oak pastry boards with blank resignation. The blades with pointed tips faced an uncertain future (anyone in their possession was one step closer to death), while their round-tipped brothers, unfit for stabbing, could look forward to years and years of conversations with vegetables. Tin spoons and forks, sound asleep in the bottoms of drawers, were ready to brave long marches and freezing days and nights in any old bootleg without complaint. Tin plates that for years had been relegated to some corner of the

kitchen now clattered away, derisive and shrill, in the Mertenbachs' sink on Breitgasse 29, mocking the Meissen porcelain,
which answered the insult from behind the leaded glass panes of
the china cabinet with a scornful flash of cobalt and gold.

The sun, which rose from the sea every morning behind the
peninsula and sank every evening, exhausted by the discharge of
light, behind the morainal hills, past Karlsberg, past the steeples
of the Cathedral, was only the sun, although bright clouds were
already alight on Memling's altarpiece, where the archangel
Michael divided the saved from those damned to perdition.
Who among us sensed then that the city was slowly advancing
toward the blazing light, the sizzling fire, the smoke of burning
tar, dust of crushed brick, shards of exploding stone, charred
canvas, burned silk, torn paper, cracking wood, shattering marble,
melting copper. Mrs. Bierenstein held up her ticket to the Mu-
nicipal Theater to check her seat number; Mr. Kohl pulled on his
soft yellow suede gloves and adjusted his cuff links as he left the
house; Günther Henecke glanced over the photos of the pretty
chorus girls from *Lohengrin* in his wallet; Albert Forster's housekeeper polished the tarnished silverware with blue chalk; Hanemann arranged his books on the lower shelf of the leaded glass
bookcase; Alfred Rotke sighed with relief as he lit his lighter decorated with the seal of Berlin and the bills of exchange drawn
on his account caught the tiny flame; Martin Retz affixed his signature to a police questionnaire; and at about three o'clock on a
Sunday afternoon, wearing their white lace dresses, the Walmanns' daughters, Eva and Maria, followed their mother up the
sandy path that had been washed out by the rains, waving their
furled parasols and holding on to their hats, which were bending
in the salty wind off the bay as they climbed the grassy slopes of
Bischofsberg to get a view of the city.

And the city spread out below, dark brown studded with flashes of light that bounced off the open windows, while a delicate web of smoke wafted from the tall chimneys of soot-stained brick. The Lehr pile driver from Dresden could be seen slowly pounding at the depths of the former moat; a small flock of pigeons flew over the High Gate, and when we shaded our eyes and focused on the far horizon, pierced by the spires of the Katharinenkirche, the little Rathaus and the big one, the dome of the synagogue and the serrated silhouette of the Trinitätskirche, we could make out a strip of sea past the dark haze that stretched from the sandbars of Frische Nehrung to the cliffs at Adlershorst, and we knew for certain that the city would stand forever.

| *Flannel, Canvas, Silk* |

"MRS. WALMANN!" Liselotte Peltz, a petite, fragile woman with a pink turban wrapped around her forehead, stood outside and called up to the half-open window, sounding worried. "What are we supposed to take with us, did they say what we're supposed to take?" Mrs. Peltz lived across the street at Lessingstrasse 14, in the same building as the Schultzes and the Bierensteins. For several days her radio had been sitting on the shelf like a mute ebonite coffin, stuck between a little blue vase of dried asters and a photo of her husband in his Luftwaffe uniform.

"Don't take anything you don't need," Elsa Walmann answered through the half-open window, "only what's absolutely necessary, Mrs. Peltz, nothing else." Seeing that Mrs. Peltz was already on her way back home, she went into the dining room. Mr. Walmann was next to the window, kneeling on a large pigskin suitcase, trying to shut the bag despite the trailing flannel shirtsleeves. A few silk lace blouses were lying on the divan with the embroidered Chinese motif, alongside some Tyrolean sweaters and white knee-highs of thick wool. "That's no way to do things," Mrs. Walmann sighed, but it wasn't clear whether she meant her husband's futile struggle with the ocher suitcase or the disorder in the room where she was accustomed to receiving guests at the dark walnut table, where a crystal vase with a pale-red paper rose was on permanent display.

Outside the window, on the other side of the street, the Hardenbergs were passing by with little Erwin, pulling their belongings in a handcart covered with red bedding and tied down with string. A black shadow came streaking out from behind the trees, and the family threw themselves on the ground against the iron picket fence. The cart toppled in the snow as the shadow roared over the houses in the direction of Zoppot—the explosions were far off and muffled, as if someone were beating a soft glove against the top of an empty jar. The Hardenbergs ran back to their cart, and once again Mr. Hardenberg fitted his shoulder in the strap that was fastened to the chassis, the wide strip of strong webbing that Kolwitz's uncle had brought yesterday from the shipyard. Erwin kept the wobbly load from tipping over, and slowly they went on their way toward Kronprinzenallee.

Elsa Walmann turned away from the window.

Now her husband was fastening a belt around the suitcase: "Why don't you see what's up with Hanemann." She went upstairs, opened the door, and looked in; Hanemann only nodded. There wasn't too much time left. When young Axer Bierenstein stopped in that morning to see his mother, he reported that the Russians were nearly at the old Polish border and were bound to start moving up the coast toward Zoppot. The Volkssturm units were pulling back from the edge of the Gutenberg Grove, Müggau, and Pietzkendorf and regrouping in Langfuhr. Fortunately, Adolf-Hitler-Strasse was still open; you could follow the tram tracks down Kronprinzenallee to the viaduct, cross over the railroad siding, and head straight down

Ostseestrasse to Neufahrwasser, where the transport ships from Wilhelmshaven were already at the breakwater; there's still a chance you can make it on board...

Mrs. Walmann had calmly taken everything in, even though Axer's uniform had been stained with lime and he had been looking at his mother with fearful eyes. Now the windowpanes she had cleaned so often with her own hands—over the objections of the housekeeper—were shaking with the reverberating explosions, and it was no longer clear in which part of the city the relentless rumble was increasing, perhaps somewhere out by Schidlitz—or even closer in. Nor could they tell where the heavy salvoes were coming from that occasionally cut through the dull thudding (Axer had claimed it was the *Prinz Eugen* firing into the hills from the bay, to cover the port at Gotenhafen). Every few minutes, formations of three to six planes with white numbers on the fuselages flew over very low, barely clearing the huge birch tree in the corner of the yard, and the people heading for Kronprinzenallee took cover behind tree trunks and brick quoins, but the shots—a long series from the cockpit guns—burst farther on, where the thudding seemed to be increasing most, probably out past Espenkrug, though when she looked toward the cathedral, she couldn't see any smoke, just the occasional green flare fired from somewhere near the streetcar loop, barely visible in the sunlight.

So Mrs. Walmann took it all in calmly (though every detonation caused her heart to skip a beat), since she was sure they'd get a "white" pass for the transport ship *Friedrich Bernhoff,* thanks to her brother Otto Erhardt, who'd spent a year working in the Danzig Senate. They had to be in Neufahrwasser by six o'clock at the latest...

"Dr. Hanemann," she said, resting her hand on the door lever, "please hurry. And don't forget your warm coat—you know, the one with the sheepskin collar; believe me, it will come in handy." Hanemann peered up for a moment; a small parcel wrapped up in waxed paper was lying in his open leather bag alongside a bottle of cologne, some bandages, a thick wool turtleneck sweater, and a towel: "You'd better go on downstairs; the children will be getting worried."

Ach, those children! How many times had she told them not to go out in front of the house? But how was she supposed to keep her eye on those two rambunctious girls in their little mouse gray coats, who kept chasing each other up and down the stairs of the entryway and darting out into the garden every few minutes? Then they would come back in, all heated up, puffing tiny white clouds: "Mutti, we're hot." "So stop running around," she'd answer impatiently, "you're supposed to be downstairs in the laundry room, I told you that you could play. Or better yet, sweep out the hall." But they wouldn't hear of that. They kept scurrying over to the iron fence and calling out to the children who were walking alongside carts and strollers piled with bedding—"Gerda, Fritz, you're leaving?"—adding proudly, "We're about to leave, too." Then they ran around the courtyard, throwing snowballs at Mrs. Peltz's drab cat, who had no intention of coming down from the porch roof and merely used his paw to knock the white balls off the snowy incline onto the path.

Eva and Maria laughed, oblivious even to their father's summons. Another plane marked with white numbers flew over their house, practically scraping the top of the giant birch; people passing on the street hugged the wall in funny poses, seeking the shelter of the stone cornices. Eva and Maria interrupted their game behind the arborvitae only for a minute, craning their necks to look at the dark shape disappearing over the rooftops—after all, how long can anyone stay afraid, and besides, the planes hadn't hurt anybody. "Come back inside at once!" their mother shouted, as soon as the clamor of the plane died away, but the girls sensed a strange softness in her voice and, pretending not to hear, stayed hidden in the thorny branches, laughing silently at the joke they had played on Mutti. "Those girls..." Mrs. Walmann shook her head. "Maybe we should lock them inside the other room?" But right away she realized that was a silly idea, since today all doors had to be kept open so that everyone could make it out to the courtyard without delay, just in case something happened. "Mutti, we're so hot in these coats. Can't we take them off?" the girls called from the fence. "Don't you dare! Come back inside!" she answered from the window. She had made them dress in three layers: woolen sweaters, light jackets of pale blue gabardine, and winter over-coats with rabbit-fur collars. "The sea fog is very dangerous, you know," Otto had said, "especially at this time of year, once you lose your body heat...." And so they had wool, gabardine, and that heavy, mouse gray loden.... Footwear was another matter; even the fur-lined shoes they had on now weren't good for long treks, and their yellow leather ankle boots, the ones with the snaps and the thick felt lining, were still at Mr. Bierst the cobbler's. But there was no sense in trying to track them down, not after Bierst and his son had been in that Volkssturm truck on Friedrich-Allee, the one hit by a mortar as it came around the curve—everybody on Lessingstrasse had been talking about it.

The girls went, whispering and giggling, into the hall to hide, and she calmed down a little. She wanted to be by herself: now that the worst had finally come, even Alfred's presence annoyed her. So she just said quietly, "Maybe you could move to the kitchen?" He walked out, carrying an empty suitcase made of cardboard, and carefully closed the door behind him.

She stood in the middle of the room, in front of the mir- rored armoire they had bought at Müller's warehouse on Breit- gasse a few days after their wedding, but when she saw her grayed face in the walnut frame she quickly opened all three doors. Her reflection vanished in a flash.

The left side of the armoire was filled with dark wooden shelves—first a layer of white and pale blue towels, then sheets and pillowcases, followed by shelves crowded with linen, cre- tonne, and cotton blouses, folded into squares and smelling of dry wood and starch. A large red duvet cover, strong and finely woven, with fabric-covered metal buttons, lay spread out on the floor by the window in the corner of the room, waiting for Mrs. Walmann to pick out what was absolutely essential before she tied the four corners together into a bundle. Her heart twinged as she sank her hand into the cool white linens, the crisp flowery chiffons, the soft flannels, the airy cottons, her fingers feeling subtle differences she had never before noticed, for now, as she knelt in front of the lowest shelf, it seemed to her that even with her eyes closed she could discern the softness of the fabric, the coarseness of the weave, the sleekness of the thread, that she could feel which blouse was Eva's and which Maria's, which sheets were from their double bed and which belonged to the girls. Lifting the stiff, starched edges, she slid her hand inside the sheets, up to her wrist, until her fingers uncovered the Walmann family monogram, an uppercase *W* embroidered by Grand- mother Anna, like a track left by a chicken that had stepped in violet ink.

And everything smelled of dry fir, because the armoire, al- though it looked like walnut, wasn't walnut at all but merely had a blond-grained walnut veneer, applied at the Johann Kneipp woodworks in Bromberg (the name of the company could be seen in black letters inside one of the door panels). The gentle fragrance of the wood permeated the sheets, and Mrs. Walmann, fighting to hold back tears, caressed the yielding linen, which was already somewhat worn, and frayed in a few spots along the edges.

But now there was no time to rearrange the pillowcases, to glide her palm along the starched sheets, smoothing out the wrinkles. Now she had to disturb the perfectly level strata, take out the absolutely necessary things, and toss them onto the red cloth spread beneath the window. But her fingers kept running along the edges of the bed covers and blouses, unable to decide, so, in an attempt to stave off the terrible moment just a tiny bit longer, Mrs. Walmann turned to the right side of the armoire, where her dresses and coats were draped on wooden hangers next to her husband's coats and suits. "Only what's absolutely necessary . . ." She realized that was how it had to be, of course. But what would they do if they got to Hamburg and found that Aunt Heidi and Uncle Siegfried's home, where they were supposed to stay on their way to Hannover, was nothing more than a pile of snow-covered rubble? (After all, Hamburg had been bombed as well.) Alfred should wear his long post-office coat with the metal buttons: it was a well-known fact that being in uniform always made things easier. But what about her? She reached for the wine red coat with the ruddy fur collar, the coat they had bought at Hartmann's on Langgasse, even though the one hanging next to it, navy blue with pearl buttons, was a lot warmer—but it looked so much worse. Right away she thought in horror about the tanks already outside Dirschau, and about what the Russians did to women, so she quickly grabbed for the oldest dirty-gray coat she owned, one she had inherited from Grandmother Henriette, a battered, oversize coat of thick wool they had kept on the bottom of the armoire for years—that's right, that would be best, that old worn overcoat with the mended sleeves, so long out of fashion...Elsa Walmann shook her head: "My God, what am I doing? What am I afraid of! After all, by tonight we'll be at sea, far away from Danzig. Otto said Hamburg was only a few days' sail from here."

With a strong yank she pulled Maria's warm flannel shirt out from under the sheets and tossed it on the red ticking.

| *Reeds* |

BY FIVE O'CLOCK they were hurrying across the viaduct near the station at Langfuhr, ducking as they ran, while the shells went screeching through the dark sky, high above the trusses, in the direction of the airfield. Earlier that morning, Axer Bierenstein had told them a Russian battery was already in place in Emmaus or Schidlitz, where it could fire at the western edge of the district. The Walmanns planned to go under the bridge to Schwarzer Weg, then down Marienstrasse to Max-Halbe-Platz, and from there to the tram tracks on Ostseestrasse—but did that still make any sense? The apartment buildings around the marketplace were burning with a bright, nearly smokeless fire, and flaming strips of cloth were soaring over the houses—curtains, perhaps, torn from windows by the wind, or large sheets of paper flying in swirls of sparks. Mrs. Walmann was wearing a fur cap fastened to the back of her hair with a silver pin; her coat was unbuttoned; a rucksack was strapped to her back. She was leading Eva and Maria by the hand, a few steps behind Mr. Walmann, who was carrying the large bundle on his back as he pushed the old iron stroller with the squeaky, rusted axles. Every time the wheels hit an uneven spot on the icy sidewalk, the ocher suitcase tugged at the leather ties and threatened to tip over. Through the railing of the viaduct, off to the right, in the empty space close to the station, they could see the pinkish gleam of the tracks that ran from Danzig to Zoppot; a few twisted rails jutted out of a black crater near the freight dock. Several steps farther down, a truck from the Todt firm was smoldering away on the platform with a dull, emberlike glow.

Hanemann turned around and looked back at the viaduct. The Russians weren't there yet; these were still Germans, overloaded with packages and suitcases, hurrying ahead, tripping over the clumps of snow. The Walmann girls walked on in silence, only muttering a reply each time their mother asked how their feet were holding up in their squeaky shoes, still not broken in. When they again stopped to catch their breath and she adjusted the girls' woolen scarves for the third or fourth time, Maria complained: "But we're so hot!" Nevertheless, once they were well beyond the viaduct, passing among the houses along Magdeburger Strasse, where the fire over Langfuhr disappeared behind the dark, looming hulks of the buildings (still unscathed), and all that remained of the glow was a heavy, moist spiderweb swaying over the rooftops, the girls began to feel afraid, and they pressed against their mother, and only then did Elsa Walmann burst into tears.

She walked on, holding the girls against her, and the tears streamed down her cheeks. At least it was good that Alfred didn't look back, focused as he was on avoiding the piles of snow that were blocking the sidewalk. She saw his bent back, the dark bundle rocking from side to side, fastened to his shoulders with straps taken from an old rucksack that had seen the Great War and the battles on the Somme. The undulating glow was too dull to cast any shadows as it crept along the eastern sky, a pale, sickly pink. Dim figures could be seen moving down the street between the long facades on either side, the houses pitch-black except for the occasional kerosene lantern glowing in a tiny basement window. Overloaded with knapsacks, hauling sleds freighted with packages and wrapped with wire and string, they trudged on in silence beneath the pulsing sky, making their way toward Brösen and Neufahrwasser, where the transport ships were supposed to be waiting by the breakwater. But as soon as they reached the avenue, where the streetcar tracks ran straight to the sea, they saw a brilliant column of fire shooting into the sky, and halted in the trodden snow. Hanemann went up to Mr. Walmann: "The grain elevators?" Mr. Walmann shook his head; he knew the area well, since his brother lived close to the water tower. Then he adjusted his shoulder straps and muttered: "Probably the warehouses in Neufahrwasser." This was far worse than if it had been the grain elevators, since it meant the mouth of the channel was on fire and the gunners in the Müggau heights would be able to see the western half of the port as clear as day; now it was only a matter of time before they managed to move the guns off the sidings near Weichselmünde and the Island of Holm to the eastern edge of Brösen, then the woods, and finally to Westerplatte.

But neither of the men said that out loud, because what more was there to say? They had no choice but to head for the port as fast as they could, and even if their worst fears were realized, there would still be nothing more to say, especially since the girls had shaken off their earlier terror as soon as they'd caught sight of the fire far away over Neufahrwasser, as if they found the bright pillar of light holding up the sky with its amber glow much less threatening than the black streets near the viaduct, walled off in darkness by the looming buildings with their lightless windows.

So they went on, paying more attention to their footing on the icy pavement than to the ominous glare above the port, joining the long line of fellow wanderers in the middle of the avenue, the black figures toiling on toward Brösen, stepping carefully in the slippery snow, supporting themselves with canes, umbrellas, bamboo ski poles, pieces of lath hastily cut for the road, while the shells flew high overhead, puncturing the darkness with their monotonous whistle, on their way to the snow-covered airfield bordered on the north by the Glettkau woods. A massive cloud of smoke hung over the plain between Langfuhr and Oliva, lit from below by distant fires, as if all of Gotenhafen, and not just the eastern edge of Zoppot, were ablaze.

Beyond the crossing, not far from the water pumps, Mr. Walmann managed to flag down a truck, from the Hinz & Weber firm at Hochstriess, on its way toward the waterfront. Hanemann stood behind the cab of the large Merzbach and peered through a slit in the flapping canvas, watching the fire that was pulsing over the port get closer and closer, while Mrs. Walmann sat huddled in the corner of the cargo bay, caressing Marie's hair, and her husband, barely visible in the dark, held Eva in a tight embrace. The old Merzbach skidded over the frozen ruts, so that the passengers had to hold on to the iron bows recoiling under the cloth cover. A sudden turn brought them onto a street alive with flashes of bright light that sent shadows of leafless trees dancing up and down the pavement, while flames soared skyward through an exploding roof off to their right.

The wild, disconcerting flashes made it impossible for Hanemann to see where they were. They passed a long, neo-Gothic building set behind the trees, its windowpanes flickering red with reflected fire, and around the corner they saw the motionless hulk of a burned-out tank, its turret hatch torn open. Their driver braked sharply, steering clear of the wooden crates that littered the street; brass cartridge-cases went clinking under the wheels of the truck. The crowd parted before them, but when they reached the open iron gate, they got stuck among the bundles, suitcases, and tin boxes strewn about the street. The entire yard was packed with people loaded down with bags and bundles. Here and there a bayonet flashing on the end of the rifle marked a member of the Gendarmerie; an officer wearing a long overcoat and a tin gorget was stationed at the entrance. Their driver waved a "yellow" pass, but even the official stamp and signature proved ineffective, so thick was the crowd milling about the yard between the brick-wall enclosure and the warehouse with the vaulted roof, where earlier bombs had left holes of starry darkness in the milk-colored panes.

Actually, Hanemann had expected much worse—panic, children bawling, women shouting—but for the moment the crowd, as he peered at them through the slit in the canvas, was quiet and still. And somewhere, farther off, had to be the water, although the *Bernhoff* was nowhere to be seen.

The driver leaned out of the cab: "I have to back up!" The two men jumped into the snow to help Mrs. Walmann as she handed down the girls, who were more terrified of the crowd than of the surging fire and the sparks skipping across the broken roof on the other side of the street. As soon as they felt the prickly, nauseating stench of burning petrol mixed with soot, the girls stopped their noses with their fingers, still in their woolen gloves. "Hold on to me," Mrs. Walmann shouted, "so we don't lose each other!" So they stuck to her as closely as they could, clinging to her coat. "Alfred, find out how long we'll have to wait here." Mr. Walmann headed for the gate, but Hanemann held him back: "Why don't you stay here." He made his way through the shivering crowd to the gendarme with the tin gorget, but all he found out was that the evacuees were being conveyed aboard the transport ship on tugboats, since the *Bernhoff* couldn't possibly venture into port as things were. "But that will take hours!" Hanemann couldn't help muttering. The officer didn't even look at him. "What do you want? Listen, if the *Bernhoff* were to sail up here to the channel..." So they might be stuck there for hours? Mrs. Walmann was frightened. At least the girls were warmly dressed, but the idea of their having to stand in the cold for hours on end, their little shoes flocked with trampled snow...

All they could do was find a place on the loading dock by the warehouse, close to the building, where the tin roof overhang kept the concrete free of snow. They nestled in among the people wrapped in blankets and furs, where the girls could sit on the suitcase and lean against the bundle. But when Eva and Maria heard the woman next to them whispering prayers, and when they saw her, shrouded in her reddish fur, staring wide-eyed at the fire across the street, they felt so spooked that they huddled close together, like two little sparrows shivering with cold. And only then, as they sat in the frosty air that pinched their cheeks and puffed out of their mouths in tiny white clouds, did they begin to be truly afraid. Mrs. Walmann put her arm around them, but what could she do? Mr. Walmann stroked his wife's back, and even though no one was hungry yet, he reached into his pocket and pulled out two slices of bread wrapped in yellow waxed paper. When the girls started chewing the slightly bitter, grainy dough, they slowly regained their good humor. Mrs. Walmann patted her husband on the hand for having thought of that.

Meanwhile Hanemann pushed past the people sitting against the wall and made his way to the end of the loading dock, stepping over cardboard suitcases, rucksacks, packs of bedding wrapped in paper, crates with makeshift metal handles. From there he could make out the black line of the channel's other bank. He looked into the darkness beyond the breakwater, straining to see if anything was moving, when suddenly the air shook, and the roar of exploding shrapnel merged with the screech of shattering windowpanes. The crowd rocked back and forth on the square, apparently more terrified by the screams of a wounded woman than by the long series of explosions thundering over the channel. A rain of bomb shards pelted the water and pinged against the glass roof of the warehouse. The girls cried in terror at the sight of the dark smudge trailing the legs of the woman being dragged by her mother, who was calling for help. Mrs. Walmann took them in her arms, their father shielded them with the bundle, but they went on screaming, huddling against their mother's coat, deafened by the din, the shriek of flying iron, the tearing rattle of tin being ripped by shrapnel. One after another, the shells flashed over the harbormaster's tower.

They were still overshooting, not quite hitting their mark. The observers in the Müggau heights looked through their scopes at the line of tiny flashes going off between the numbers 5 and 10, blossoming silently over the warehouses and crane trusses at Neufahrwasser (the echoes of the explosions took a few moments to reach the gunners), and then a new order was given, the sights were moved one or two millimeters to the left, the gun crew reloaded the howitzers emplaced on the Zigankenberg, and the next missiles went flying straight into the roofs on the right side of the blaze.

The people between the brick wall and the loading dock crawled under small tin carts, took shelter beneath the iron gantry, scrambled for the gate, trampling anyone lying in their way, and with each new explosion, another painful cry pierced the din, and a body was dragged away, leaving a long black trail in the snow. The middle of the yard was deserted; right next to the tracks was a ripped-open suitcase, its muslin nightshirts now in ribbons that rose and fell with every blast. The exploding fragments raked the yard, kicking up clods of snow. Then, suddenly, all was silent.

A man behind one of the gantry columns choked on his sobs as he gripped his leg, which was wrenched into an odd position; a woman's voice called out cautiously: "Günter! Günter! Where are you? Come here, I can't stand it anymore, get me out of here..." But the black figures stayed hunched over the snow, no one believed it was over, though the gunners on the Zigankenberg seemed to have stopped for a moment, perhaps to adjust their sights from Target 102 to Target 104 in Neu Schottland, which had already been shelled. The hush over the square seemed amplified by the fire that was roaring in all the windows of the neo-Gothic buildings along the street. Then the fragile silence was broken—whispers, calls, a woman's voice. "Dr. Hanemann, are you all right?" The reply came from the edge of the loading dock: "Everything's fine, Mrs. Walmann"—and she sighed with relief, her girls still huddled beneath the pile of clothing. "You better come back where we are, don't stay so far over." Her words had a rebuking warmth that brooked no contradiction, so that Hanemann couldn't help smiling as he brushed the snow off his clothes and started picking his way back through the discarded suitcases and crates strewn about the deserted dock, but before he reached the Walmanns he saw something move in the darkness over the water, out there on the left, past the floating crane. Something darker than the sky was looming near the channel, a shape was advancing toward the breakwater light, and Hanemann realized it was one of the tug-boats returning from the *Bernhoff.*

So he jumped down from the loading dock and called out in the direction of the iron doors, "Mrs. Walmann, hurry!" And Mrs. Walmann, hearing the change in his voice, understood at once that there wasn't a moment to lose, that she had to prod her husband to lug the suitcase and bundle while she dragged her terrified girls to the edge of the water, because she wasn't the only one who had heard the urgency in Hanemann's voice, that presage of hope that reverberated between the warehouse and the brick wall enclosing the yard. Others heard it as well, and the black figures left the shelter of the iron columns, crawled out from beneath the carts, dashed from behind the ce-ment platforms, and began racing toward the bank. But Mrs. Walmann was quicker; she and her girls had already reached the landing and were climbing the steps, holding on to the wooden post so they wouldn't be knocked into the water, and Mr. Wal-mann joined them, tossing his bundle over the railing and slip-ping under the beam onto planks that smelled of trampled snow, tar, and lengths of wet line.

It wasn't long before the others reached the landing, but the officer with the gorget raised his pistol and fired a few rounds into the air, and the crowd stepped back. "Get your things!" Mrs. Walmann called out from the landing, when she realized that in her rush she had forgotten Hanemann's leather bag. "You can still make it!" So Hanemann, driven by the warm power of that voice, automatically made for the stairs at the front of the load-ing dock.

He hadn't reached the second step when a flash went off to his left, above the tall crane. A loud blast tore the air; the ex-ploding shell sowed iron shards across the black water by the mooring. Bits of metal clanged against the tin roof of the warehouse and the overhang along the loading dock. A hail of glass splinters. Hanemann ducked as he jumped to the wall. The tugboat was already at the landing. A cistern had caught fire across the channel; the purplish blaze sparkled in the water like quicksilver. Hanemann could feel the warmth on his face, could smell the petrol. Outside it was bright as day—even the waterfront behind the warehouse was lit by the flames from the opposite bank. Hanemann squinted. Rails? A switch? Reeds? Scaffolding? On the bank overgrown with reeds he made out the wreck of a small ship, propped on a wooden scaffold. The brightness across the water rose in the sky; the cattails around the hull glowed a fiery red...

In the light of the flames, Hanemann examined the rusted side, his eyes settling on the faded letters that spelled the name *Star*. He felt a twinge in his heart—nothing big, only the light prick of an icy needle, but that tiny cold touch unleashed a wave of heat that stifled his heart. Mrs. Walmann called out from the landing: "Dr. Hanemann, what are you doing, for God's sake, hurry!" He picked up his leather bag but walked slowly, one step at a time, still feeling that light touch of cold and the painful, scalding wave. The crowd on the landing, the tugboat's stack churning clouds of smoke lit by the glow, the screams, the shouts, the wailing... thirty steps to go, twenty... "Dr. Hanemann, faster!" cried Mrs. Walmann. "For God's sake, hurry. We're about to cast off!" And just as Hanemann reached the landing, again, off to the left, this time very close, over the roof of the warehouse, a flash...

When he opened his eyes he saw a hand right in front of his face, covered with snow, stiff, and strangely twisted. His head was spinning, so he rolled over onto his back and stared up through half-closed eyes at the sky, deep and black and full of tattered clouds moving now to the west, now to the east. Fighting off the pain, he slowly raised himself on his elbow and looked in the direction of the mooring. But the landing was deserted, and there was no sign of the tugboat. A breeze wrinkled the water in the channel. The black gantry, the iron rails, an overturned cart. Far off, on the other side of the channel, the cistern that had been hit was still burning. Spraylike signal flares drifted slowly over the cranes, lighting the way for the paratroopers. Flickers. Soundless, red. A zigzag shadow on the snow. The constant noise of fire. Distant shots. From where? Müggau? Or was that an echo? The wind chased a child's rabbit-fur cap across the snow.

The next tugboat pulled up to the bank, the crowd crawled out of its hiding place under the gantry and pushed its way onto the landing, but Hanemann stayed on the loading dock, leaning against the warehouse wall and watching everything as if through a milk-glass windowpane. He didn't even sense the cold slowly closing in around his back, because he still felt that needle in his heart, that strange mixture of sharp heat waves and icy shivers, swelling and ebbing away.

And that was how Lieutenant Remetz from the Hochstriess barracks found him at around ten o'clock—huddled against the wall. Remetz had taken his official Benz to drive his wife and daughter to the pier, where they were to be taken aboard the *Bernhoff* on the little motorboat that belonged to the harbor guard: they had "white" passes signed by Colonel Voss himself. And even though the lieutenant insisted that he join them, Hanemann declined.

As his body stiffened into a warm numbness, the pain began to dissipate. Hanemann remembered his leather bag, but there was nothing left but singed yellow tatters. The whole area was covered with unraveled bundles, packages, cases, scattered heaps of clothing, charred sheets of paper wet from the snow.

At eleven o'clock, a black car with military plates took him to Lessingstrasse 17. Lieutenant Remetz surmised that they were going back for something valuable Hanemann had left behind and that Hanemann would try to make one of the transport ships the following day. As they drove up to the gate, the houses on both sides of the street were completely dark. Only the clouds drifting over Langfuhr were glowing brighter than the sky. The center of town was burning, and probably the area around the train station.

Remetz promised to come by the next morning, no later than eight, but the black car with the plates from the Hochstriess barracks never again stopped in front of Lessingstrasse 17.

| *Brittle* |

WHEN HANEMANN reached the gate in front of his house, he thought he saw a light flickering at Lessingstrasse 14, the house owned by the Bierensteins. He walked past the arborvitae and turned and crossed the street.

He pushed open the heavy doors and stepped into the entrance hall, automatically scraping the snow off his feet on the iron grate. He struck a match and held it up until it singed his fingers. The little yellow flame wavered in the chilly darkness and went out. Hanemann wondered why he had come, if he was merely trying to assuage his heart—but what difference did it make now?

Still, he had seen that light...

He wanted to go back to Number 17, through the double row of arborvitae to his own door, and he would have done so if he could have stopped thinking about the landing in Neufahrwasser, that white space between the warehouse and the brick wall around the yard. The scraps of paper, the black smudges in the snow, the landing, the suitcases, the crowd, the piles of clothing, the shouts, the gentle voice of Mrs. Walmann. That was what kept him from leaving, what stopped him there, on the stairs, in the dark entry hall under the oval window, where the colored panes muted the glare over Langfuhr into a feeble glow. Here, on the right—the Schultzes' apartment.

He dragged another damp match across the edge of the box, there was a sulfurous flash, and he held the match high against the brown paneling, his palm cupped pink around the tiny flame. The darkly varnished door, with the floral ornamentation on its oak frame, glinted and glistened in the flickering light. Above it, a stucco relief emerged from the shadows that slanted across the wall—a Madonna and Child, nestled within a wreath of olive branches.

But what he saw next... deep gashes and gouges on the Schultzes' door, right along the jamb. Flashing bits of broken metal around the latch housing. Fresh yellow scratches, black dents and bruises, as if someone had tried to pierce the brass with a knife. So they're already here, they've already been here; while he waited by the waterfront at Neufahrwasser, they had been breaking into an apartment on Lessingstrasse, cursing under their breath as they grappled with the brass reinforcement, as they pried at the metal escutcheon beneath the latch before finally ramming the door with their shoulders and bursting inside, struggling to keep their balance on the slick linoleum with the white and yellow checkerboard pattern. He wanted to go back home, to avoid the sight of the ransacked wardrobes, the huge heaps of linens dragged off the shelves, the drawers ripped out of the chest and tossed into the middle of the room, the rug trampled by muddy boots and stained with clods of melting snow.

But the thought of the Schultzes... They had left at noon; he'd watched them turning onto Kronprinzenallee, just beyond the chestnut trees. Günter with a little rucksack. A stroller. A wooden suitcase. Mrs. Schultz's red hat. She had turned around. A brief glance at the building.... Hanemann grabbed the handle; the door yielded softly to his hand. Dark-red door drapes in the entry room. Tea-colored wallpaper. Shadows. The match went out, he groped his way toward the kitchen, something crunched beneath his soles. When he could see the window—its rectangle glowing dimly in the dark, the thin cross of its frame—he again reached for a match.

The yellow flame faltered, brushed by a little fog of breath; the shadows jittered as they rose from the devastation, crawling out of the broken furniture; and a moment later, when the little tongue of fire climbed higher, he was able to see the Schultzes' kitchen. He'd never been inside, but he knew it well; after all, how many times had he walked across the garden and glanced through the window on the ground floor at Lessingstrasse 14, and seen the white interior and Rosa Schultz standing there, silently saying something to her husband or yelling at Günter, a boy with a sunny face who looked at her obediently, though he was probably thinking the whole time about how he could get out of the kitchen without hurting his mother's feelings and go to his room, where he had a cardboard cutout of a Heinckel 111 suspended by threads from the ceiling—something Hanemann had also seen once or twice before. Now Hanemann stood in the door of the kitchen, staring at the table, the Schultzes' rectangular kitchen table with its greenish brown oilcloth—the wood all hacked and slashed, the rubber-coated cover in ribbons that dangled to the floor, a floor littered with the white shards of cups and saucers, dinner plates, salad dishes, serving platters...

Like a sea of crushed ice.

And whereas a moment ago he had felt disgust and hatred for the people who had forced open the door, dragged the linens out of the armoire, trampled the bedding, ripped the upholstery in their search for hidden gold, he was now confronted with a worse, more painful sensation. Earlier words and gestures he had either overlooked or simply preferred to ignore suddenly resurfaced and began to fuse into a repulsive whole. No, it couldn't be . . .

Because why would the Russians, who were searching the abandoned houses for gold, for silver spoons, for rings, crosses, bracelets, brooches, necklaces, sugar bowls, coins, typewriters, sewing machines, adding machines, fountain pens—why would they shatter the mirror in its oak frame, why would they shred the drapes with the light-colored tassels, slash the tea-colored wallpaper with a knife? He lit a candle he found on the windowsill. Everywhere he looked—the kitchen, the entry room, the main room—it was the same: torn curtains, tabletops gouged by some sharp instrument, broken crystal panes in the china cabinet, shredded quilts, slit pillows, slashed bedding, trampled towels, sheets doused with kerosene, vases overturned, curtains ripped to shreds. It didn't make any sense. Was it possible that the people who had broken in had taken revenge for not having found any gold? That they took the china out of the cabinet and smashed it on the floor in retribution? But what about the bathtub? The washbasin? The shattered tiles above the kitchen sink? The broken chandelier? Such fury required fierce effort and patient rage . . . So why would they do it?

Hanemann picked up the torn drapes and went into the main room. Something clattered beneath his feet; he lowered the candle, and saw, gleaming on the ruined carpet, Erich Schultz's bayonet, his bayonet from the Great War, the parade bayonet with the eagle-head pommel, but the long, serrated blade lay broken in two beside the hilt. Hanemann picked it up. So it wasn't them after all. It wasn't the people looking for porcelain, silver, silver-plated dinnerware. It was Erich Schultz himself, smashing the china with his own hand, his own heels stomping on the brittle glass...

Hanemann stood in the door, surveying the scarred furniture, the scored wallpaper, examining the wounds to read what had happened just hours before: how Erich Schultz had taken his bayonet and flailed away at the rows of glasses lined up on the cabinet shelf, how he opened the cupboard under the window and hurled the dinner plates and salad dishes to the floor, crushing the delicate faience with his heel. But that wasn't enough, not for him, so he knocked over the chairs and ran the blade through the plush upholstery...The screech of tearing damask, the squeal of springs, the ripping fabric. Rosa Schultz had grabbed his hand: "No, don't do it! We're coming back!" But he just shook her off and struck at the chest with slanting blows, crushing the carved mahogany frame on the glassed cabinet, smashing the crystal pieces that adorned the shelves, snapping the miniature columns of the dresser. Mrs. Schultz had stood in the doorway, hugging Günter, watching with terrified eyes, following the flashing bayonet, but her husband was blind to her tears; he stepped into the entry room and calmly and deliberately began to bash the metal pommel against the mirror until it burst into starry lines. Then he tore down the curtain and opened the door to the bathroom. Mrs. Schultz tried to pull him away, but he whispered sharply, "They're not getting anything, you understand? You think I could live in the same house once those eastern pigs had stayed here? You're not going to bathe in the same tub where some swine of a Polack has just bathed along with his louse-ridden wife. You'll see"—he lowered his voice—"the whole place will be covered with lice. You're not eating off the same plate where they've had their filthy muzzles. We're not leaving them anything, you understand, not a thing!"

And he stomped on the white linen shirts that were strewn around the linen cabinet, as if he wanted to stamp out the invisible bugs that were already—he could see them—swarming in the hems of his cuffs and collars.

Hanemann waded through the broken glass, moving from room to room, checking the bathroom, the porch, and he could hear that sharp whisper and the cracking glass, could see the white enamel chipping under the heavy blade, until finally the metal clanged flat against the edge of the bathtub and broke in two, and Hanemann—sick with disgust—turned around, went outside, and, avoiding the arborvitae, returned to Lessingstrasse 17. A fresh white snow dusted his footprints on the path.

A draft blew through the Schultzes' apartment, catching the down from the shredded pillows. Swirling feathers. A hushed sprinkle of snow drifted in through the broken windowpane. Frost. Bright squares shone on the walls of Günter's room where the photos had been removed. The ashes of the burned pictures stirred inside the kitchen stove. The torn curtain swayed, like aquatic plants on the bottom of a river. The crystal glass of the chandelier rang in the darkness. And in the shattered mirror, the light over Langfuhr faded and surged...

| *Stella* |

THAT SAME DAY, underneath the windows, just past the arborvitae, a step away from the iron picket fence...Hanemann had been there, Heinrich Mertenbach was sure of it, he'd been there the whole time, in the apartment on the second floor, no doubt about it...

They'd left Langfuhr at dawn, the sun a low ember over the air hangars. A blackened streetcar lay stretched across Kronprinzenallee like a charred fox cage, and everything was completely quiet as they walked along the tracks. The din over Danzig had faded during the night, as if by the end of the day both sides had had enough of loading, aiming, firing, cleaning barrels, and oiling bolts, had put down their weapons, and were waiting for the sun to light the smoking plain. They'd left Langfuhr—Heinrich Mertenbach, August Walberg, and Stella Lipschütz—and were following the tracks, tripping over the ties, stumbling from rail to rail, falling into the snow and staggering back on their feet. All were wearing Todt uniforms stained with oil and kerosene, with no packs or gear except for gas-mask bags, which instead of masks contained ethyl alcohol from the shelves in Dr. Darnhoff's office on Brösener Weg 12. Heinrich and August had rescued the thick glass bottles at the last minute, when the fire was already up to the window and they had to make a run for it. They fled down Magdeburger Strasse, crossing the viaduct over the freight siding at Langfuhr, then straight along Adolf-Hitler-Strasse, which was empty because everyone who wanted to get out of town had left during the night, so that by then they were the only ones trying to escape, and it wasn't until they reached the curve of Friedrich-Allee that they were joined by Stella, a tall girl with copper hair stuffed under a black forage cap.

It occurred to them that if the planes started up again, the airport would be the primary target, so they decided to backtrack to the viaduct, take Kronprinzenallee, sticking to the residential neighborhoods between Pelonker Strasse and the streetcar line to Glettkau. This was more a matter of instinct than of reason, because everything was spinning before their eyes, the buildings on Kronprinzenallee were floating on a soft snowy wave, sinking and surfacing like the cliffs in the foamy waters of the Rhine. When they passed the burned-out streetcar, August let go of a bottle, which shattered on the iced-over rail, a pink trace of moisture seeping into the snow. They locked arms, Stella in the middle, barely alive, her coat too big, unbuttoned, dragging in the snow. August said something about the boys from the Volkssturm who'd been hanged yesterday at Johannisberg Strasse, but the others just burst out laughing. Stella tried to stop his mouth with snow, and he pushed her away, angry with himself for not being able to hide his fear. He shouted up at the air, waving his fists and taunting, but no plane appeared. The sky over Langfuhr was empty.

They reached the first houses—wooden villas with Chinese-style roofs draped with a thick layer of snow—and were amazed to find buildings there, in the middle of the city, that had survived without a scratch; even the dove white layer blanketing the street was unmarred. They trudged on without a sound, oblivious to the cold that was sticking to their shoes. August said something about his mother, who had stayed in Königsberg, swore that he'd reach her in time, but what time would that be? "High time!" said Heinrich, in a fit of laughter.

They knew that if they followed the tram tracks they'd eventually make it to Glettkau, and if the pier by the hotel hadn't been hit, they might be able to get on one of the small Westermann boats—the *Ariel,* the *Merlin,* or the *Mercury*—which as of the day before were still taking people to the steamship anchored in the middle of the bay. Just stay calm, keep an even step, stick to the tram tracks, but they pitched into another snowy swell that lifted the villas overgrown with ivy on the left side of Kronprinzenallee, the sparkling powder came sprinkling onto their faces from the maple branches, and Heinrich stopped in his tracks, puzzled that the villas with the split-level roofs, the glassed porches, and the rounded mansards had suddenly turned into a long iron picket fence studded with wavy flame finials. Not until much later did he realize that it was Lessingstrasse, beautiful Lessingstrasse, immersed in silence that was unbroken but for the occasional, unhurried pecking of the machine guns guarding Müggau or Kokoschken, rattling away far beyond the morainal hills.

Lessingstrasse? But they'd been following the tracks... Heinrich adjusted his cap. The sight of the untrammeled white made everything in him go quiet, as they walked down the empty street, stepping without a sound, and the street gave way beneath their feet, softly, like the down duvet on his parents' huge bed, the one he used to jump on as a child—much to his mother's dismay—from the tall chest, sinking into the bedding with a moan of springs before being tossed back up into the air. The street had a similar warm bounce; its white swells crested under their feet, lifting the arborvitae, the junipers, the black spruce trees, setting afloat the redbrick villas, the gates, the metal turrets, and the tall iron picket fence. Shadows, frost, fire, his mother's distant cry, the flames dying out, the ice glistening in the gutter...Just the day before yesterday, the Mertenbachs' home on Breitgasse had been suddenly flooded with a bright, nearly white blaze, when the jars of ethanol his father kept in the basement caught fire and exploded with a loud hiss, shooting a tight cluster of sparks through the barred window and onto the street. Now, in the silence that was unbroken except for the distant rattling, all that remained of the fire on Breitgasse was a faint dark afterimage stuck under his eyelids. Now, two days later, it all seemed to Heinrich like one of those phantasmagoric scenes from the old book about the Great War, where the names Elsass and Lothringen rose out of the rubble of Gothic characters. So now their home on Breitgasse just didn't exist? Everything burned to rubble? The pillow embroidered with Sophie's monogram, Mother's secretary desk, the rush-bottomed chairs, Father's patent-leather shoes, the pen case with the eagle engraving, the agate inkwell, the violin, the armchairs from Thorn, the rugs, drapes, mahogany chest, bamboo étagère, white and pink towels, the lamp with the green shade, the leather-bound volume of Grimm's Fairy Tales, the Arabian sewing box, the poplin coat, the leather ball, the tennis racket marked "Astra"...Heinrich's eyes filled with tears, he rested his head on Stella's shoulder, and they walked like that, down Goethestrasse, half dozing, half laughing, wrapped in each other's arms, the gas-mask bags banging against their hips, as the street dipped and swelled beneath their feet. Behind them, in the east, the pale yellow sun rose in a haze over the hangars, the huge cloud of smoke dissipated in the white sky over Danzig, and August, whose bag was already empty, propped up the other two, now from the right, now from the left, afraid that if they crashed into one of the white drifts along the iron fence, they would fall in the snow and sleep forever and his mother would never see him in Königsberg.

But their legs wouldn't land where they wanted, and suddenly, as if felled by some sleep-inducing breeze, all three crashed into a bright fluffy drift, right below some pickets with flame-shaped finials, and only then did Heinrich realize, through a fog, that Stella was with them, the same Stella who'd passed him so many times on Magdeburger Strasse, on her way back from school, the same Stella who was now laughing out of control, cheeks flushed, eyes half-shut because the snow was crusting her eyebrows, Stella who was lying on her back scooping up the cold powder, which was so dry that it didn't feel cold at all. She pelted them with crumbly snowballs; they turned away and grabbed her hands in self-defense, but she, still convulsing with laughter, just tossed her head from one side to the other, shaking off a powdery white cloud, not entirely aware who these two were, these two disheveled boys squeezing her wrists so hard she couldn't move, though it wasn't painful at all—she was simply feeling lazier and lazier...Another wave of pinkish light rolled over August, the street seemed to tilt back and forth, he tried to catch his balance, but his head plunged to the ground. In evil merriment he started stuffing snow inside Stella's unbuttoned coat; she elbowed him in the chest so hard he staggered, then grabbed his hair and pulled until he felt burning needles in his temples and cried out like a child. He raised his hand to hit her back, but it was strangely heavy; drowsiness surged into his eyes, veiling everything, then he bent forward, softly, like a flower being cut, all his joints seemed to melt, and leaned over her so that his hair touched her breasts. Her first instinct was to push him away, and she crooked her knee to hit his face, but suddenly she was overcome by a hollow, bubbly laughter, and borrowing a gesture from her mother, she garnered August's head to her breast and purred, her eyes flashing with irony, "There, there..." She stroked his wet, caked hair, spreading her fingers in disgust even as she held him to her with condescending tenderness, and he snuggled his cheek against her breast, not realizing where the warmth was coming from, the mixed smell of wet wool and kerosene, the moist, bristly heat. Then he climbed higher, his lips level with hers, and she pulled her head back, but that tiny, less than resolute gesture only egged him on: he was hurt by her rejection and angry with himself, and as he struggled with the pinkish fog that was once again clouding his eyes, he hugged her hard, dragging his lips across her warm neck. She shuddered at the moist touch and laughed, banging her forehead against his cheek. They thrashed about violently, the snow stuck to her hair, and the cold stung his eyelids, giving him a start. Quickly, like a bird, he reached inside her tunic and felt for her stiff bra, and suddenly she pressed her lips to him with all her might, blindly seeking his...

Heinrich lay next to them, his cheek buried in the snow. He could feel them with his hips as they moved away, as they sank into sleep. By the time he opened his eyes, the sky was bright, the tops of the arborvitae crackled with little drops of ice, and he could see the dark spruce, the iron pickets with finials like undulating flames, the wall of the house behind the fence, the glistening red bricks, the window on the second floor, and through the window, behind the glass...

"It was Hanemann, I'm sure it was Hanemann," Heinrich Mertenbach told me years later in a small gallery in Worpswede, as we talked about the city that no longer existed. "It couldn't have been anyone else, I'm sure it was him, I'm absolutely positive, because I'd seen him a few times at my father's office. Besides, people had talked so much about that horrible thing that happened. I'm convinced it was him, even though the windowpane was dark enough to reflect the arborvitae in front of the house, so I couldn't make out the face ... I was lying in the snow, I could feel the others with my hip, could hear their rapid breathing, and there, above, behind the window ..."

But if the features were blurry, the expression was not: Heinrich Mertenbach had never seen a face that showed such pain. Back then, however, as he lay in the snow, next to Stella and August tangled in their coats, when he came to and rolled over on his back, with the idea of sinking even deeper into the downy cold, the glimpse of that face set something off in him, triggering a wild fit of laughter, hostile and aggressive. Engulfed in the pinkish fog, he failed to put two and two together, and it wasn't until much, much later that he realized ...

That Stella—the same Stella who was fleeing with them from Langfuhr to Glettkau, the girl with the oversize coat from Todt (he could still remember the smell of wet wool stained with kerosene) and the copper hair that lay spread out on the snow right next to his cheek—that Stella was Louisa Berger's sister.

Afterward, when they began to feel the cold, they crawled out of the snow. Coated with the frost, they moved along the iron fence that bordered the gardens on Lessingstrasse, grabbing on to the icy pickets for support, trudging ahead, their feet feeling the ground beneath the powdery snow, passing through the drifts blown high against the buildings, until they finally reached the poles with the white insulators and felt the tracks. Hadn't Heinrich kept telling them the streetcar line would take them all the way to Glettkau? August tripped over the ties and gave a triumphal shout, and Stella buttoned up his coat, whispering, "Come here, my little boy, you can't catch cold now, don't make your mama mad..." But the thought of his mother waiting in Königsberg was too much, and he shoved her away. So they walked along the ties, their shoes plowing through the powdery snow, past the streetcar loop at the bend in the avenue. When they reached the park, they saw trucks with scorched covers rolling down the wet black pavement of Adolf-Hitler-Strasse, the flapping canvas marked with large letters spelling "Drogen" and "Chemikalien," or with advertisements for the Wernitz furniture store in Bromberg. The cabs were packed full of unarmed soldiers and women wrapped in woolen shawls, their faces dirty with soot, flushed and sleepy. Stella stood on the curb, waving her cap, but it took half an hour before a huge Merzbach with a smoking stack stopped beside the walls of Lazarus Hospital.

With some difficulty they clambered into the truck bed. A few others like themselves were already stretched out on the boards, in outsize coats and tattered Volkssturm jackets, their heads swathed in bandages and dirty scarves, lying still. Stella's red hair fell over her shoulders, she gave a vulgar, sassy laugh— pretty white teeth, cracked lips—before collapsing onto the floor. She swigged away at the gas-mask bag, the pinkish liquid burbling inside the glass, dribbling down her chin, until they took it away from her. The truck passed under the viaduct near the station, rattling the pockmarked platform, then turned onto Seestrasse and, after passing the millponds, pulled up to the hotel in Glettkau.

They jumped out onto the packed snow. Small groups of people with suitcases and rucksacks were heading through the dunes toward the pier. A fog hung over the sea, white and turbid, like vapors in a bathhouse. They went down to the beach, walking on the wet sand mixed with trampled snow. A horse with a torn bridle lay dead in the buckthorn; they passed piles of crates, empty overturned strollers, torn pillows and duvets leaking eiderdown, the body of an older woman wearing a nutria coat, wedged under the burned wreck of a Daimler-Benz. Again they felt the pinkish wave surging inside them; they locked their arms and walked across the beach, the sea tilted in front of them from west to east and from east to west like the deck of a ship; they felt the creosote-treated planking under their feet, heard the clatter of their iron heel plates, saw the landing littered with suitcases spilling their contents in the wind—silk blouses, stockings, nightshirts. August laughed out loud: "Königsberg!" Because on the western side of the landing, over the heads of the people jammed against the railing, he spotted a tugboat puffing away, with a great red *W* on its stack. "Here, for Königsberg!" he shouted, craning his neck. Beyond the tugboat moored to the landing, he saw a long, flat-bottomed grain barge, its open bays filling fast, as the people on the pier waited their turn to board. "Königsberg! I'm for Königsberg!" August shouted. Now all they needed to do was push their way to the end of the pier, but the pink wave tilted the sodden sky above them, and the planks sank and rose with a gentle quiver at every step. As they moved into the crowd by the gangway, a voice called up from the boat below: "Here I am, Rudolf, down here!" Somebody's child screamed, the wind scattered the clouds of black smoke from the slanted stack, just five or six more steps to the gate and Stella collapsed on the icy boards. She rose with difficulty and started running back toward the beach, but August and Heinrich caught up with her right away, even though the sky was listing once again, this time in the direction of Brösen. They took her under her arms and led her back to the boat, screaming and flailing, as if to fend off the nonexistent blows. A gendarme pushed back the crowd; Stella dug in her heels, they shoved her to the edge of the pier: "Jump! What are you waiting for? Go on, jump!" But she held on to the balustrade so tightly they couldn't tear her off—it was as if she were frozen onto the whitewashed railing. Her lips were quivering. But it wasn't the barge she was looking at, or the people lugging their bundles over the gangplank; her eyes were fixed farther out, at the two pilings jutting out of the water a few meters off the pier, the two huge copper-plated posts, where even large ships could tie up, she stood there staring at the pilings and the blackish green depth, clinging to the railing so hard they couldn't pull her off, until Heinrich slapped her in the face. Then she spread her fingers, they pushed her off the pier, and she fell into the cargo bay into a pile of straw that was used for bedding. They jumped in after her...

Two planes came flying slowly from Brösen, and a few bombs fell on the beach by the hotel—a flash, dark craters in the snow, motionless bodies at the entrance to the pier, fire, a burning car, scattered eiderdown. But the barge full of people was already casting off: the children started to cry, the wet line connecting the barge to the tugboat snapped taut, the fumes from the slanted smokestack drifted back into the cargo bays... They sailed north, listening to the explosions grow ever fainter. Stella fell asleep with her head tucked under her arm; they covered her with a frayed duvet and a few army blankets. The sea was smooth and deserted, though little could be seen in the grainy clouds of white. The distant rumble faded. Fog. They dozed off, leaning against wooden crates marked "Hinz & Weber." Next to them, a man in a postal uniform with his head wrapped in a knit woolen scarf was praying silently. It wasn't until around one in the morning that they spotted a shadow in the fog, some two or three hundred meters off to the right. As they came closer, a gigantic ship loomed out of the mist. The cold felt increasingly biting. Gray frost sat on caps, hair, and coats. A wooden plat-form was lowered from the deck above, and somebody shouted that women with children should be let on first, but no one moved, so finally they just forced people onto the rocking struc-ture, which made several trips up to the deck, the hemp lines squealing and banging against the iron hull.

The shouts woke Stella. Half-conscious, she raised her head. High on the side of the ship, which towered over the barge like a huge wall, she saw a row of faded letters gleaming with ice. Straining and squinting her bloodshot eyes, she was able to read the name: *Friedrich Bernhoff.*

| *The Word* |

THERE WAS A QUIVER in Father's voice: "Look, the sea!"

"The sea?" Mama just shook her head. "What are you talking about, Józek? That can't be—we're still in Gdańsk. We'd have to be near Sopot to see the Baltic." She knew for a fact that Gdańsk was on the Mottlau River; they'd learned it in geography, at the Marianist school in Warsaw. But seeing that little strip of azure behind the airfields made Father's heart skip a beat: he'd never seen a real sea before.

The street they were walking down was named "Kronprinzenallee," according to an enameled sign with scary Gothic letters, which was posted on the wooden shelter at the tram stop. The rails were hidden deep in the snow; they stumbled on the icy ties. They stepped over fallen signal poles and had to walk around a burned-out streetcar that was blocking the tracks. The city leafed out before them like frost on glass. The spiky steeple of a church, a brick smokestack, a row of poplars coated in frost. Over Pelonker Strasse, flocks of jackdaws flitted among the linden trees hung with balls of mistletoe. The silent flapping of wings, the cold sheen of fog. Mama found it spooky, but Father didn't want to go back. After all this? That didn't make any sense! On the other side of Pelonker Strasse, the southern edge of the district was ringed with hills—a dark expanse of green pines, speckled with gray beeches, extending in a long, leisurely line from Langfuhr (or, as we would know it, Wrzeszcz) toward Gdynia, and it was probably that view that decided everything. One look at those hills was enough to make your heart tremble, imagining how beautiful it would all be in spring.

So Father walked on, more and more convinced that they had finally found what they were searching for. He looked right, off to the east toward Brzeźno, at the white airfield and the dark line of pines, and then to the left at the linden trees along Pelonker Strasse and the gentle hills with beeches stretching off in the distance. Maybe, he said to Mama, maybe we should stay here for a while, maybe even forever—no, he didn't say that yet; he preferred to treat the days that lay ahead as an open promise. And I was walking with them, upside down and fast asleep, tucked away under Mama's heart, with my little fist under my chin and my feet comically twisted around, in the warm gulf of water, that tangle of veins that connected me to her. After all, I was the reason Mama had to keep stopping to catch her breath, since the bulge beneath her coat, where I was rocking to the rhythm of her steps, was every bit as heavy as the brown suitcase Father carried in his left hand while he helped Mama with his right, easing her way.

They trudged ahead, the powdery snow grating under their feet against the slick ice lurking underneath—Mama had to hold on to Father's elbow so she wouldn't slip—until at last they reached the first homes. They peeked through iron fence pickets and open gates marked with Gothic numbers; around pine, spruce, and birch trees; through tangles of ivy and strands of creeper, and peered at the three-windowed garden villas that recalled summer homes around the Wannsee; trunklike buildings with stained-glass dormers; white houses with glassed-in porches...

The houses, the streets, the courtyards, the little squares shaded by giant chestnut trees, where the snow lay clean and untrodden—all abandoned by those who had fled or burned or drowned, all slumbering in the silence of the frozen morning. The neighborhood was in no rush to give up the secrets it kept hidden behind the hedges of hornbeam and arborvitae. Not far away, in the center of town, by the train station where the black-lettered signs still said "Danzig," green trucks were rumbling through the snow-covered ruins, startling the flocks of crows that were busy picking the meat off fallen horses, while men in heavy woolen coats and military jackets drifted among the houses that had been left standing, carrying canvas rucksacks, wooden suitcases, bundles wrapped in cloth.

But here they seemed to be at the very edge of the city: the forest started just on the other side of Pelonker Strasse and stretched all the way to Zuckau, Müggau, and Kokoschken. Here they were far enough away from the main artery that would soon be renamed Grunwaldzka, where the convoys rolled by every few minutes on their way toward Gdynia: heavy trucks with flapping covers of bleached canvas, horse-drawn trailers hauling field kitchens, tanks with the turrets turned backward, their armor splattered with lime. This neighborhood seemed out of the way, secluded; the flood of people moving west just passed it by, and Mama and Father were able to choose the house where I was to be born.

So they moved from house to house, stopping by gates overgrown with creeper... At Number 6 a narrow path led to a dark villa with a rounded mansard roof. Father adjusted his rucksack and was about to cross the stone threshold into the little courtyard, but Mama tugged him by the sleeve: "Wait, let's look a little further." So they went on through the snow, leaving deep craters in the pristine white, and stopped at Number 14, by a wooden fence with a carved pattern of upside-down hearts. They stamped the powder off their feet, Father opened the gate, and a startled cloud of waxwings and bullfinches darted from the thorny branches where they had been pecking at the red berries.

Father considered the roof to be more important than anything else (he had hoped to find a metal roof, ideally copper), so they craned their necks to inspect the saddle-shaped tiles, warily eyeing the black stains of moss where the snow had slid to the gutter. In the sunlight, the house showed off its splendors—the plaster ornaments, the graceful angel heads of white cement, the dazzling displays of color from the stained-glass window... but all in vain, because as soon as Mama stepped into the hallway with the dull blue stuccowork, she jumped back right away, without really knowing why... Over the letterbox marked "Briefe" was a copper plate, with names written in shiny, slanting letters: "Erich Schultz," "Wolfgang Bierenstein," "Johann Peltz."

So they walked on, past a bend in the street, until they came to an iron fence next to an arborvitae hedge, and a house of glistening red and olive brick. "How about here?" Father asked. Mama never forgot that moment. The house was by no means the prettiest, it lacked the airiness of the white villas with the glassed-in porches, but its sloping roof, firmly mounted on stone lintels, evidently won Father's trust, and, brushing off the snow with his elbow, he set his suitcase down on the concrete planter. Then he put his hands in his pockets and slowly walked around the building. The dark windows gleamed in their carved frames.

And that little turret attached to the left wall! A stairwell? Yes, it was the stairwell, and Mama must have liked the idea of a separate entrance, detached from the other apartments, away from the comings and goings of strangers. The turret couldn't claim to be much higher than the roof, but it did have a little balcony with a cast-iron balustrade that gave the house a pretty crown. Maybe that was what decided things; perhaps that fairy-tale spire encouraged my parents to indulge some childish urge to forget all the terrible things they had experienced. Because they were ready right then and there to stop what they were doing and run up the stairs to the top of the turret and look out, and maybe, just maybe, they would be able to see the entire neighborhood, the airfields past Kronprinzenallee, the forest, and even the sea . . .

The dark front door had a milk-glass window, covered with a wrought-iron grate in a sweet flag motif; one of the triangular panes was etched with a Gothic 17. Father picked up the suitcase and stepped inside, followed by Mama, and both immediately liked what they saw. A beam of light came through the window, scattering into a rainbow that flashed across the green tiles and up the winding staircase, where the brass handrail spiraled down to end like a snail's shell. Mama couldn't help sliding her hand along the surface that had been buffed gold by a thousand touches, just to see how it felt, to check if it wasn't too high—as casually as if she went up and down those stairs every day.

The railing was just right, not too high, not too low, so they climbed the steps, which had gold-tinged brass edging that was worn in the middle—Father in his black lace-ups with the sheepskin lining, Mama in her lacquered ski boots with the nickel hooks—and the stairs creaked very lightly. The pale green paneling did a beautiful job mimicking the solemn veining of marble. Mama ran her fingers across the slippery surface, patterned with thistle leaves and cornflowers, tracing the shapes or perhaps checking to see if it was all real, and Father, seeing how tenderly she did this, leaned over and kissed her on the neck just behind the ear, a little saucily, cockily, perhaps to mask or hide his own emotion. Mama, who had been engrossed in the silence, let out an impatient sigh, but a little smile appeared on her lips, understanding and ironic. Halfway up the stairs was a landing with a round stained-glass window that overlooked the garden; the frame sparkled with light from a circle of bright blue set in the middle. They looked out at the large arborvitae, the birch tree and the blue spruce, and suddenly they heard voices.

They stopped in midstep. At first they couldn't make out the words, and after a moment everything went quiet. Father hadn't paid any attention to the floor before; now he noticed a few brownish clods and some wet smears...Mama was about to head back down, but Father instinctively reached for a sooty iron poker that was sticking out behind the metal coal bin by the wall—as if cut to the quick by the possibility that the turret with its view of the airfields, the forest in Brzeźno, and even the sea had been taken away from them just like that, by someone who'd been quicker, who'd beaten them to it. For a moment Mama tried to wave him back downstairs, but Father was so intent on what was happening upstairs that he didn't notice her anxious gesture. Now the voices sounded louder, but they still couldn't distinguish the words.

On the second floor they saw a large green door, slightly ajar, with a brass escutcheon and a large lever shaped like a lion's paw. Cautiously they peeked inside, past the dark entry hall and through a white sliding door that opened onto a large room with a decorated plaster ceiling and a crystal chandelier...

They saw a man silhouetted against the window, caught in the glare, so that they couldn't make out his features—they only saw that he was tall and wearing a light-colored shirt. Then he was blocked from their view by another man's back. Mama didn't approve of eavesdropping or spying in any form, so she held her finger to her lips, to signal to Father that he had no business there, but Father merely shook his head. The man's back moved again, a shadow blocked the glare for just a second, the tall man in the light shirt turned around...

That was their first glimpse of Hanemann.

My parents' instinct was to step inside and politely announce their presence with a loud "Hello," but they stopped in their tracks.

A man stepped up to Hanemann. Swarthy, with a wet-looking face, fur cap with earflaps, the straps dangling below his ears, woolen gloves. The man stood facing Hanemann and poked him in the chest, very nonchalantly. Mama squeezed Father's elbow, but Father gently freed himself from her grip and crossed the threshold, careful not to make the floorboards creak. The others didn't hear a thing. From inside the room came the crack of a lock being opened, followed by a strange crunching sound. Father caught sight of a tall, yellow leather boot: someone was crushing shells that were scattered on the carpet—fragile Japanese shells, near an open lacquered box...

At that point Mama really began to be afraid, but not of the shadows that were crossing in front of Hanemann. What scared her, what terrified her was Father, who was beginning to shake with tiny tremors of rage; he gripped the poker so hard his fingers turned white. A second, shorter man in a military jacket without epaulettes now appeared next to the one with the fur cap, who had picked up a celadon teacup with a gold rim. Holding it right in Hanemann's face, he crushed it in his fingers like a hollow Easter egg. Crack. The porcelain shards sprinkled onto the carpet. Hanemann blanched, and when Father saw that, he stepped through the open door.

The men turned around, more surprised than scared, while Hanemann just half-closed his eyes. Father stopped at the doorway. Carried away by his rising spleen, he tilted forward, brandishing the black poker, ready for anything, and uttered the single word: "Out!"

Oh, Father, how you grew into a giant, how powerful you must have been when you stood there on the threshold of Hanemann's room, brandishing that iron poker, and uttered that single word—my heart would melt every time I pictured that moment. Because when you stood there, my short, disheveled father with your grayish cowlick, oblivious to Mama tugging at your elbow, you looked exactly like the man in Memling's triptych, armed with a spear and a mighty scale for weighing souls, separating the righteous from the damned before the latter are cast into the infernal abyss. And to anyone who tells me that the Archangel Michael is nothing but a fiction we've invented to assuage any doubts that the Last Judgment might never come, all I have for an answer is a friendly smile, tinged with pity.

"Józek, stop!" Mama whispered, and tugged on his elbow, but Father didn't hear her in his wonderfully charged state, which radiated from him like a heavenly light as he raged in the doorway. And although I always wanted him to go on raging as long as he could, I had a nagging suspicion there was something Mama hadn't told me, because Father's heavenly light probably looked a little different from the way I pictured it. Because Grandmother once told me that whenever Father got mad, his face would flush with a red that turned a beautiful purple as it ran to his cheeks and all the way up to his forehead, setting his ears completely on fire.

But even if your ears were a fiery ruby red, I'll never forget that moment, that wonderful moment when you stood in the doorway to Hanemann's room. I wanted it to last forever, my heart couldn't get enough. Because when you stood in the frame of that white sliding door, tilting forward, ready for anything—the world recovered its glow. That was a moment that made me want to be alive, made me want to live!

Mama tugged at his sleeve for him to stop, because she saw right away that the two men threatening Hanemann were carrying guns under their sheepskin coats: one move and that would be the end of us. But Father was carried away by his exaltation, or maybe something worse—some atavistic Finno-Tatar reflex that lay slumbering in our eastern blood and suddenly caused him to shout so loudly that the glasses rattled on the shelves of the cabinet: "Get out!"

"What are you doing, can't you see it's a kraut?" said the man in the fur cap, not too loudly, once again poking Hanemann in the chest.

Perhaps it was the man's mindless, disdainful gesture, or perhaps it was the sneer in his voice, that set off the explosion that had been seething inside my father. Father didn't move at all, didn't take a single step—he merely leaned forward, glowering with rage, his lips white, his cheeks purple, the blue veins popping out on his temples: "You goddamned son of a whore, get the hell out of this house!"

When Mama repeated those very words to me, many years later, she hid her embarrassment in ironic half smiles, but she was clearly proud. And I understood that from the moment those words were pronounced—or, really, shouted—Father, Mama, and I could claim our home here, at Lessingstrasse 17, that those words established the house where I would be born. They sounded nothing less than glorious. I could listen to that tale over and over, the tale of my beginning.

Father shouted the Word, his face flushing red, then going white with rage, and sounded so terrible that Mama let go of his sleeve, and the man in the fur cap just stood there, first looking at his companion, then at Father. He set down the lacquered ballerina and muttered: "OK, what are you shaking for? Come on, Jędras. He can drop dead along with the kraut as far as I'm concerned. There's nothing here anyway. Just a bunch of papers."

They walked out the room, ostentatiously slow, in defiance of Father. The taller man was about to say something, but he just turned around, kicked a piece of shell that was lying on the rug, and shoved Father away from the door. The men stepped into the hall. Father started to rush after them, but this time Mama succeeded in holding him back. He wanted to shout something, wanted to have the last word. He was seething, still brandishing the poker, but Mama held him firmly, until he simply wilted, like a weed pulled out of the ground. Then she whispered to him, "Józek, calm down, they're gone," and led him to the armchair, where he collapsed onto the leather seat. He was trembling all over. Mama knelt beside the chair and caressed his hand, while he kept his whitish fingers tightly wrapped around the sooty black poker—the quivering scepter of an abdicating monarch.

Even so, as often as I pictured that moment, I never felt the urge to reproach him for getting so carried away. I would grow tense just listening to Mama tell the story, but then, as I imagined that little man trembling and panting and swallowing hard, his Adam's apple bobbing up and down, all the tension would abate and dissolve into a blessed tranquillity, followed by the growing certainty of victory. I could feel him slowly regaining his strength, feel his humble power, able to withstand anything. Had Father won? I had no doubt, although it could have been the sight of Mama in her blessed state that placated the men and persuaded them to leave Hanemann's apartment (that version of events was equally dear to me, since it suggested my own modest contribution to the victory). Father's breathing slowed down, and he began caressing Mama's hand, as if he wanted to absolve some guilt he had just called to mind. They braided their fingers together, one hand caressing the other, and she burst out sobbing like a little girl: the tears came streaming down her face, but they were probably tears of joy, since Father delicately wiped them off her cheek, and she pressed her smiling face against his hand.

Outside in the hall, from the middle of the stairwell that was echoing with the steps of the men climbing down to the ground floor, a voice reached them, full of contempt: "First they burn us out of our homes and steal everything we have, and this one decides he's going to be all nice and caring..." "To hell with him," the other voice answered. The two men were walking slowly, adjusting the bags they were carrying on their shoulders, full of clinking metal. They had no need to rush, there were plenty of houses left, houses and houses...hundreds in Old Oliva and across the tracks in Oliva itself, houses full of armoires, cabinets, trunks, crates, baskets, barrels. And each time Mama reached the part where the front door of Lessingstrasse 17 slammed shut and the entry hall was so quiet you could hear a pin drop, I knew for sure that the house was ours.

The only thing I could never figure out was why Hanemann answered those men in German when they showed up at his door.

| *Lavender* |

MY PARENTS WENT downstairs, where they found an unlocked door with a brass nameplate saying "E. A. Walmann." The rounded door handle was cold and smooth, with a goldish hue; it yielded gently to their touch and the door opened. Mama remembered the exact moment: the dark vestibule with the green linoleum, the flash of the large mirror facing the doorway. Father started across the threshold, but Mama held him back, pulling on his rucksack: "What do you think you're doing, going in with your shoes on?" He took off the pack and untied his shoelaces. They left their shoes by the door and went inside in their stocking feet.

It was cold in the apartment. The only light in the room was coming through a door, off to the right with a milk-glass pane, which presumably led to the kitchen. They saw their hazy reflections in the mirror. Father spoke softly, as if afraid he might wake someone sleeping in another room. "What's your guess, how many rooms are there?" Mama noticed two hooks mounted in the upper jamb, evidently for a child's swing, and felt uneasy.

She took down a bundle of keys hanging next to the gas meter: two small ones made of brass and a longer one made of iron, on a wire ring. Pipes from the central heating ran just under the ceiling. The linoleum was clean, only a few dried footprints near the door.

Father put his arm around Mama: "Come on, let's first take a look at the kitchen." But Mama thought of something else; she reached into the rucksack and took out a tin soap dish and a linen towel.

The door to the bathroom was painted with white enamel. The narrow windowpane was coated with frost. The sill had a drainage groove for any rain that managed to come through; now it was filled with a thin stream of ice. She detected a fragrance in the air, one she wasn't used to—lavender, she thought, mingled with the tang of the cold interior. She felt as if she had checked into a hotel and was examining the bathroom: she had the same curiosity about the color of the tiles, the same fear of finding rust stains in the tub, that quick glance at the mirror above the sink to check for signs of wear and tear. Except this wasn't a hotel. Once, when she was little, her grandmother had sent her to borrow something from Mrs. Bogdanowicz, their next-door neighbor on Nowogrodzka Street in Warsaw. She found the door wide open and cautiously stepped inside. Suddenly she heard a man's voice just behind her: "And what are you doing here, walking in like that without knocking?" She was so startled her heart practically stopped beating. She turned red up to her temples and couldn't say a word; she felt her ears were on fire, even though Mr. Bogdanowicz was only pretending, just to give her a scare. Now, in this apartment, as she stood in the bathroom looking at the tiles, she had a similar sensation. But who could come in now? They'd shut the door behind them and latched it with a chain.

She was about to put her own soap in the iron mesh basket that straddled the edge of the tub when she saw that there was already a piece there, dried up and flattened with use. When she noticed a few hairs stuck to it, she felt a slight revulsion, as if she'd found a dead snail, but it turned out they were only hairline cracks, so she took the pink sliver out of the basket and held it in her fingers for a moment, not knowing what to do. Finally she placed it on the shelf under the mirror, next to the two glasses and the empty box of Vera tooth powder. She put her own bar of yellow-gray soap in the basket and quickly rinsed her fingers. Without thinking, she reached for the faded hand towel on the hanger, but when she noticed a blue embroidered *W* she stopped. She took down the towel, placed it in the linen closet, and hung up her own—white, with a green stripe. When she had finished she again held her hand up to her nose.

The tub was clean, though the bottom had been worn matte by frequent scouring. In the strainer, however, she found a clump of blond hair. A child's? She fished it out and dropped it in the toilet.

The bath had a large faucet with a wide, flat mouth, and butterfly knobs labeled "Kalt" and "Warm," their nickel finish chipped in a few places. The showerhead looked like a phone receiver attached to a shiny metal hose. She turned it on to rinse out the tub; as the water ran across the white enamel, the milky reflection of her face faded in and out of the tiles that glistened on the wall.

Lace-hemmed curtains in the kitchen window, white windowsill. Wooden floorboards. First she turned on the brass spigot, to see if the kitchen, too, had running water. A needlepoint depicting a windmill was hanging on the wall beside the table—blue thread on white linen; seeing that the Gothic legend was a little crooked, she straightened the edge of the embroidery. Father noticed how tenderly she smoothed out the fabric, and smiled at her. He was standing beside the open stove, tapping the iron grill with a poker: "Well, the stove looks in order." The burner rings were on the stovetop. She could smell the damp cinders, the gray ash. The tiles of the oven were off-white, almost cream-colored, and completely smooth. Squinting at the pipes, Father said, "Look, this is for the central heating. And over here is for baking. But we'll probably have to burn cordwood. Because the firebox is very small."

She opened the doors to the mahogany chest, rattling the leaded glass panes. Among the cobalt glasses and ceramic jars labeled "Pfeffer," "Salz," and "Zucker," she saw a gleaming white oval tureen with a hand-painted Chinese seascape—blue brushwork and a brown-sailed junk—and a lid shaped like a pagoda. When she lifted the lid she left a fingerprint next to the Rosenthal emblem—a dark pattern on a film of dust, like a round postmark on an ivory-colored envelope.

She began taking things out of the rucksack, one by one, and setting them on the white oilcloth that covered the table. The thick sweater she had worn during the uprising in Warsaw, the ski pants Mr. Z. had given her when the Ukrainians moved into Żoliborz, Aunt Hela's tin cup from Koszykowa Street, the bottle with the porcelain stopper (the leftover tea long since cold), two teaspoons, a knife (labeled "Gerlach"—from the nuns in Szymanów), Father's shirt from UNRRA, a coarse linen sheet, a light blue nightgown she had managed to save from Nowogrodzka Street, three or four gray russet apples wrapped in paper...

Father turned away so he wouldn't have to see how thoughtfully, how gently she was unpacking the few possessions that had survived. He went down to the basement and brought up some coal in an old Maggi tin, then took a tidy stack of yellowed *Völkischer Beobachter* newspapers out from under the cabinet, broke up a few pine splinters for kindling, and lit them. The stove had a good draft, and the wood caught fire right away. The tiles absorbed the heat, Mama put her hands on them and mumbled something that Father pretended not to have heard, but when he asked her to repeat it she just shook her head and smiled and closed her eyes.

In the middle of the apartment was a large room with a walnut armoire. A round mirror was mounted in the door; she was startled when she saw her own reflection. The walls were a pretty tea color. A picture hung over the sofa—fiery red clouds in a gilt frame—sunset over the beach at Glettkau, a white pier with pilings, a pleasure steamer pulling in to dock. Stepping closer to study the painting, she saw a signature in the lower right-hand corner: *L. Schneider.* Very gently she touched the canvas: there was a tiny bit of dust, which she blew off her fingertip. Standing by the window was a Singer sewing machine; she ran her hand over the curved, cold body, then, feeling more and more tired, she sat down on the sofa, and only now, as she rested her head on the soft upholstery that smelled of plush fabric and dried seaweed, did she take a deep breath. The table was decorated with a paper rose inside a slender crystal vase; her first instinct was to throw the flower away, but then she took it out and set it on the bamboo étagère. Later she moved the rose to the armoire, where it would lie for many years, flattened by suitcases and packages, until it lost all its petals and leaves and nothing was left of the green tissue stem but a few tarnished wires.

The armoire was full of white and blue linens, evenly arranged on the shelves. More lavender? She lifted the edge of a freshly pressed sheet and peeled back a little of the cool material—no, it was wild rose, a few brittle petals sprinkled on the smooth fabric, which was embroidered with the same *W* as the hand towel. Later on she, too, would scatter petals from the rosebush, which grew under the birch tree in the corner of the garden, on all her freshly pressed sheets and pillowcases.

Father lit a fire under the kettle in the laundry room, and when the water was hot enough, he tossed in the sheets and pillowcases he had removed from the armoire, despite the fact they were already clean and freshly starched. But even two full hours of boiling couldn't dispel their cool, fresh scent, so different from the sheets Aunt Marysia had given Mama. And in the evening, as they lay on their newly made bed in the middle room— Mama in her nightgown from their home on Nowogrodzka Street and Father in his striped UNRRA pajamas—the smell of their sheet from the outskirts of Warsaw collided with that of the monogrammed bedcovers that Elsa Walmann had bought in 1940 in Julius Mehler's shop at Ahornweg 12, two incompatible scents upsetting their sleep. Their own sheet still smelled of travel, smoke from the train, the canvas rucksack, the winy old russets they had bought when the train stopped for an hour in Malbork, while the freshly pressed duvet cover with the blue embroidered *W* had the chalky odor of empty homes and of singeing by a hot iron that had left just a trace of cinnamon on the stiff white material. The fabric in the middle felt cooler; the scent seemed strongest at the edges, which were hemmed with lace.

They lay in bed, unable to sleep, listening to the steps of the man who lived on the next floor. Next to the door was a photo: two girls wearing straw hats and crinkled batiste dresses gazed at them somberly. They were standing on the pier in Zoppot next to a man in a postal uniform and a young woman in a frilly dress with a rounded collar. Father got up and carefully took the picture off the nail, exposing a rectangle in the wallpaper where the tea color was a little lighter. He blew away the cobwebs and looked at the back of the photo, which was labeled "Ballerstaedt. Photograph-Atelier." A date had been inked in: "Juli 1938." Then he stashed the picture in the lower drawer of the walnut armoire, next to some notebooks filled out in a child's even hand, a Westermann world atlas, and a bundle of postcards from Bavaria, tied with a waxed string.

It wasn't until later, at midnight, when Mama was standing in the bathtub while Father washed her back with warm water and rinsed her growing belly, where I was slumbering away with my little fist tucked under my chin—it wasn't until then that the steam melted the sprigs of ice on the windowpane, and we all felt a little more at home.

WHAT A HOUSE! To get to the turret with the balcony you had to climb some black steps under the pointed roof with the zinc ball finial; in good weather you really could look out and see the airfield, the pine forest in Brzeźno, and, off in the distance, the azure line of the sea. The roof had dark red Prussian tiles, lined with moss in true Vistula Gothic style, and each window was anchored by a row of olive-glazed bricks. The large, two-storied porch overlooked the garden, where a path of packed black earth ran alongside trimmed boxwoods to an ornamental iron gate. A dense yew gave some shade to the flower beds, which were bordered with cobalt-glazed tiles; farther out was an enormous birch and twin hedges of arborvitae. A tall blue spruce grew in front of the house; its ash-colored trunk was branchless all the way up to the gutter.

Dębinki, Traugutt, Tuwim, Morska . . . the recently renamed streets sounded like faraway countries when Father came home in the evenings and talked about his job at Antracyt, the coal and coke company where he'd been working since January. The owners had a mine near Gliwice: two shafts, a loading dock, and a coke oven. Bunker-style warehouses on the Vistula at Nowy Port and its own freight siding in the port at Oksywie! The first invoice forms Father used were green with purple columns and a letterhead that said "Herbert Borkowski. Drogen u. Chemikalien-Grosshandlung. Danzig. Brabank 4."

Father earned almost thirty thousand zlotys, which was very good, and Mama earned six thousand teaching at the nursing school, so they had no cause for complaint—considering what they'd been through, it was paradise. But in July two men walked into the countinghouse on Morska Street and said to Father, "You have to sign here that the firm is being placed in receivership."

Father just looked at them. "I can't sign that because I'm not the owner. The owners are in jail."

The men nodded their heads understandingly. "In that case you won't be working here anymore."

"In that case I won't."

At one point Mama asked, "What did they put the owners in jail for, Józek?"

"What do you mean what for? For being capitalists."

Delbrück-Allee was no longer Delbrück-Allee. Now it was Skłodowska-Curie Avenue. The old Volkssturm barracks on the way to the Academy had been converted into a chapel, and only a few of the gas streetlamps by the cemetery were working—there were cases of nurses being attacked as they came off the night shift. The students Mama passed on the street, young men in trench coats and fatigues without insignia, called out to one another: "We're going up to the gallery!" Which meant: We're going to our class in comparative anatomy, to the auditorium in the building at the corner of Zwycięstwo Avenue, where not so long ago the Germans made soap out of people they murdered. The Warsaw School of Nursing, which had been established with support from the Rockefeller Foundation under the aegis of the Hospital of the Infant Jesus, had been moved from Koszykowa Street in Warsaw first to the town of Biały Dunajec and then to Building E of the Academy in Gdańsk. Mama was very proud that they had hired her. The Academy also employed a number of doctors from Vilna—surgeons from the medical faculty of Stefan Batory University. Mama listed their names with respect: Drs. Michejda, Piskozub, Jóźkiewicz. But also with a tinge of resentment, because many of the nurses at the Academy were German *Krankenschwester,* around thirty years old. They all wore the same long blue dresses and white aprons with the ties crossed in back, and they all kept their hair parted and pulled back. The Polish doctors liked working with them, perhaps even more than with the Polish nurses. Meanwhile the *Krankenschwester* treated their Polish counterparts as if they didn't exist.

Germans also worked as lab technicians in the x-ray facility located in the basement. Until one day in September, when Mama saw three or four trucks parked outside Building C and the technicians standing on the sidewalk with their bags and baggage.

An extensive network of bomb shelters had been built under the Academy. "We just assumed there were Germans living below us," Mama said later. "One of the women at work saw a German come out of the building and run away." All the nearby woods were mined, and a number of children were blown up in the hills and ravines. From the roof of their hotel, the nurses could see the shipyard standing idle, the ruins of the city center, the Mottlau River, the town hall missing its spire, the churches without steeples. The official story was that Gdańsk had been burned by the Germans...

Some time later a group of Swedish nurses arrived from Uppsala, bringing food, clothing, and nurses' uniforms. On December 13 they celebrated St. Lucia's Day. Occasionally Mama received huge, fifty-pound packages from UNRRA, with chocolate bars and Camel cigarettes that she exchanged for coffee or tea. A friend of hers, Mr. Szczepkowski, worked in the UNRRA office on Morska; she knew him from the transit camp in Pruszków, so now and then she was able to wangle something for Hanemann as well.

But Hanemann was reluctant to accept things from UNRRA. He preferred going to the market at Podwale Grodzkie every few days, where elderly women wearing hats with veils or turbans wrapped around their foreheads stood by the brick wall, behind whatever items they had laid out on the ground—china services, silverware, typewriters. The first time he went there he saw Mrs. Stein, standing next to the containers of crushed ice that the fishermen from Jelitkowo or Brzeźno used to lay out their fresh cod. She was wearing two coats—one heavy, one light—and a cashmere scarf around her neck. She was trying to sell a porcelain box, a lamp with a blue shade, and some forks with a flowery S monogram, which she displayed on a copy of the *Dziennik Bałtycki*. She had anchored the corners of the newspaper with pieces of brick. As she stood in front of her wares, Mrs. Stein kept holding a batiste handkerchief to her mouth, since the wind coming from the fish market was kicking up dust.

She was surprised to see him: "You mean you didn't leave?" Hanemann explained that he was planning to but still didn't know when. "You mean you're not working at the Academy? You used to be . . ."

But he didn't want to talk about it. He asked what sold best and whether one could make a living selling things at the market.

"The people who come in trucks from Warsaw take everything. They pay good money, too." Mrs. Stein preferred to take dollars, although that wasn't always a possibility.

The next day Hanemann unrolled a sheet of canvas next to Mrs. Stein and set out a few knives and forks, a number of books, and a little silver. That afternoon a man came and bought the lot for two and a half thousand zlotys.

Things went on like that until one day in September, when Mrs. Ch., who lived nearby at 12 Obrońców Westerplatte, knocked on the door at 17 Grottger Street, formerly Lessing- strasse 17. Hanemann, who didn't know Mrs. Ch., was some- what surprised by the visit, but he invited her inside and offered her a seat. Mrs. Ch. wanted to know if Hanemann would tutor her son in German. Hers wasn't the first such request: In July, Hanemann had received a visit from Mr. Wojdakowski, who lived at 7 Aleja Sprzymierzonych, a tall, blond engineer whom the shipyard administration at the former Schichau works occa- sionally sent to Eastern Germany, to Rostock and beyond, to look for machine parts. Mr. Wojdakowski told Hanemann he wanted to improve his German, which, as he put it, he had pur- sued in high school with some success; Hanemann agreed to tutor him. Then, as word began to spread, other people began seeking him out.

"We should have Andrzejek learn some German," Mrs. Ch. had told her husband. "You'll see, they'll be coming back, to- gether with the English and the Americans. German will come in handy." Mr. Ch. didn't share her conviction, but he agreed to pay for the lessons, with the result that Hanemann no longer had to ride out to Podwale Grodzkie with a roll of canvas and a bundle of silverware.

So he no longer saw Mrs. Stein standing by the brick wall at the marketplace, next to the container of crushed ice, although he did call on her a few times on Ahornweg, which was now called Klonowa Street. These visits weren't always enjoyable: Mrs. Stein was invariably bothered by the shouting and bickering that came in from the courtyard. Most of all she couldn't stand the smells in the entrance hall. Yellow stains blossomed on the walls of the stairwell, growing in number every Saturday night. That would never have happened earlier, when Constable Gustav Joppe, son of the Johannisthal shipyard owner, walked his beat along Mirchauer Weg. On Steffensweg Mrs. Stein had seen two workmen affixing an enameled plaque to the Horovitz's house inscribed with the words "Stefan Batory Street." Mirchauer Weg was now Partyzantów, and Hochstriess had been renamed Słowacki. Kronprinzenallee was Aleja Sprzymieryonych. The Langfuhr district was known as Wrzeszcz, Neufahrwasser as Nowy Port, and Brösen as Brzeźno. The new names were hard to pronounce and difficult to remember. "When are you leaving?" Hanemann asked Mrs. Stein, to interrupt her complaining, since that didn't do any good anyway. But Mrs. Stein only gave evasive answers. Everything was so difficult. She was waiting to hear from her daughters, who were staying in Düsseldorf, but they weren't doing so well. Mrs. Stein didn't want to be a burden. In the past she had often worn light-colored coats and throws; now she dressed in somber colors, brown or black coats, secondhand and dusted with moth powder.

Nevertheless, once when he ran into her on Mirchauer Weg, she was in the company of a gray-haired gentleman with a cane and returned his bow with a smile. She was wearing a new black hat with a silver pin. Hanemann watched them for a moment as they headed toward the former Adolf-Hitler-Strasse to board the streetcar. The man spoke in German, as she did, but with a distinct Polish accent.

| *Black Spruces* |

IN THE EVENINGS, Hanemann occasionally put his papers in order or rearranged the books on the shelves, but he would quickly grow bored. Then he would sit in the armchair by the window, open a book at random and attempt to read, not always successfully. Perhaps he was distracted by the voices coming from the garden or by the rustling of the wind or by the tin rooster clanging away on the turret at the Bierensteins'—in any case, his thoughts would drift across the pages and wander their own way.

These weren't sentimental journeys back to places or people he once had liked or even loved. Years ago, in a moment of impatience, his mother had said to him, "I don't think you have a heart." At the time that statement had wounded him deeply, because even though his mother may not have meant to hurt him, her words had hit a nerve and touched something he himself was struggling with, something that, concealed, gave color to his life. Now, sitting at the window and watching the sun settle on the tips of the pine trees and the tall black spruces, he felt a cool emptiness opening inside his chest, which brought to mind the blurry image of his mother as she accused him of a lack of feeling. But that same sensation also brought a pleasant feeling of relief, to which he yielded without struggle, with what was even for him a strange indifference. As if he were dreaming with open eyes. The absence of people, the silence, the day cooling off—in the waning light of evening he truly felt close to the world, as if he could reach out and touch the air floating in from the garden, as if his skin—though he knew this was impossible—could sense not only the cooler breeze but a certain bright translucence flowing in from the window and the spiraling specks of dust.

Absence of people? Rather their distant, unobtrusive presence—the voices coming through the window, mixed with the light that filtered through the birch leaves, set just the right tone for his solitude. It didn't matter if the voices weren't happy. And he was glad that the sounds outside didn't simply disappear in the afternoon hubbub of the city, that they remained distinct, rising above the murmur of trees and the rhythm of footsteps, then fading in the pinkish sunlight: a woman's voice, resonant and wise despite the mundane message, a boy answering that it wasn't yet time to go in, or a girl feigning sobs because it was still early and the sun—just touching the canopy of the forest—was still well over the Cathedral.

The shadows outside the window grew longer, and the commotion died down on both sides of Grottger Street. Mr. Wierzbołowski closed the gate behind him, the iron clanged against the post, the metal fencing rattled quietly, and as he walked up the concrete steps to the Bierensteins' house, his shadow flitted across the white drapes in the porch window, because his wife, Janina, who was waiting for him to come back from the Anglas chocolate factory, had already turned on the light, even though the clouds over Wrzeszcz were just beginning to darken and the sky over the park was still full of sunshine. Now she stood by the window, resting her elbows on an embroidered cushion, and watched the children coming back from the meadow near the Cistercian chapel carrying a kite made of gray paper and crisscrossed strips of molding, with a long tail of string and bows of tissue paper that came swishing over the ground. In the middle of the street, under the linden trees, Mrs. S.'s boys were banging an iron bar against the flint and granite cobblestones, striking bluish sparks, but at this time of day no one seemed to mind, because even if Mr. Dłuszniewski did call out "That's enough of that, now" as he watered his stocks and dahlias from a great tin can, he didn't shout very loudly—and more from a sense of obligation than to break up a game that he had probably enjoyed quite a bit when he was little.

Now and then, though, Hanemann's thoughts returned to that other world, and instead of Mr. Dłuszniewski watering his flowers from the large tin can, Hanemann saw Emma Bierenstein in a long, crinkled dress, her hair coiffed like Ruth Weyher's in Pabst's *Secrets of a Soul*, wielding dainty silver shears to snip brightly colored gladioli. And in the window where Mrs. Wierzbołowski was watching the children, he saw Rosa Schultz wearing her beige turban and a blouse of grayish green batik, carrying a basket of freshly laundered linen up to the attic to dry. But these visions came without sorrow or regret; in fact, he was grateful for these new people now living in the homes between the streetcar line and the beech woods in the hills—grateful that they were so different (because they were), and hopeful that their otherness would evolve into something truly good that would soothe his restless heart. Those moments when words and gestures faded from the gardens and porches, when people paused on the walkway to shield their eyes as they glanced at the great red sun sinking in the woods behind the Cathedral, those moments when even the ravenous need to live grew quiet and the certainty of a safe night's sleep dispelled all hate—in those moments everything inside him came together and settled like delicate layers of ash.

And later, around six o'clock, the bells of the Cathedral began ringing in the center of Oliva, soon (but always with a moment's delay) joined by the bells of the Cistercian chapel, and that distant ringing drowned out the chatter on the streets before fading away in the tangle of linden, pear, and apple branches—and then the old places, homes, rooms, faces resurfaced: images of a city that no longer existed. But they were far away, distant from his heart, as if his memory were simply shuffling a pack of yellowed photographs before they were tossed into the fire. Anna's voice came out of the blue: "You can't go on living like this . . ." But now, her words could no longer hurt him. After all, why couldn't he go on living like this?

Hanemann closed the book that was resting on his knees. He shut his eyes and ran his fingers over the coarse green cloth of the jacket. Losing himself in the tinny murmur of the birch leaves, he submitted to the play of images from the past, now purged of everything that was painful. As the splotches of sunlight and the shadows of the trees rocked more and more slowly across the facade of the Bierensteins' house, not only he but everything around him fell into a dreamy hibernation, as if unsure what to choose: restless desire or death. Even his heart—so he felt—seemed to slow its relentless march inside his chest. Noises, murmurs, the beautiful and the unfamiliar were able to fully inhabit his soul just for an instant, because his memory was not there to dull the clarity of the impressions. With almost no effort, it had freed itself from what he considered an imposed and irritating obligation to record and preserve everything he saw or heard. And inside he felt an emptiness—not the void that causes fear, but the benevolent emptiness we feel when nothing separates us from the things of this world.

Then, without thinking, a little taken aback by his new freedom, he reached for the bronze centerpiece with the two dolphins (the black letters on the base read "1909 Palast Kaffee"); he examined the porcelain box with the garden scene painted on the cover; he picked up the pale statuette of a shepherdess holding a lamb and moved it from under the lamp labeled "Alsace-Lorraine" to the other end of the table; he checked to see if he could repair the crack in the alabaster fisherman with his prize scaly catch. It wasn't that these pretentious bibelots glistening on the shelves of the display cabinet and the mahogany étagère were vestiges of a past he was yearning to return to, the city that no longer existed. He had always found the whole rococo business a little ridiculous and had made fun of the way his mother fussed over the blue and gilt porcelain, the way she stacked the Rosenthal and Werffel cups into little pyramids in the china cabinet and populated the glass shelves of the walnut chest with throngs of Chinese dancers, Japanese beauties made of majolica, Persians in lacquered costumes. He couldn't abide those dainty shepherdesses gracefully herding their golden-fleeced sheep, or the aggressive ebony samurai warriors, or the proud alabaster grins of fishermen showing off enormous sea perch with shiny golden scales. That entire world of porcelain and majolica always seemed silly to him—possessive and senseless. He was convinced that the only reason she spent so much time arranging all the porcelain boxes and figurines, and the jardinières studded with turquoise and rimmed with gold was to impress her guests. But their own sitting rooms were chock-full of similar baubles, so that the whole thing made no sense.

Now, however, at twilight, as the sky over the hills cooled

off after a scorching day, with the sun a distant fiery glow, he saw in those petite, delicate forms a childlike courage, a naive willingness to ignore the world, like the brave front children put on so they won't be scared of the dark. A benign, insolent defiance of power and authority. And when he picked up those bronze and pewter trinkets, those pieces of majolica and ivory, he felt a growing distaste for Nolde, Kokoschka, Kollwitz, though at one time he had been enamored of their paintings, of the raging red and corpselike violet that had crowded the walls of those small galleries in Berlin. Because when you deciphered their nerve-racked code, weren't all those aggressive pictures claiming that life was nothing but pain, that there was no way out, that mercy and compassion did not exist?

He stared out at the beech woods splotched with dark pines, then up at the sky where clouds were floating along like tufts of pussy willow—and all of that, transformed into the indifferent music of color, seeped into his heart, assuaging his former fears, while his soul guarded itself against a more complete image of the past. Any recollection of the larger landscape was chased away by a restless shiver. His eye chose to dwell on single, solitary objects—an ant climbing up a lampshade, a grain of rice stuck between the floorboards, a maple leaf with rusty edges clinging to the windowpane, a hawthorn branch jutting over the sill, dewdrops on a spiderweb in one corner of the window.

His mind guarded itself against the image of the whole, because the whole included those other images as well—that dark sea, the dock, the enormous clouds, the long beach between Neufahrwasser and Zoppot, water the color of lead, the white pier at Glettkau, and the pretty excursion boat with the black lettering on the hull...

And when those pictures did return, his heart turned away from the fading lights of dusk. His thoughts moved back into the past, slowly revisiting the dark landscapes, the Black Forest he had escaped to years before, when it all happened, to wander aimless and alone, full of grief and pain. Now that he felt nothing in his chest, he retraced his wanderings among the giant trees that had looked like the columns of a black cathedral. He walked along the streambeds and felt the cool stone cliffs reaching up to the sky and enclosing him in their damp darkness. He remembered the feel of the fog when the mountains opened before him to reveal a valley covered with broken trees and awash in bracken, and on a mossy overhang he discovered a solitary cross. His memory took him back to Rügen, where he stood on the steep escarpment at the edge of the pine forest and watched the golden crags plunge into the foamy brown sea with a deadly murmur. And as he fell into those somber, pulsing recollections, it occurred to him that what had happened back then happened just so he could become frozen in this state of slumber, half-alive, this hibernation that took his soul and anesthetized it against the voices of the world. He could live that way, he knew it. He wanted to live that way, although his heart resisted, with a tremor of resentment and disgust. Instead of fighting those feelings, however, he let himself sink in their black water, drinking in their bitter spite, though he had no idea on whom he might exact revenge.

| *The Lebenstein Clinic* |

IN THE MIDDLE OF December a Danish sailor whose ship had put in at Gdynia visited Mrs. Stein in her apartment on Klonowa, carrying a letter from Martin Retz addressed to Hanemann. The letter came as a surprise, since Hanemann had assumed that his former assistant was no longer alive. Retz was writing from Hannover, where he had moved after staying with his relatives in Bremen and where he intended to set up a practice.

Most of the letter was devoted to past events, however.

"My main reason for writing," wrote Retz, "is to tell you about the *Bernhoff.* They raised anchor a little before midnight. The gendarmes used purple lamps to light the entrance to the hold. At first it was hard to find a decent place to sleep, especially since part of the hold had been taken up by cadets from the submarine training school and mechanics from the Schichau shipyards. So I spent a while roaming around, tripping over people who were sprawled out in the half dark. Fortunately all I had to carry was my doctor's bag and a red plaid blanket from my landlady, Mrs. Wirth—you probably remember I stayed at her house until the end of January. The metal deck was extremely cold; I was lucky that Mrs. Wirth had also given me a pair of fur-lined shoes, which had belonged to her late husband Edward (I'm sure you remember him, that tall man who worked as a counsel for Hersen). Anyway I'll always be grateful to Mrs. Wirth for thinking of that—what a wise woman—on the same day I left Danzig. After a while they turned on some lights they had hung from the ceiling in the cargo bay, and people started calling out to one another. They put whatever they had on the deck: thick woolen blankets, goose-down quilts, coarse canvas sheets, and covered the wooden platforms with coats, blankets, furs. The bay was packed with families sleeping or dozing away. All in all, a pretty scary sight, but no one grumbled or complained...

"At one point I heard someone shouting from the other end of the hold: 'Dr. Retz, over here, come join us.' I turned around and saw Elsa Walmann and her daughters sitting on a wooden crate, while her husband Alfred was spreading out some bedding for the girls. I was surprised they recognized me, since they'd only seen me when I went to pick you up at Lessingstrasse. But believe me, sometimes even the slightest gesture of recognition can seem like the most heartfelt greeting.

"I fell asleep without any trouble, though to this day I don't know how that was possible. At around seven in the morning the cadets started dispensing hot coffee; I rolled up my blanket, and Mrs. Walmann asked what I knew about you. She had the worst misgivings, since she had seen several shells explode right in front of the warehouse just as the tugboat was pulling away from the dock. 'A number of people must have been killed right then and there,' she said. 'Dr. Hanemann had been heading toward us, but then... When we reached the Bernhoff, I turned around, and my heart froze when I saw that huge fire raging around the buildings on shore . . .' She talked about you as if you were dead.

"At around one o'clock I went on deck with Alfred Walmann, despite the fact that Mrs. Walmann preferred that we stay where we were, since the worst thing that could happen would be our losing one another. The weather was very cold: the *Bernhoff* was sailing through a thick, icy fog, and its pipes and railings were covered with icicles, its sides coated with ice. All of a sudden we heard some shouting and crying from down alongside the ship, and a moment later we saw a big barge full of screaming people. They tossed down a rope ladder, but no one seemed eager to board, which wasn't very surprising: there were lots of women with children, and they were all afraid they'd fall in. So the sailors had to use the derrick to lift whole families like sacks of wheat. The children were doubled over from the cold; they didn't want to climb onto that flimsy platform and had to be set there by force; they were howling terribly."

Retz had assumed they were heading for Hamburg, and figured that even if the *Bernhoff* took a zigzag course to evade any submarines, the journey shouldn't take more than three or four days. After he and Walmann went back down to the cargo bay, he wrapped himself in his blanket and sat on the crate. There was nothing else to do but doze away the time like everyone else. A few people were propped on their elbows, nervously listening to the rumble of the motors. They were afraid of torpedo attacks. Now and then Retz thought about how he had nearly drowned back in twenty-nine, when he was on vacation near Brösen, and cold shivers ran up and down his spine. He also remembered what had happened to the *Gustloff* and the *Steuben*.

When the refugees from the barge were taken belowdecks, the bay was even more crowded. Mrs. Walmann went aft in search of more space, but things there were just as cramped. In the corridor she ran into Liselotte Peltz. They were happy to see each other, although Liselotte seemed strangely reluctant to join them. On her way back, Mrs. Walmann saw her former neighbor, who was wrapped in a reddish fur, furtively gnawing at a slice of brown bread.

The girls kept quiet until about two o'clock, when they started to complain. Their mother tried to control them, but without much luck. She set some bread on a linen towel and shelled a hard-boiled egg. Mr. Walmann tried to cheer the girls up with a funny song about Heidelore, which he quietly whistled through his teeth. Then Elsa Walmann took out an apple, slowly peeled it, and cut it into four parts.

Mr. Walmann asked if Retz knew how far the Russians had advanced, but Retz hadn't been sure: "I told him I thought they'd reached Köslin, or maybe even farther. 'And what are you going to do now?' he asked. 'Me?'"

Walmann's question had caught Retz off guard, since for two days he'd felt as if he'd been lugging his body around from place to place like so much baggage. But that disembodied sensation had its advantages, too, since it allowed him to see everyone, including himself, as if through a glass pane. But now he needed to give an answer: "Well, doctors are always in demand." Mr. Walmann agreed and then paused for a moment before asking, "I'm curious: Do you think a person can remember the taste of tobacco when he dies? What do you think?" Retz had said nothing, just rummaged through his pockets, but couldn't find the prunes Mrs. Wirth had given him the morning before.

Although the fog they were sailing through was fairly thick, at around three o'clock a small airplane broke through the clouds and strafed the deck. They called for a doctor, so Retz took his little bag to the forward bay, where a space had been set off for a field hospital for wounded soldiers. They were tearing sheets for tourniquets and bandages. Down in the hold everyone was talking about submarines. People started pacing anxiously among the crates and bundles. At around three-thirty a tremor went through the ship. Four shadows came flying out of the fog and spouts of water shot up on both sides of the hull. Undeterred, Retz went on bandaging the chest of someone who had been shot in the lung. After the fifth or sixth explosion another tremor shook the ship, the deck tilted, the nickel-plated instruments slid off the table, the wounded started crying out, and the alarm bell went off. Retz smelled burning petrol; the medics ran on deck; he didn't know what to do. Finally he managed to get a few to turn back, then the ship tilted once again. He called a soldier with a rifle, but the people escaping from the forward hold shoved him aside to the wall. It wasn't until the soldier fired into the air that some of the wounded could be loaded into a lifeboat. The lines squealed, and the raft was lowered into the water.

The hull of the *Bernhoff* was listing more and more to starboard. Retz watched from the lifeboat as clouds of dirty yellow smoke billowed out of the superstructure in the middle of the ship. A moment later he caught sight of the Walmanns standing on the stern, barely visible behind the dark streaks of fire. Mr. Walmann was trying to get to another lifeboat that was hanging from the davits behind the second bay, but the flames were blocking his path. Mrs. Walmann was standing among the screaming women, both girls pressed close against her. Then the ship stopped tilting and stood frozen like a cliff over a lake, but the people kept backing away from the flames, closer and closer to the rail, because the air above the deck was undulating from the heat. When the fire had almost reached the aft superstructure, a few men jumped into the water. The girls clung tightly to Mrs. Walmann: Alfred Walmann first tore Maria from her mother's grasp and pushed her off the deck, then did the same with Eva. The girls hit the water and never came up. Mrs. Walmann began to scream, but all Retz could see was her open mouth—her cry was drowned in the howling of the wounded. Walmann dragged her to the rail, but she held on so tight he couldn't pull her hands off. He jerked hard, they both lost their balance, then he pushed her overboard. She somersaulted into the water and never surfaced. He jumped in after her but couldn't reach the spot where she had disappeared because the burning petrol was floating on top of the water. As the fire reached the people still on board, they started flopping into the water like scorched fish. Walmann made it to the raft; he shouted something to Retz and tried to grab hold of the transom, but a seaman was using an oar to fend off all those struggling to get on board, since the boat was already full of wounded soldiers. That's how Retz remembered him: a twisted face being hit by an oar...

Reading Retz's letter, Hanemann experienced a strange rush of feelings.

He was amazed that someone had thought about him that night aboard the *Bernhoff,* that someone had spoken about him—although what was so odd about that? For a moment he felt guilty that he hadn't been there with the others. He reproached himself for not having held them back at the dock; had he done so, things would not have turned out the way they had. But he shook his head, realizing right away how ridiculous he was being: how could he have known it would end like that? They had had a better chance than the ones who stayed behind; after all, thousands of people had made it to Hamburg, Bremen, Rostock, Wilhelmshaven. For a split second he imagined the bottom of the sea, the gray sand somewhere off Bornholm, the birdlike print of a child's hand, a gleaming array of tiny bones…Eva, Maria…But he sensed something else, too, in his brooding sorrow; he felt his heart grazed by some unsettling, tender emotion. Pity? Then a cold wave of frustration. He looked at Retz's letter, unable to sort out his feelings. He wanted to sympathize, wanted to accuse himself, wanted somehow to erase his guilt. But what if it turned out—he thought suddenly—that theirs had been the more intelligent decision, that night when they boarded the tugboat and set off toward the ship hidden in the darkness?

He put off answering Retz for several weeks. Finally, at the beginning of February, he wrote a polite note consisting mostly of questions, since he didn't want to write more about himself. He didn't receive a reply until that summer, when a short letter arrived from Miss Hildegarde Müller, assistant to Professor Jürgen T. Wolff, informing him that Dr. Martin Retz had passed away in March at the Lebenstein Clinic in Bremen, where he was being treated for lung cancer. Dr. Retz had endured great pain but had borne his suffering courageously, winning the respect and gratitude of the medical staff from Department III C.

Hanemann stared awhile at the lilac-colored card in his hand, the card imprinted with the label "Lebenstein Clinic. Bremen. Bahnhofstrasse 33." Miss Müller had a beautiful script: even, slanted, with no unnecessary ornament. Her signature resembled a handful of black grass.

So that was the port where the steamer *Friedrich Bernhoff* was headed on that winter night as it left the channel at Neufahrwasser, while the rockets were flaring over Brösen, illuminating the harbor with a garish blue light, and the observers in the Müggau Heights directed the gunners on the Zigankenberg to move the sights of their howitzers two millimeters to the left…

| *Summoned* |

THE SUMMONS CAME on Wednesday. Hanemann signed the receipt without looking at the postman, handed back the copying pencil, closed the door, and turned the key. Footsteps disappearing down the stairs. The look in the man's eyes. Hanemann had no illusions: this was the look for those who had fallen into disgrace.

At eleven he took a streetcar downtown into Gdańsk.

"Mr. Hanemann..." A man wearing a dark suit opened a cardboard file. The room was hot, the window ajar. Hanging on the wall was a white eagle on a red background. "You recently received a letter from Denmark?" Hanemann nodded, quickly adding up the days: the Danish sailor had visited Mrs. Stein on Klonowa Street last week, at exactly noon on Friday; today was Thursday.

"What kind of letter was it, if I might ask?" the man leafed through pages written in green ink. Blotting paper, an inkwell in a wooden holder, a lamp with a wrought-iron shade. Hanemann explained that the letter was exclusively personal.

"And who sent it?"

Hanemann paused a moment. "My former assistant, Martin Retz, who is currently living in Hannover, where he intends to open his own practice."

The man raised his eyebrows. "You claim this letter came from Martin Retz, your former assistant at the Anatomical Institute, and that it was exclusively about personal matters, but if that's the case, then why wasn't it sent through the mail?" Hanemann admitted that he couldn't answer that question, but he guessed that Martin Retz had taken advantage of the Danish sailor's offer in order to save a few marks.

The man shrugged his shoulders. "Are you suggesting that someone is opening your letters and therefore you prefer not to use our mail?"

Hanemann felt his heart beating faster. "That never occurred to me."

The man rose from the desk and went to the window, through which they could see the dark structure of the Marienkirche, the charred tower of the Rathaus, and, to the left, the space on Reitbahn off Karrenwall, where the New Synagogue with its brass sugar-bowl dome had stood until it was demolished, in thirty-nine. A few workers were standing on the dusty plaza, stacking bricks pulled from the ruins. On Złota Brama Street, a poster had been hung on one of the buildings that were still standing; the paper had been torn, leaving only the words "... reactionary dwarfs..." Hanemann had seen posters like that on walls in Oliwa and Langfuhr as well, but he didn't really know to whom they were referring. Undoubtedly people the new regime considered to be enemies.

"Mr. Hanemann, it's not just about the letter"—the man turned around, fingering a green penholder for a moment. "Tell me, why is it you didn't leave?" Aha...so that's the reason they called him in… "Surely you read our newspapers, so you know that your fatherland hasn't changed as it should have, except in the east, where we're happy to see some very visible improvements. But Hannover is another matter… People who deserve to be put on trial are returning to power… and you receive letters from them. Perhaps you ought to reconsider your decision…"

Hanemann stared out the window at the pine scaffolding around the Rathaus tower. Over on Hundegasse—now Ogarna Street—some workers were laying shiny fresh red tiles on the roof of a building.

"Are you listening to me?" The man's voice sounded impatient.

Hanemann looked down at his hands. "My sister was killed outside Dirschau in January of forty-five. I don't have any family on the other side of the Odra. So why should I want to go there?"

The man began to pace the floor. "Are you suggesting that we killed your sister?" Hanemann half closed his eyelids: What did this person really want? The man stopped at his desk. "We're concerned by how well you speak Polish; after all, you Germans consider us a subhuman race." Hanemann made a face. He had had enough of the conversation. For a moment he was relieved at the thought they might pack him onto a train and ship him somewhere west—at least for the moment no one was saying anything about the east. What difference did it make where he lived? He wasn't going to lift a finger in his own defense.

"I have no plans to leave. However, if I'm thrown out…"

The man cut him off: "No one has any intention of throwing you out. The point is that you should simply consider whether it might not be better for you…"

Hanemann felt more and more irritated. "You're surprised I speak Polish so well. But I can assure you that the reason is completely coincidental, just like the fact that I speak German. My mother's family came from outside Poznań. I've always had Polish friends: before the war, when I studied in Berlin, and later in Gdańsk. But that doesn't mean anything. I speak French well too: my father came from Alsace."

The man eyed him closely. "You really are a curious case, Mr. Hanemann. And one more thing: Why didn't you go back to the Academy? I'm sure you realize that several of your countrymen are still employed there. I'm told they maintain the x-ray apparatus. And there are a number of nurses . . ."

Hanemann didn't move. "I have no intention of returning to the Academy. There's no need to go into the reasons, which certainly wouldn't interest you."

The man smiled. "Who knows . . . By the way: how do you plan to make a living, if you insist on staying here?"

Hanemann thought about his home on Lessingstrasse. Although he hadn't counted on them to leave him alone, he had hoped against hope that they might. After all, why was he any different from his neighbors? Only a slightly harder accent, or so he believed. He had imagined that he'd vanished in a sea of people and that no one would pay any attention to him. His herringbone coat was the same as Mr. K.'s, who'd just had his things carried up to the second floor of the Bierensteins' house. And when he looked in the mirror, Hanemann saw a man like any other you might meet on the streets of Langfuhr, or Wrzeszcz as it was now called. But now he was beginning to regret that he had stayed, that he hadn't had the strength to go to the train station, with or without a suitcase, when the last Germans from around Jäschkentaler Weg climbed aboard the cars labeled "Gdańsk-Koszalin-Szczecin." He had counted on being able to blend in with his surroundings. And here this man was eyeing him like an entomologist examining an insect under a magnifying glass. Hands, feet, shoulders—everything was larger than life, like the little hairs on a bee's abdomen, viewed with a powerful lens. Hatred . . .

"But you know perfectly well how I'm earning my living."

The man smiled. "There's no need to get angry. Of course I do. I just wanted to make sure you were being frank with me." His hair was smoothed back and shaved high over his ears, there were scratch marks on his neck, a tight collar, a necktie with a thick knot. "Go ahead and keep doing what you've been doing. We don't care." Hanemann still didn't know why he had been summoned. The man rested his hands on the desk. "Of course, if you aren't more careful about the kind of contacts you keep, you might land in trouble. Someone with your qualifications would be of great interest to Fascist agents: they're bound to approach you." Was this a threat, then? The man looked at his fingernails.

Hanemann turned his head. "I have no intention of approaching anyone."

"There—right away you get so irritated." The man gave Hanemann a condescending look. "And besides, you're being unreasonable. There could well be times when it would be necessary to let someone approach us. The evil we don't know is a hundred times worse than the evil we can recognize. After all, you knew some interesting people, presumably pretty well, too—Albert Posack, Erich Brost, Richard Tetzlaff, to name a few. Not to mention Rauschning. But that didn't mean anything, right? Supposedly you just talked about music . . ."

So they know about that as well.

"Of course," the man went on, "the Social Democrats weren't the best choice, but you did prefer them to the brownshirts. Supposedly you even made a few strong statements in the presence of Greiser or Forster. Is that right?"

So they know. They probably have people from the Free

City, there's no sense in trying to hide things. But who? Almost all his neighbors on Lessingstrasse were from far away. Mrs. Stein? Nonsense. Maybe the high school teacher, Mr. J.? That was ridiculous. Nervously, he shuffled through the faces in his memory. But then he calmed down: What difference did it make where they got their information?

The man leaned against the window frame. "So you no longer have the letter from Hannover?"

"No," he replied automatically, although it wasn't true.

"You burned it?"

"That's right, I burned it," Hanemann's voice stiffened.

"That's strange," the man said, moving to the desk, "burning a letter from your former assistant that was exclusively personal. Why? I don't believe you. I'm sure you still have that letter. But that's not important. Go on and keep it. We don't need it." The man closed the cardboard file and tied up the covers with a gray ribbon. "That's all for now. So I understand you don't intend to leave Gdańsk anytime in the near future?"

Hanemann felt a cold twinge near his heart. "No, I don't."

"That's good. Because if the need arose..."

"I have no intention of leaving," Hanemann repeated. "You can rest assured that you will always be able to find me on Lessingstrasse."

"You meant to say Grottger Street?"

"Yes, on Grottger Street."

"Fine. Well, that's all for now. Here's your pass. Just leave it at the door." Hanemann took the printed form. "If you need to contact me for any reason, just ask for extension twenty-seven. Lieutenant Karkosz." Hanemann said nothing. "And one more thing. If you decide you want to visit your former assistant Retz in Hannover some time, I think that might be possible. Just something to consider. We wouldn't pose any obstacles."

Taking the Number 2 streetcar back to Lessingstrasse, Hanemann carefully weighed every word he had heard on the fourth floor of the building on Okopowa Street, and couldn't help concluding that the passing of time was only an illusion. It was incredible to think that just a few years earlier he had been taking the Number 3 streetcar back to Lessingstrasse after a similar meeting, though the tone of that encounter had been a good deal friendlier, since it was his friend Johann Plesner who had invited him. Johann had the same boyish quality he remembered from their student days in Berlin, although he had exchanged his white doctor's coat for a steel green policeman's uniform and now held the important and respectable position of police commissioner for the Hakelwerk district. Johann had invited Hanemann to his home at Breitgasse 4, where his mother served them an excellent Rhine wine in the sitting room. The warm smell of birch wood burning in the tile stove, which had been built in the days of Frederick the Great, did wonders to relax body and mind. All those recollections, friendly disputes, the old student jokes! Sip by sip, the wine vanished from the glasses, and small wedges of walnut torte appeared on the decorative platter in the middle of the table. At that point Johann had suddenly become very serious, his voice very matter-of-fact. He mentioned a group of specialists in Dresden, experts in Slavic linguistics who enjoyed the enviable support and confidence of the Reichsführer himself. But with all due respect, wasn't Hanemann just as fluent in that difficult language spoken by the Slavic people living a little to the east? Or perhaps even better, since for all their expertise, the specialists probably spoke that language with an accent that was a shade too hard, too clipped... And Pomerania was full of native speakers who would notice, and whose growing presence in the region posed a threat to the ancient Teutonic culture—a culture great enough to shelter all of its descendants, including those who had lived among the eastern tribes for generations. (After all, which of us can claim absolute racial purity?) Hanemann's own family background was proof, for despite whatever Slavic blood ran in their veins, his illustrious ancestors had always found a welcome in the grand Gothic house of eternal Germany.

Hanemann listened to the entire speech without setting down his glass and without breaking his smile. Oh, that Johann—would he never change? Always that cool sparkle at the bottom of his true Bavarian eyes. But Johann proceeded to catalog all the achievements of the house of Hanemann as doctors in the service of the King of Prussia and his army, and then moved on to more contemporary matters. Nor can we forget, he continued, about the difficulties our national mission faces here, in this very city that the British and French have ironically declared to be "Free" according to that damned Versailles! There are times when it can be good to approach people who are clearly disinclined toward us, just in order to get to know . . . Johann had in mind Chief Brzostowski of the Polish Post Office in Hakelwerk, who had recently moved to Oliva, where he rented a room in Greta Schneider's house, close to the streetcar loop.

Now, as the Number 2 streetcar passed the Anatomy Building on its way to Wrzeszcz, and the dark walls of the Institute appeared outside the window, Hanemann averted his eyes. He didn't want to look at the gray facade. On the other side of the street, he saw a green Russian tank mounted on a stone pedestal, freshly painted, with a white eagle on the turret. So that was the tank Mrs. Stein had been talking about . . . Several carnations, red and white, were strewn on the steel plating. Next to the treads two children were playing in the sand. An elderly lady sitting on a bench was calling out to them without a voice.

The day promised to be beautiful and hot.

| *Gutenberg Grove* |

"I WOULD HOLD THE BOOK in one hand and slowly read out loud, patiently moving my finger across the long rows of Gothic letters, because my parents really wanted me to shine in front of the exam board in Poznań, to show them that I knew how to read the old script, in addition to having a good accent. Each time I tripped over a new word, Hanemann would point his yellow Kohinoor pencil at the syllables I had to repeat. Not that it helped much: the Gothic *M* looked like a braided black ribbon, and I kept mistaking it for a *W,* and the double *S,* that mischievous little sign, insisted on looking like an *F.* And this despite the fact that I'd been able to practice everything ahead of time, in Father's room, where he had a Protestant prayer book from our family's home in Powiśle lying next to a Cyrillic Bible. The prayer book was printed in Polish, but with Gothic type.

"Even so, the lessons had their rewards," Andrzej Ch. went on, when we met years later at the university of Bremen, where he'd found a job after finishing his doctorate in German and where he taught seminars on Central and Eastern European culture for young men from Bahrain and women from Thailand. "It was painfully difficult," he explained, "for a sixteen-year-old boy from Bohaterów Westerplatte Street: my eyes would trudge across the thorny Fraktur type, the interlocked chains of Gothic characters, but in time the pain became mixed with pleasure, and eventually I discovered a colorful world I hadn't known existed the first time I visited that apartment on the second floor of 17 Grottger Street. Because whenever Hanemann had had enough of the tedious grammar, which I have to confess I did not always prepare for as thoroughly as I should have, when he was bored with all the repeating and reciting, he would smile his little smile and invite me to what he called the Gutenberg Grove—and he wasn't talking about the woods of the same name near Jaśkowa Dolina.

"He would step over to the mahogany case with the leaded glass panes and pull a volume out at random, usually off the shelf housed works from the thirties, books bound in linen, edged with leather, and brown with age. He would look at the book and decide whether it was right for the moment, and if it was, he would hand it over to me—not to translate (it was far too early for that!), but to hold, to feel its weight, to touch the yellowish paper with the odd name 'Java' and feel the dark gilt edges, to give a glimpse of what was yet to come.

"One day he picked out Rauschning's *Revolution of Nihilism*. It was a beautiful edition, printed in Zurich, with a black Gothic title on a red jacket. But what could it possibly mean to me, only sixteen years old? When Hanemann saw what book he'd chosen, he shook his head with a bitter half smile, as if something truly valuable were hidden between its covers. However, he had a different book by the same author, *The History of Music in Old Danzig,* which was another matter—I loved looking at the frontispiece, a sepia print of the Marienkirche organ. Hanemann started to read a passage from the first chapter, in a calm, measured voice, slowly so that I would understand as much as possible, and the long German words filled my ears, there in the second-story room at 17 Grottger Street. I didn't understand much, since the piece was full of technical terms from music history, and the subject didn't really excite me, but he kept on reading anyway, because, as he put it, you need deep water to learn to swim. Later, when he began to translate into Polish, I suddenly felt how the melody of the history of church music in old Danzig clashed with the melody of the translation—a clash I'd never sensed before, either reading to myself or even out loud. Little by little, I began to understand what foreignness really was, began to realize that differences in tone matter much more than differences in meaning precisely because tone is so palpably close to us. We cannot escape our voice no matter how hard we try: it's locked deep inside us, jealously guarded by our body.

"But those were all mere attempts, first approaches that promised more than they delivered, and I had no choice but to be patient, as long as I felt this physical distance from a foreign concept of beauty that I accepted partly on faith, although more and more words began to resonate inside me with double and even triple meanings. In time, the complex sentence structures became transparent, but the words remained decidedly too long. What were my Polish ears to make of words like *Einführungsfeierlichkeit, Elementarunterricht,* or *Haushaltungsvorstand*—which sounded like the train rattling across the mile-long bridge over the Vistula at Tczew? All these initial forays taught me respect for German, but even when I immersed my ears in the sounds, my heart remained completely numb to any charms of accent or intonation, and it was with only a cold interest that I listened to

Hanemann's voice, trying to detect new twists of syntax, which though ostensibly laden with meaning seemed empty to me, like a scaffold waiting for the home to be built.

"That was usually the way things went. But one September day, as I sat there, patient but indifferent, ready for the next trial, Hanemann selected a book bound in green linen. His hand hesitated for a moment, unsure whether to keep it or return it to the shelf, but then I saw something in Hanemann's face I'd never seen before, a barely perceptible softening of features, and then, just when I was sure he was going to put the green book back in its place, he quickly handed it to me.

"It was a good 1905 edition of Kleist's letters, edited by Erich Schmidt, Georg Minde-Pouet, and Reinhold Steig, a book I enjoy picking up to this day. Hanemann's calm, muted voice began reading the letters of a poet named Heinrich to a woman named Adolfine Henriette Vogel, and I immediately felt the strange words, which up until then had been only a cold, artificial pattern of meanings, begin to reach my heart. These words contained a dark maturity that I had dreamed about but never actually seen, a maturity that was strange and solemn, dangerous, not without pain—a maturity pervaded with a childishness so fierce that it was scary. It attracted and repelled me at the same time. A strange, somber tone came flowing out of the pen of that poet named Heinrich, and I felt as if his words were growing inside me. Then it dawned on me that they were simply resonating there, because—and this took me a while to realize, too—Hanemann was not reading the way he usually did. At times he seemed to forget that it was only a linguistic exercise designed to lead me through the labyrinth of German syntax.

"I couldn't fully grasp the life that opened up before me in the fragments he was reading, Kleist's last letters, confessing his love to Henriette, but I could tell that they had a strange power, highly unsettling and contagious, yet also calming. Various contradictory forces were at work, which shook the infinitely sensitive soul of that odd man who wrote to Mrs. Vogel. His was a struggle I could sympathize with; feelings I had worked hard to muffle and contain as weak and unmanly resurfaced. Emotions I had always been ashamed of now appeared in a new form, strangely powerful and still. Love, hate, and hope were fanned to the extreme, and somehow these feelings, which are so amorphous, so chaotic that they generally inspire fear, acquired a crystalline beauty in the voice of this poet I had never heard of before. Of course, I wasn't able to describe it like that at the time—all I felt back then was a vague tangle of passions: obsessive desire, love, trembling, the yearning to die young, but all of these 'sick emotions,' as Goethe once called them in a strongly worded letter, struck me as pure and natural, signs of a heart that was truly alive.

"When I asked to hear more, Hanemann told me about a boy—and I mean a boy—in the uniform of a Prussian officer, injured and insulted, at odds with everyone, cast off by family and friends, a boy who finally found support in a girl who was as sensitive as he was, and her support was stronger than the whole world.

"I dreamed about death, and never before or after did such dreaming seem so sweet as when I pictured that boy and girl on the banks of the Wannsee on November 21, 1811, those two souls who first wrote those wild and beautiful letters that Hanemann was reading to me in his changed voice, then took their own lives beside the bright, clear water. Something opened up deep inside my soul that had been imprisoned; I sneered at all the cold people devoid of feeling, scoffed at their caution, their scheming. I was prepared to give in, to yield to that same undertow, no matter how the world might condemn my action. I felt myself falling into the sweet darkness of that faraway lake, but with half my mind I knew I was doing something I would later bitterly regret, so I completely missed the fact that I was not alone, that Hanemann, too, had found something in the voice of Henriette, something deeply, achingly personal and shameful that connected him to me, a sixteen-year-old boy. And today I would probably say that both of us were traveling to a faraway time, sunny and good, that we had never inhabited but that nonetheless existed, it had to exist, because it was there in the letters, opening up before our eyes.

"It must all have been connected with past events I knew nothing about, because one afternoon, when I was looking at an album of photos from the Free City, I came across a brownish picture of a man wearing a white jacket and a woman in an ankle-length dress of dark crepe de chine. They were walking down the middle of a pier toward an invisible photographer, and behind them you could see the harbor pennant and a white excursion boat with the name *Star* visible on the hull. 'But that's you!' I shouted, full of joy at my happy discovery—and Hanemann came over to where I was sitting, leaned over the brownish photo with the caption 'Glettkau. Pier and mooring,' and I saw the same barely perceptible softening of features I had seen when his hand first picked out the book bound in green linen.

"And while Hanemann slowly read Kleist's last letter, with muted voice, I kept seeing the brownish photo with the Gothic caption. Glettkau... what kind of name is that? A pier on the Baltic? Where could that be? And then I realized, of course, it's Jelitkowo, but the pier's no longer there. The images from the past merged with my own recollections of places I knew so well. The muted voice, the room in the green half dark, the window opened at an angle, where every breeze from the garden sent ripples through the curtain, the whisper of the birch tree shading that side of the house—all of that made it impossible for me to resist the impression that Hanemann was talking about someone he knew well as he told the story of the boy and the girl who killed themselves beside the Wannsee, even though they had died so long ago. And as he told their story using the words of that faraway letter, as he led me through his private Gutenberg Grove, not far from the real one on the edge of Jaśkowa Dolina, where I had wandered so many times, the deep blue Wannsee opened up in a forest of red maples like an eye gazing at the heavens, the deep blue water was ringed by a narrow green meadow, and in that meadow, under a dark spruce, Henriette Vogel was writing a letter to Ernst Friedrich Peguilhen, lightly guiding her pen across the vellum paper with the prince's watermark: 'I am enclosing 10 Reichstaler with the request of placing an order for a beautiful pale blue cup, gilded on the inside, the edge to be white with a gold arabesque trim, and with my name on the top, in accordance with the latest fashion. If you would deliver this commission to the bookkeeper Meves at the porcelain factory, with instructions to deliver the cup to *Louis* on *Christmas Eve,* but my dear friend you will have to hurry or else the cup will not be ready in time. May you fare well and be happy.' And on another letter, a postcript: 'Fare you well, then, my dear friends, and remember in joy and sorrow these two unique souls soon to embark on their great voyage of discovery.'

"Hanemann's voice made it sound as if that extraordinary woman were speaking right to him, as if he himself were the mysterious Herr Peguilhen whom I had never heard of. His speech was quiet, calibrated to a tender sensitivity which guaranteed that these faraway greetings and requests would not be lost in nothingness, and then I heard another voice, accompanying Henriette's, the voice of an unknown Prussian officer who didn't want to be an officer, the voice of a boy who had been forsaken by everyone: '...that I have a friend whose soul soars like a young eagle, I have never seen the like of her in all my life, she understands my sadness as something higher, deeply rooted and incurable, and therefore, even though she has in hand the means to make me happy here on earth, she wishes to join with me in death...and you will understand that my sole and joyous care will be to find a precipice deep enough for us to leap into.'

"Listening to Hanemann's voice, I saw them both, Kleist in his bright blue tailcoat and Henriette in her white and pink dress, gently ruffled by the warm breeze from the Wannsee, while high above the smooth table of the deep blue lake, high above the surrounding forest, a bright, narrow path opened up between the clouds, just like the one I liked to run down from the sandy rocks in back of the Cathedral, and I wanted so much, I yearned, to be one of them, to feel that airy joy, the exaltation trembling in Henriette's words, and the stunningly calm certainty that the path that passes between the clouds just as it passes between the cliffs in Caspar David Friedrich's paintings, that this bright narrow path does not lead to nothingness but climbs straight up to a blaze of light, which isn't the sun but an ephemeral mist like a cloud of pollen, full of winged souls holding hands. And down on earth Henriette was running through tulips and bellflowers with tiny leaves, as distinct as if they had been painted by Philipp Otto Runge himself. Everything came together in one big picture: the yellow cliffs of Rügen vanishing over the horizon; the Brandenburg Gate; the wild, unbridled gallop of a horse with fluttering mane, in which an old man with a windblown beard and fiery green eyes holds on to a boy whose face is flamed with fever, and around them, whirling through the air like butterflies, an array of drowned women with bare white shoulders and tattered muslin garments, flashing in the windy stream. And all those swirling colors and lights flowed straight into my bloodstream; I felt them hit my chest and found myself waking in my dark room at Obrońców Westerplatte Street, where the minute hand was almost showing six o'clock and a new day was about to begin with a painful racket, a day full of promise that I might again catch sight of Anna, whom I sometimes saw on the steps of our school, sitting with a red-haired girl who was always laughing, and maybe everything would work out and it would all be sweet and painful and heart-breaking and forever..."

Fraktur

AT DUSK, THE STUCCO on the wall of the Bierenstein house, cooling off after the sweltering day, cracked silently into a web of thread-thin lines. Inside Hanemann's room, invisible layers of dust settled on the books. The marbled paper in the margins of the pages patiently yellowed, sprouting rusty stains and splotches where touched, while the covers aged pale and gray beneath the jackets. Dark clouds drifted over the beechwood heights toward the Cathedral.

At that time of day Hanemann would move his armchair next to the window.

Years earlier, whenever his mother finished reading another bedtime story from the Brothers Grimm, she would put the heavy volume back in the bookcase, wish him good night, and leave the room. No sooner was the light out than Hanemann would feel the letters—yearning for adventure and eager to escape their confinement, waiting for the chance to run around inside the book—break out of their paragraphs, join together in happy black garlands, and weave a new tale never heard by human ears. Then in the morning he would dash to the bookcase, pull the book from its shelf and open it as quickly as he could, to catch them off guard. If only he could catch them once before they came back from their nighttime revels to the empty page! And if his mother could see it! What he wouldn't give for that!

Nowadays when he opened a book, he knew that the letters wouldn't slip out of his fingers like spiders running out from under a lifted rock. But occasionally he had the same wish: that what was written was not written forever. The story he kept coming back to was a simple one, since the man who wrote it was only recounting what he had seen and heard. The title was set in Fraktur at the top of the page: "The Testimony of Johann Friedrich Stimming, keeper of the New Tankard inn near Potsdam." The even rows of characters, pressed into the paper from Koblenz, formed a tight column of Gothic script. Hanemann lifted the red-ribbon bookmark and smoothed the page. Once he began to read, even the distant noises of the city could not distort the hushed voice of Herr Stimming:

"On Wednesday the twentieth of November this year, at two in the afternoon, two strangers rode up in their own carriage from Berlin, a lady and a gentleman. They put up at my place and asked if they might eat. They explained they only wished to stay a few hours, as they were expecting some people from Potsdam to come for them. They asked for a room and we showed them one downstairs on the left, but the lady was not satisfied with it and preferred to take an upstairs room. So they were shown a room upstairs, whereupon the lady asked if they might not be able to take an adjoining room as well, and we immediately agreed. Then the woman went to the window and asked if they might be able to obtain a rowing boat, to cross to the other side of the lake. My wife explained that we could probably find such a boat but that it would be difficult; however, it was easy to reach the other side of the lake on foot. The lady was very pleased to hear it. She then asked for a sofa and, since we had none, requested that two beds be made up, one in each room, as the people they were expecting might come during the night, and would then be able to rest...

"At five the next morning the lady came down and asked for some coffee, which both of them drank, and at seven requested another serving, and soon it was nine o'clock. They had the girl clean their clothes. When asked if they would like to eat, they said they only wanted to drink some bouillon, and would eat all the better for it in the evening.

"They then asked for their bill, which they paid, and for a receipt. Afterward they requested that a messenger be sent to Berlin to deliver a letter, and he set off at twelve o'clock. When asked what they wished to eat in the evening, the gentleman replied that they were expecting two men that evening and they would certainly have an appetite. 'No,' said the lady, 'I thought we had decided they would be satisfied with an omelet, just like us.' 'In that case,' said the gentleman, 'we'll eat all the better tomorrow afternoon,' and then both repeated that two guests were coming that evening.

"Then both went out and spoke about the setting and the beautiful surroundings, very pleased and playful, so that no one noticed anything unusual...

"They came into the kitchen, and the lady asked my wife if she would bring the coffee to that beautiful green clearing on the other side of the lake; it had such a lovely view. When my wife expressed her surprise, since this was so far, the gentleman said very obligingly that he would happily pay the people for their trouble and asked for eight groschen worth of rum as well.

"Then they both went to the clearing in question, and when my wife asked if they wanted the room cleaned in the meantime, they declined, saying they would prefer 'that everything be left the way it was.' The lady had a little basket on her arm, which was covered with a white cloth, which is probably where they had placed the pistols.

"When we brought the coffee and rum, they asked for a table and two chairs, which were also sent over. Then the gentleman requested a pencil and asked how much he owed for the coffee. This made us think he was an artist who wanted to sketch the surroundings. I sent the pencil over with the message that the coffee could be paid for later. Both guests walked up to meet the servingwoman, and the lady handed her the coffee dishes, with the money for the coffee and rum in one of the cups. The lady then said, Here are four groschen for your trouble, and added that she should give the other money to the innkeeper, wash the cup out, and bring it back. The woman left, and both guests hurried back to the table.

"The servingwoman had gone no more than about forty steps when a shot went off, followed by a second one, thirty steps later. The woman believed that they were shooting for pleasure, since both guests had been so playful and merry, throwing stones into the water, running and jumping, joking with each other. When the servingwoman brought the cup back to us, we found it odd that they would want the cup returned without any coffee. But the servingwoman took it and carried it over. When she reached the clearing she found both people, lifeless, in their own blood.

"Dumb with horror, she ran back to her apartment in shock, and when our girl saw her running like that she called out that the two guests had shot themselves and were lying there dead.

"We, too, were stunned by the news. We first went to the rooms but found the doors locked fast. We pushed our way into one of the rooms through a side door, which had been barricaded with every chair available. Nothing was there except a sealed package. Then we ran to the clearing, where we found both dead, the woman leaning back, both halves of her jacket flung open, her hands folded on her breast. The bullet had entered her left breast, pierced her heart and passed through the left shoulder blade. The man was found in the same spot, kneeling before her, having fired a fatal bullet through his mouth into his head. Neither appeared distorted; rather, each wore a happy, contented expression.

"At six o'clock two gentlemen arrived from Berlin; one climbed out of the carriage and asked whether the two guests were still here. When he was told that both were dead he asked whether it was really true. We told him that both were lying in their own blood on the other side of the lake. Then the other gentleman stepped out as well, the husband of the deceased. He came inside, threw his hat into one corner and his gloves into another, and was completely inconsolable over the loss of his wife.

"When we asked about the gentleman who had shot himself together with the lady, we learned that he had been a friend of theirs, a Herr Heinrich von Kleist...

"We then waited until eleven in the evening, and since no one came from the police, we went to bed. The next morning the husband had a lock of his wife's hair brought to him, and both men traveled back to Berlin. At noon the first gentleman, who had accompanied the lady's husband, returned: a certain military councilor, Herr Peguilhen, who now had a large grave dug close to the bodies, promising to send coffins from Berlin, so that they could be buried next to each other.

"On November 22, at ten in the evening, they were both placed in their coffins and laid to rest."

When nothing remained of the day but a warm rectangle of sunlight crossing the windowsill, Hanemann put the book away. The gold letters gleamed on the green linen of the cover. The air in the garden was weightless and still bright, and even a fuzzy golden brown butterfly, restlessly beating its dark little wings against the windowpane, did not disturb the tranquil twilight. Footsteps were coming up the street. The clear, high sky slowly died out over the arborvitae.

A pigeon's shadow flitted across the wall of the Bierenstein's house.

Warm, living hands.

Fear.

The Oak Leaf

NOW AND THEN Mr. J. would stop in for a visit. In the Free City he had taught at the Polish gymnasium (which he'd paid for with interrogations in the Victoria-Schule and the Stutthof concentration camp); now he taught German at the lyceum on Topolowa Street. Hanemann had known him for a long time, and although he felt that Mr. J.'s visits weren't without ulterior motive, since he probably came not only to exchange ideas but also to hear proper German, with which he otherwise had little contact, Hanemann was happy to receive him. He would set Mr. J. in the leather armchair and offer him a glass of red wine. To say that they were close friends might be going too far. But each time I saw them walking down Grottger Street or strolling toward the Cathedral, I had the impression that there was something else that connected them other than the fact that they had known each other when the city was governed by the High Commissioner from the League of Nations.

I sensed the same thing with other Poles from the Free City. Like Mr. J., they sought out opportunities to speak the language of Goethe. They also tended to treat the "new Poles"—whether they came from the former eastern provinces or from Warsaw—with a polite reserve, as if the years spent in the Free City, where hostile elements made their lives a constant daily struggle (as they always emphasized), had not only strengthened their character but also marked each who had survived with a kind of stigmata of superiority. Mr. J. considered everything the new Poles brought to Gdańsk to be watered down, weak, of dubious quality. After all, they had come in on the heels of a huge army and found everything waiting for them in Langfuhr and Oliva, but what if the Germans came back? Would these Poles from Warsaw or Lublin or Wilna show the same fortitude and strength of character that the Danzig Poles had shown in the days of the Free City? Mr. J. had grave doubts.

Although both men undoubtedly had causes for general resentment, they kept them well hidden, while certain traits they had in common were immediately evident—the same timbre of voice, the same serious approach to matters that might seem trivial to the uninitiated—and they clearly shared other, less visible qualities as well. As a result, they could move from one theme to another without any conscious effort or plan. They talked mostly for simple enjoyment, conversing rather than debating complicated issues. The pretexts were accidental: an everyday event, a photograph, a particular book. Mr. J. liked to focus on the old German writers because he didn't know the new ones. Hanemann wasn't always able to answer his questions.

One afternoon—it must have been in May—Mr. J. spotted a collection of Kleist's letters lying on Hanemann's desk, a beautiful volume bound in green linen. He picked it up and opened it at the little red ribbon. Looking at the photograph of the young man in the Prussian uniform, Mr. J. said, "You know, we have a similar story with a Polish author and artist." He wondered aloud what drove people to such extreme actions...

Hanemann raised his eyebrows.

Mr. J. flipped through another few pages of Gothic print and smiled. "I even knew him a little. Well, I didn't exactly know him, but once when I was in Warsaw, a friend of mine from the teachers' union, who was acquainted with various writers—including the poet Czechowicz—and a number of painters, took me to Bracka Street so I could commission a portrait from one of his friends. As it happened, I wasn't very pleased with the way it came out, but that's immaterial. Anyway, everything was destroyed in the fires, so not a trace remained. But that's how I met the man, and I think that his story was a little like this one." Mr. J. tapped the green linen cover.

Because back in the days when Hanemann was stopping in at the little galleries on Winterstrasse or in Siegfriedplatz to see the latest paintings by Nolde, Kokoschka, and Kollwitz, back when he was reading *Der Sturm, Die Aktion,* and watching productions staged by Max Reinhardt, Mr. J. was taking advantage of every trip to Warsaw or Poznań—partly out of snobbism and partly out of curiosity—to see exhibitions of "difficult" painters. Now and then, among the works of Czyżewski, Pronaszko, Waliszewski, or Chwistek, he would find a painting by the man he had just been talking about—typically convulsing with strident colors. Mr. J. didn't exactly like the pictures, but so what? Everybody knows how hard it is to judge something you don't understand. So they sat in the second-story room talking about remote events, their slow German speech accompanied by the muffled rustling of the birch tree outside the window, and years later, when Mr. J. told me about his encounters with Hanemann, I had the strange impression that their quarrel over Kleist and Henriette really served to mask a different disagreement, one they were probably unaware of. Besides, were they really quarreling?

The story Mr. J. told Hanemann happened a few days after the war broke out. Hanemann couldn't picture the places on a map; he only knew they were somewhere east, across a large river, where the land was flat and marshy . . .

A few days after the Germans laid siege to Warsaw, a Polish commander ordered all men to abandon the bombarded city— this alone sounded suspicious to Hanemann: What kind of general would give an order like that? But the detail also whetted his curiosity, so he listened carefully as Mr. J. went on.

The painter boarded one of the trains heading east, in the company of a young woman. They had no idea where they were going, perhaps Romania, perhaps farther. "Just two people without a home racing into the unknown" was how the same woman put it later, as Mr. J. listened to her in a Warsaw apartment. Stations were on fire, planes kept strafing the tracks, they stopped for hours at a time. Every chance he could, the painter reported to the recruitment centers in the stations—he'd had an officer's rank in the Czarist army from the old days before independence—but even younger volunteers were being sent away empty-handed, since there were no weapons to issue. The couple ran into some people they knew who were also making their way east: Maja Berezowska, Bolesław Miciński. The names didn't mean a thing to Hanemann, but he paid close attention, aware that Mr. J. was choosing his words carefully, so as not say too much.

The painter and the young woman got off in a small village in the middle of the forest. His liver and kidneys were swollen; he'd drunk some bad water from a well, he was in great pain, she wanted to help him, but what could she do? The pain grew worse. His legs and hands began to swell. "Everything is starting to fall apart, and it won't stop until it's all over," he said to her, holding her hand. "You don't know what savages they are. You're helpless. You're weak. You're a child. You'll die without me. It's better to die together. Besides, your blood and mine are all part of the same system. If you leave me, I'll lose what little strength I have left."

On the morning of September eighteenth, the day after the Russians invaded Poland (which he knew about), he said: "Today's the day, we're taking off." She kissed his hands, hoping to postpone the decision. They left the house and walked toward the forest. On the way he took some painkillers. They sat down in the sand, under a huge oak. "Here," he said. He began saying farewell to his friends, his mother. He tried to pray, starting with "Our Father," but broke off because he couldn't remember the words. Then he told her he wanted to marry her. She'd once said that the only way she'd agree to get married was under chloroform. His fingers touched her eyelids, forcing them to close. "I now pronounce us man and wife."

He took out his entire cache of luminal, nearly forty tablets. He opened a bottle of water, poured it into a cup, and dissolved the tablets. "Here, this is your share." She drank it without fear. He had two razors, and gave one to her to use when the luminal started to take effect. He showed her where to slit her throat. Then he tried to open the veins on his left wrist. But that proved difficult; the blade kept catching on the tendons. There was barely a trickle of blood. He smiled: "Looks like that's not going to work." She tried to help, without success. He rolled up the sleeve of his jacket and started cutting away at his elbow. She felt herself slipping into darkness. As if through a fog, she heard him say: "Don't fall asleep before me, don't leave me alone." He wanted so much for things to be ideal, for them both to lose consciousness at the same moment.

That was between twelve and two in the afternoon. She didn't wake up until dawn. When she looked around she saw him lying next to her. A pocket watch was lying in the sand by his right arm; he'd apparently gone on checking the time until the end. A small stain on his neck showed that he had cut his carotid artery. She reached out to touch the stain but saw that her shoulder and part of her sleeve were soaked with blood. Every layer of clothing was wet. Even though she was unable to stand on her feet, she felt she had to bury him; he couldn't stay like that, defenseless. So she started crawling around and scraping away the wet leaves, moss, and earth, until she finally managed to scratch out a shallow, shapeless cavity.

Years later, the same woman who had used her fingers to dig a grave for the painter said to Mr. J., "He kept thinking about the other Miciński—Tadeusz. Do you know who that was, ever hear his name? A great writer, very great. Peasants hacked him to pieces with their hatchets back in 1918, outside Czyryków. They thought they'd caught a Czarist general. There's no grave. And that's what he wanted, too, to be graveless just like Miciński. He thought that was wonderful: everybody knew Miciński and respected his work, so even if there were no material remains, he was everywhere. And there I was trying to dig a grave for him, just a step from where his body . . ."

Mr. J. put the green book back on the desk: "Do you find it strange that I'm telling you all this?"

Hanemann smiled: "No. All I think is that we can never really know what's lurking inside us."

Mr. J. shook his head. "He just didn't want to accept the world that was coming. Exactly like Kleist."

"You think?" Hanemann looked out the window. How many times had he heard that Kleist had committed suicide because he was so deeply wounded by the German defeat, because he couldn't stand the spirit of the Prussian army, because his parents had rejected him, because he couldn't cope with his nerves, because he'd read too many Romantic poets... That for one reason or another he ran away with Henriette to the Wannsee, where he wrote those beautiful letters of farewell and then shot her in the heart and himself in the mouth. And that she had run away with Kleist to escape being eaten alive by cancer, to escape an empty life with her accountant husband, throwing herself madly into the whole affair like a dying person happy to learn that the whole city's on fire, because when the whole city is burning, our own pain is less.

But was it true? The birch branches swayed outside the window. Hanemann didn't take his eyes off the gentle tremble of the leaves. "Just like moths," he thought. He could still hear the painter's last words: "Don't fall asleep before me. Don't leave me alone..." Like an echo. The damp forest. A black glow. Dew on moss. That was all he really remembered of Mr. J.'s story. Just those few words.

"Have you by any chance read *The Prince of Homburg?*" he asked Mr. J.

The teacher raised his eyebrows. "*The Prince of Homburg?* That lovely patriotic story of a young German who dreams about saving Germany? The glorified warrior and all that? I always had mixed feelings about that particular play. The rabid ambition of a young German aristocrat who dreams of defeating his enemies. You know, back in the Free City I saw where fantasies like that can lead."

Hanemann waved his hand. "There you go again. Prussian drill and the sensitive soul of a German patriot. That's all just window dressing. But there's a scene in that play—a very sad one that the Germans can't abide—where the Prince of Homburg, a German officer, is about to be shot for insubordination on the battlefield. He falls to his knees and begs a German princess to spare his life. He wants to live. At any price. But then all of a sudden he changes his mind and agrees to die. Does this mean he suddenly recognizes the right of the state to execute him? Or is it a different revelation? That when he disobeyed the elector and won the battle he had been acting as himself for the first time in his life. And he understands that this one moment of self-fulfillment is going to cost his life." Hanemann paused. "So who can say what led to that suicide by the Wannsee? Maybe one of the wisest things you can know is exactly when to die..." Hanemann paused for a moment, then added, "What did they care about the world that was coming?"

Mr. J. didn't know what to make of Hanemann's speech. He sensed some hidden tension, perhaps a secret disdain for all who live normal lives and have no desire to scale such lofty spiritual heights. Then again, he might be wrong. In spite of what he had heard, Mr. J. had never been all that drawn to Kleist, and as for Henriette Vogel, her little gesture of sending her cuckolded husband a cup adorned with her name struck him as unusually cool and calculated—love anguish or no love anguish. Wise? What wisdom was there here?

The similarities had made him think that... But in reality the two stories were so far apart, what could they possibly have in common? And as he and Hanemann went on talking, Mr. J. felt far closer to the aging painter, dying somewhere in the eastern marshes. His death was more—he paused a moment, searching for the right words—painful, more serious than what happened by the Wannsee. The reasons were perfectly clear, understandable and forgivable. But to die by a beautiful lake after writing an extravagant letter and eating an exquisite breakfast? And not in response to some humiliation? Or out of a refusal to admit defeat? A fear of sickness? The story of the Prince of Homburg was moving, no doubt about that, but Mr. J.'s reading was different than Hanemann's. To know exactly when to die? What a bizarre idea. Because that moment doesn't belong to us. Freedom? Reviewing his own life, he could recall neither great peaks nor flashes of revelation. His own past seemed more like a plain pitted with dark chasms that he had miraculously avoided. But did that mean he should regret that it was flat? Mr. J. felt that fate had been extraordinarily kind to him; after all, he had survived Stutthof, although there had been moments when only a tiny quiver in his heart kept him from throwing himself on the wires. By chance he had survived, and so he was able to spend a lovely May afternoon relaxing in Hanemann's beautiful room at 17 Grottger Street, talking about the good old days with his friend like two old school chums. He didn't consider this any particular achievement on his part. He had considered survival a matter of duty—to his mother? To himself? The people he knew? Did it matter? Though now and then he did feel a vague twinge of guilt.

But what about Hanemann? Mr. J. suspected that his story of the girl and the painter who had died in the eastern marshes hadn't affected his German friend very much, that Hanemann hadn't found anything in it that would steep the soul in the same light as the tale of Heinrich and Henriette. No, Hanemann probably just saw it as the story of a deserter pursued by a mighty army into a dark corner of the world where he killed himself, having dragged along a girl who wanted to save him. The man ran away from the Germans and right into the Russians, and then he slit his veins. These were not the actions of a man who was free but those of a man who could not accept his fate. A weak man.

Mr. J. peered at Hanemann's face, half hidden in the growing dark, but Hanemann was silent, staring through the window at the beech woods looming gray beyond the houses across the street.

| *Tuckwork, Pearl Buttons, Silk* |

BUT THE FACT THAT they knew each other from the days of the Free City wasn't the only reason Hanemann enjoyed talking to Mr. J. "You see," Mr. J. once explained to me, "I was there, back then at Neufahrwasser, on the pier, on the morning of August fourteenth. A colleague from Krakow had come up two days earlier for a meeting of the teachers' union, which we were holding in the Polish gymnasium. I'd offered to take her on a boat ride from Neufahrwasser to Zoppot—what better thing could I suggest on such a fine August morning? She'd never even laid eyes on the sea. She agreed to try one of the little Westermann excursion boats, so on the morning of the fourteenth we took the number-three streetcar to Brösen. The morning was warm and dewy, the boardwalk was wet, it must have rained in the night. A few minutes before eight, the sun was already over the tower at Weichselmünde, and everything was quiet except for a steam crane puffing along in the port, past the bend in the channel. The Althausen Company had had it towed all the way from Kiel; it had arrived the previous Wednesday. (They even wrote about that crane in the *Danziger Volksstimme*: I remember the big green pictures of the tugboat *Mercury*.)

"We walked through the park, and when we got to the landing we found a few people already waiting. I spotted her right away—white dress, white gloves, resting her hand on her parasol's ivory handle, looking in our direction as if she were expecting someone. No, she wasn't alone, she was with another young woman... Let me think... A light blue dress... Maybe a necklace. Earrings? The boat was already at the dock, black letters on the white hull spelled out *Star*; a round porthole, a light hanging from the mast, they still hadn't let down the gangway. People behind us were talking, laughing. A couple was coming up from the streetcar stop—the woman was wearing a brown cape and a hat with purple roses made of gauze; the man had on a white corduroy jacket with a black handkerchief in the breast pocket, just like the brokers at Hansen's trading house on Breitgasse.

"Then the crew from the *Star* let down the gangway, an iron grate with a rope railing strung between posts on either side, but somehow no one seemed eager to board. We still had a couple of minutes. And there was that sun! The air was light, clean, with a little patch of fog above the fort, the water was smooth, there were wagons of cotton waiting outside Schneider's warehouses, workers shouting on the docks, the distant screech of a streetcar turning in to the depot. The conversations were more full of warm, lazy silences than words, although a few people were telling stories or laughing at jokes, a little sleepily, as if the day had yet to begin in earnest. There was one elderly couple, a lady with a plume in her hat and a man with a panama and a pince-nez. I remember a beautiful woman with a cashmere shawl draped over her shoulders, a girl in a batik blouse... We could hear the motor rumbling inside the hull, dark smoke was floating up from the funnel with the Westermann logo—a great red *W*—and seagulls were squawking around the mast, but we didn't head for the gangway until an officer in a white uniform with black epaulettes rang a bell and said, 'Shoving off in four minutes. Please take your seats.'

"She was walking in front of me. Tapping the tip of her parasol on the tarred planks of the dock. The sun was glaring over Weichselmünde, and she had let down her veil. The swish of her dress. I nearly forgot I was with somebody else. Her heels struck the ground, clanging on the iron gangway; she tripped, I grabbed her elbow. She looked at me and smiled: 'Thank you . . . I'll be all right . . .' I could feel the warm silk of her sleeve, the stitching of the tuckwork. Pearl buttons along the cuff. I slowly withdrew my hand and smiled back. She climbed on deck. 'It's these heels . . .' She lifted her skirt. The tip of a white shoe. We walked past her. My companion stood at the rail and watched a tugboat with a black smokestack steam down the middle of the channel: We could make out the white letters *Minerva*. The wind came up. The long, soft wake of the *Minerva* lifted the side of the *Star*, and my companion held her hand to her breast. 'My God . . .' She blanched and closed her eyes. 'I had no idea, my heavens, I thought it would be a little boat ride, but I don't think I can . . .' 'Would you like to get off?' Her hand was looking for a hold. The rocking slowed as the wake from the tugboat faded with a slurp on the shore. Once more she held her hand to her breast. 'I'm afraid I can't . . .' 'Would you like to get off?'

"I carefully led her across the gangway onto the landing. 'Better now?' She nodded, but kept her hand by her breast. She couldn't look at the water. 'I'm very sorry . . .' 'Please, don't mention it,' I stroked her hand, 'Why don't I take you around the Old Town? We can just hop onto the number three . . .' 'You're not angry with me?' 'Angry?' I'd made so many trips between Neu-fahrwasser and Zoppot, I could easily give up this one.

The bell rang and the *Star* pulled away from the landing. The officer disappeared behind the glass of the wheelhouse, clouds of smoke temporarily blocked out the sun, the red Danzig ensign fluttered its golden crown and two white crosses. The propellers churned whirlpools in the dark green water. Slowly we headed back toward the streetcar. My companion didn't say anything; she was mad at herself for disappointing me. When we reached the park, I turned around. The *Star* was already in the middle of the channel, ready to steer to port. The passengers were spread out on the benches. I thought I saw a white parasol just to the right of the mast. A woman adjusting her hair. Was it her?"

Later that day, just before six, Mr. J. stopped at the Lipschützes' on his way back from the meeting at the Polish gymnasium, to borrow Alfred's *Brost Dictionary*. Stella told him about what had happened in Glettkau.

She had gone to the pier in Glettkau at nine in the morning, to meet her sister Louisa, just as they had arranged the previous Saturday at Mrs. Stein's. Leaning over the railing, she watched the white boat from Neufahrwasser pull in toward the dock. Smoke from the slanted stack drifted astern, dissolving into a patch of gray fog, and tiny sharp waves flashed in the sun that was climbing over Brösen. Stella shaded her eyes; next to the mast she could see a woman in a white dress, holding a parasol. Was that her? She looked a little taller than Louisa ... But the *Star* was still too far away to tell. The pier was deserted except for a few children running up and down. A little boy in a white shirt with a bamboo ball-and-stick game was chasing a little girl in a light blue flounced skirt—clatter, shouts, laughter. Their nanny, a woman in a ruffled dress with her hair smoothed back, kept calling out: "Helga! You stay away from that railing! Günther, leave her alone! Play nicely! See the boat coming in? We'll be getting on any minute." With her was an old man in a straw hat, with a pearl-handled cane that he kept rapping on the planks. Farther down, at the edge of the dock, two sailors from the shore crew were preparing for the landing, coiling the hemp lines. The taller of the two put on a pair of leather gloves and rested his elbow on the railing to watch the approaching boat— very matter-of-factly. Taking this as a cue, Stella went closer. The *Star* slowly rounded the pier and sailed toward two copper-plated pilings that jutted out of the water some dozen meters away from the landing. The wind was coming from Zoppot; a sudden gust blew the smoke back across the ship, momentarily obscuring the white hull. Once again Stella saw the same woman standing next to the mast. At first she thought it was Louisa, but no, it was somebody else, next to a man in a checked jacket. "Maybe something happened," Stella thought, sadly. "Maybe she changed her mind?"

The ship's bell rang out, the *Star* cut speed and sailed ahead on its own momentum as the engines went quiet. Slowly the boat rounded the starboard piling and began to head for the mooring. Suddenly the starboard hull (Mr. J. remembered clearly that Stella had said it was the right side) scraped against the second copper-plated piling. A dull rasp came echoing over the water.

Stella remembered that piling. She'd seen it once, when she went sailing with Heinz Wolff, whose cousin was the well-known lawyer Werffel, in a boat they'd rented from the hotel. They had scraped against it, too. She remembered the dark wood overgrown with white shells, the black moss, the seaweed waving from the rusty metal bars that gleamed under the water.

It was very deep there, deep enough to take huge freighters, the water was almost black, you couldn't see the bottom. Stella could see some faces in the portholes. Was that Louisa? In the third window? Raising her hand? Stella instinctively waved back. Finally, she's here. The *Star* pulled alongside the pier, a line was tossed from the deck to the sailor with the leather gloves, who started hauling it in: Stella watched his strong, sure arms, their quick, even movements. But suddenly the man flew forward, as if he'd tripped. The pier shuddered, everyone was knocked backward. Stella held on to the railing. From the corner of her eye she saw the end of the line slip out of the crewman's leather glove and race across the black tarred planks. The children screamed. The nanny jerked the young boy away from the rails. The man with the cane covered the girl's eyes. The line whistled and disappeared through a crack in the dock.

She leaned out over the balustrade and looked down by the pilings of the pier. As she watched, the bow of the *Star* lurched up, and the lady in the white dress toppled onto the deck. White lace-up shoes, a hand grasping at the railing, a torn dress, stays snapping off the mast, the clanging of metal chains. The boat listed, and the mast came crashing into the railing two steps away from Stella. She shielded her head while gusts of wind jerked the white parasol across the deck, and it floated into the water like a dandelion tuft. The man in the checked jacket clung to the railing, there was another lurch, and the women's screams went silent as the bow of the *Star* plunged into the water. Tin crates came floating up off the sinking deck, the dark waters swelled, a head in a hat surfaced for a second, a cashmere shawl, a white dress ballooning out like a puffer fish ... Then there was a rumble, and the pier shuddered once again. Stella screamed, she cried out to Louisa, but her voice sounded like someone calling from behind a wall. The older man took her by the hand and pulled her away from the balustrade, trying to console her. One of the shore crew tossed two life preservers into the water. The boat's superstructure tilted toward the pier as it went down; huge bubbles of air gurgled in the portholes. Then the hull rose out of the water one last time. A whirlpool of darkness. Stella saw a woman floundering on the surface, her open mouth gasping for air, until one of the loose stays caught her and pulled her under. The black smokestack with the letter *W* collapsed onto the bridge, hissing steam. Three men came running over from the hotel, the boat hook thumped against the planks...

A slight impact was all it took—according to the evening extra edition of the *Danziger Volksstimme*—for the ribs at the keel to give way. The hull broke apart, water flooded the engine room, and the *Star* capsized, all in the space of a minute: saving people was out of the question. Nevertheless, the Helmholz & Son insurance agency refused to pay the Westermann claim of eighty-four thousand marks. Two experts from Hamburg, Professor Hartmann and Councillor Mehrens, examined the wreckage, which was hauled ashore at Neufahrwasser alongside the Schneider warehouses, and determined that the seam of the hull had long been in dire need of repair, while Westermann kept the *Star* sailing between Neufahrwasser and Zoppot—often taking on more passengers than allowed. And even though an investigation conducted by Commissioner Wittberg from the Zoppot police had ruled out any wrongdoing, there were still rumors that the sinking of the *Star* had in some way benefited the company, which was said to be over three hundred thousand marks in debt to banks in Berlin and Frankfurt.

About a week after the accident, on the twentieth or twenty-first of August, Mr. J. visited Hanemann to tell him what he knew. He spoke slowly, carefully choosing his words, omitting details that might be too painful. He realized that it was only thanks to his friend from Krakow that he hadn't been aboard the *Star* when it sank; thanks to her unforeseen reaction to being on the water. But Mr. J. saw no reason to reproach himself—what for? For having caught the elbow of a lady as she tripped on the gangway of a boat that had been running for years between Neufahrwasser and Zoppot? Nevertheless, whenever he thought about August fourteenth, he preferred not to recall that particular moment. Nor did he ever mention it to Hanemann.

Only now and then, in the morning, before he left for the school on Topolowa, as he buttoned his poplin shirt, meticulous as always, his fingertips felt a kind of echo, as they remembered the touch of that silk sleeve, the dainty tuckwork, the pearl buttons on the narrow cuff.

| *Aristocracy and Decline* |

AND THE THINGS? They went about their usual business, watching from the shelves and étagères, windowsills and countertops, indifferent to our concerns, refusing to take sides, patiently yielding to our waiting hands, either to fit like a glove or slip through our fingers and fall with a shriek onto the concrete tiles. Only then did they jolt us into awareness, in the flash of shattering porcelain, the clatter of silver, the splintering of glass. In actuality they were invisible, because who ever paid any attention to the color of air, light trapped in glass, the song of drawers pulled open, or the high-pitched notes of the mahogany armoire?

But then they would be remembered, and a desperate search would ensue. A hunt for lost textures and forgotten surfaces. Regrets for having shown so little care, so little heart. For having only existed among them with no feelings, doing nothing more than picking up, wiping dry, putting down. And why? Because we just didn't feel like it? Nonsense. Because we resented their constant demand to be pampered, no matter how exhausted we might be? Were they never satiated? Were they doomed to vanish under layers of tarnish and soot?

And why do we always remember too late? At Lessing-strasse 14, in his room on the second floor of the Bierenstein house, Mr. Dłuszniewski was dying. In the past he used to bustle about, full of noise and energy, but now he lay on Emma Bierenstein's brass bed, his eyes half-closed, quietly trying to re-member what the kitchen had looked like the day he came from Pozelwa to Gdańsk. The dark, enormous interior, lit only by gleaming porcelain—had seemed so enormous, but the image crumbled like a brittle canvas. He could see the outline of the tall buffet with the carved mahogany panel that had shielded the rows of glass and crystal from the red glow over Langfuhr—but he couldn't remember all the pieces that went inside. Only his fingers could still feel them, his fingers that were beginning to grow cold as they rested on the soft down bedding. What had been on the top shelf? White and clattering? Shiny and round? A sugar bowl? The lacquered Arabian tin box where Father kept his Egyptian cigarettes? The crystal bowl mother had brought from her sister's in Grodno? His mind groped into the past like a blind man touching the face of someone close, but all his fingers felt was a cool darkness. Things that once had weight, porosity, a smoothness, a cool glassiness, changed into colorless clouds. One-sided, like the moon, and seldom full.

The heavy teakettle with the tulip-shaped spout that had come from the kitchen at Lessingstrasse 14 was now as light and slender as a new moon. The base no longer existed, only the domed lid with the rose-colored ball shined in the darkness of his memory. Sometimes its warm shape would glow in his dreams like a passing planet, but it was obscured by the parade of later teapots that had taken its place on the gas burner of the Junkers oven—one white, one green with a red rose, one light blue with a snowy star. What a succession of enamel and aluminum and cast-metal shapes! Which one had Mama used to brew her linden-blossom tea? What was on the mug in which Grandmother served us her freshly pressed apple juice? A rose leaf? A shepherdess cradling a lamb? What were the sugar cubes in when we stole them from the china cabinet? And the tea boxes? Did they have a Turkish minaret on a blue background and a note about the Dardanelles? Or was it an Indian elephant with a funny-scary, raspberry-colored trunk? And the saltshakers? The dainty cups where soft-boiled eggs lost their heads after a well-aimed whack with the little knife? The rush-backed chairs, the armchair with the wine-colored upholstery, the chaise longues that migrated first to the porch, then to the attic, and finally—after patiently enduring a quarantine in the basement, where they were fed false hopes about returning to the rooms—ceased to exist...

Disappearance. Fleeting. When had the old German armchairs vanished from 17 Grottger Street? Was it that June when Mama came back from Warsaw, and Father went to Szczecin for a few days, or maybe later? But which day, which hour, which minute? Things passed away unnoticed, like alley cats, without a trace. The crystal vases came into our lives with great fanfare, wrapped in white tissue paper and carried into the room to the triumphant strains accompanying a birthday or name-day celebration—but when did they leave? Because after some time they were no longer there. Moments of realization. A sudden opening of the eyes. Amazement. "Heniu," Mrs. Potrykus called out from the kitchen at 21 Grottger Street, "have you seen that silver spoon anywhere? You know, the one with the little flowers on the handle?" But what could Mr. Potrykus, a mail carrier with the Soviet army, say to that? That was the first he'd ever heard about the pretty spoon that had once rested down the street, in the Bierenstein's drawer—even though he'd been eating with it for years. "It's that Marcinkowska woman again. The nerve!" said Mrs. Potrykus, indignant.

Of course, we had to have visible, guilty parties, who filched their neighbors' silverware, slipping the booty into an apron pocket and sneaking off into the cloudy night. Each visit threatened a further diminishment of supplies. The drawers erupted in a clattery panic, forks snuggled against the knives, ladles clung to teaspoons. The flatware—the silver chests lined with wine red velvet imperceptibly leaked their metallic gleam. Sparkling nickel-plated shapes would vanish over a period of months, leaving nothing but a few dark depressions in the plush devoid of their inhabitants. The unfair accusations, the mutual hostility, kitchen detectives and backyard investigators, basement interrogations, the gossip whispered in line at the store. But what protection was there against the patient void that daily swallowed cities, homes, stainless-steel Gerlach knives, and forks with the unusual name *Stojadła*?

Because the minute you turned your back, the silver sugar bowl lost its lid, as if blown away by the wind. One glance out the window, and there on the shelf, instead of the crystal salt-shaker, was nothing but empty space.

And the fruit dishes, the coffee mills, the tiny pastry forks? What about the processions of spoons? The ranks of kitchen and dinner knives? Where had they gone? And all without a trace. If only we could follow their fragile paths to nothingness, those dreamy odysseys that no nostalgia can ever recover. Who will sing the voyages of spoons? On the very day that Mrs. Potrykus, appalled by the idea that Mrs. Marcinkowska was filching her silverware in the folds of her apron, uttered her unjust accusation, the Bierensteins' spoon was in Mr. Węsiory's wagon heading for the dump outside Kokoszki, together with a pile of other rubbish from Grottger Street. Years later, it would wind up at an antique shop on Długa, and from there make its way to 7 Tuwim Street, where Professor Jarochowski, an engineer at the Polytechnic, would place it in his collection of local silver. The Bierensteins' soup spoon with the thistle motif, poured at the Müller silver works outside Lübeck, had been destined for the quiet eternity of Professor Jarochowski's display case on Tuwim Street. What more beautiful finale could be imagined for that twilight of household planets, orbiting in peace and quiet, then flying noiselessly into the void?

But only a few objects were marked for such heavenly gliding—the elite, the Junkers of silver plate, the *obersturmbahnführer* coffee services of cobalt porcelain rimmed with gold, the aristocrats of nickel, silver, and copper that were able to withstand the onslaught of time, household moves, and kitchen remodeling, tolling their heavy, metallic ring on the white tablecloths spread out on Sundays and holidays. But even their haughty, gleaming ranks succumbed to attrition inside the oak drawers, displaced by a slow but relentless wave of proletarian aluminum forks and bakelite ashtrays stamped with the initials of the Workers Vacation Fund—humble mementos of the Potrykuses' trip to Szklarska Poręba, where they stayed at what had once been the Siegfried pension and was now the official vacation home for workers from the Zenit sugar factory.

And the downfalls? The shameful humiliations of canvas and wood, enamel and tin? Each morning when we came into the kitchen we were greeted by an embroidered hanging—sky blue stitching on a white background, with a phrase in German that said "Welcome Morning / May You Bring / Joy To Every Home." But time stained the white fabric with apple and carrot juice, until finally, one day, the hanging sank to the green linoleum, and from then on it was used to mop the floor. And when Mama wrapped it around the stiff bristle brush, dipping the grayed fabric into the bucket of hot water, the only words left were "Morn," "Joy," and "Home," all crushed and stretched, swimming bluish under the mop water.

And what about the martyrdom of tiles, on walls and floors and by the stove? The fading of the finish on the bed rails? The dulling of brass fixtures? The greening of copper? The black deposits accumulating on the tin gutter? The December hoarfrost? The nighttime whisper of roof tiles spending their last days in the pool around the base of the fountain? The crackle of peeling stucco? The rattling of joists and rafters? The constant trudge of rubber-soled shoes wearing furrows in the steps? The saving— of whatever could be saved. And the weight of the air causing it all to crumble. And the yellowing of the bathtubs. And the rusty streaks in the porcelain sinks. The slow death of gardens.

Mr. Wierzbołowski's shoe mallet banged away at the floor in the bathroom at 14 Grottger Street, loosening a number of octagonal tiles, which Erich Schultz had ordered in 1937 at his wife's request, from Hoesse & Son outside Allenstein—six square meters of the best cobalt terra-cotta! The house groaned from the hammering, the leaded glass in the stairwell window clattered, the pipes carried the painful blows up to the second floor and higher—all because Janina Wierzbołowska's laundry kettle had fallen onto the floor next to the tub. The cracked terra-cotta tiles from the Kister factory in Dortmund had been replaced by an oddly shaped stain of terrazzo, its waxy shine sticking out among what was left of the cobalt background. Meanwhile, the unmoored tiles, barnacled with Portland cement, drifted one by one first to the rubble heap in front of the house and then to the garden, onto the path between the rows of arborvitae, where by August they were covered with bright green moss. Later they would form a toothy border for the iris bed: Hanemann helped Father plumb the line with a wire stretched between sharpened stakes.

But the most painful changes were hidden, lurking, deceptively quiet, barely perceptible. Coming back home one late afternoon, Hanemann realized that he could no longer remember what color the Bierensteins' house had been. The old color hadn't been changed; layers of dust and soot had simply made the stucco look like ash. The navy-blue and yellow panes in the stairwell windows had lost their luster. At the Maletz's house across the street, the stucco was entirely gone in a few places, revealing the reed matting used as insulation. Window frames were painted from the inside only. The sun beat down on the hand-carved woodwork, causing it to blister and crack. Someone had realized it needed repairing, but had done nothing more than apply a thick coat of paint to cover the cracks. *Administracja* was a word frequently invoked, with sighs, as people waited for that mysterious power to declare an end to the destruction. At first Hanemann didn't understand, until he finally realized what Father meant when he said "you can't get anything."

Laundry bearing the Walmanns' light blue monogram fluttered outside the windows, pinned to lines stretched between the wall of the house and the trunk of the spruce, but the threads of the embroidery were torn, and the letters had fewer and fewer loops. When the wind picked up the drying linens, the sun showed through a few places where the fabric had been worn into a sieve.

Hanemann stood at the window and watched the fluttering white, thinking about the Bergers' house on Frauengasse. Did it have an oak vestibule? Were the steps curved? Was the threshold brass? What was in the entrance room, to the left of the mirror, next to the portrait of Councillor Wolfgang Berger? What was on the marble column between the windows in the salon? What was embroidered on the back of the red chaise longue? And the table, the beautiful walnut table—what was on the table, that day? A sparkling carafe? A bouquet of dahlias in an azure vase? A demitasse held in white fingers. A ring with a malachite eye. A head turning. Shaking of hair. Stella's dark red dress. A white saucer with an iris flower?

A cup?

Yes, a cup, the demitasse with the iris design, that thin gold line running around the lip of the sapphire bowl—do you remember that cup, Stella? Tell us, when did it vanish from our sight forever?

If someone had asked you on that day, you would simply have shrugged your shoulders. What cup? When? With all the teacups and coffee cups that pass through our hands...Who's going to lose any sleep about the warm touch of porcelain, the gentle grittiness of the base with the blue Werffel trademark? But now, Stella, now that you're no longer here, you know it wasn't very smart, twirling around the kitchen like that at Frauengasse 16, letting all the things float by like little boats of paper that disappear without a trace.

Because now what wouldn't you give to touch, for a single second, that scalding demitasse—remember? filled with Eduscho coffee, smelling so hot that you bit your lips—now that you're no longer here, now that you're lying at the bottom of the sea off Bornholm, where the great ship *Bernhoff* sank in the cold water on its way from Danzig to Hamburg, now that all that's left of your hand are a few tiny bones, as insignificant as a bird's, spreading on the ooze, the pattern of your palm pressed into the sand...

Like the trace of a leaf, Stella...

| *Hanka* |

ONE DAY I OPENED my eyes and discovered we had a Ukrainian in the house. "What do you mean, a Ukrainian?" my father would say, rolling a cigarette. He always objected when someone called her that. But practically everyone did.

Anyway, on that morning the clatter in the kitchen sounded different, and the footsteps on the green linoleum sounded different. (And what were footsteps doing there at all, since my parents were always out of the house by seven o'clock?) And there were other different sounds as well: the ring of porcelain, the chopping of a knife on wood, the rustle of paper, the swish of a brush, the rattle of a window being closed—so I tiptoed to the door and peeked through the cracked milk-glass pane into the kitchen.

Our Ukrainian was standing by the window, breathing onto a silver-rimmed glass, which she then wiped with a linen dishcloth and held to the light to make sure it was clean. Her hair was pinned behind one ear with a black hairpin. I could see her neck, bare shoulders, and dark skin—well, not exactly dark, but as if you were seeing her through a smoked-glass lens... Pushing my cheek against the pane, I watched every move of her hands as she polished the dried glass, and took in every fold of her red and yellow floral cretonne skirt, so engrossed that I was caught off guard when the door opened and the warm material actually brushed against my cheek. Two hands with slightly smoky skin lifted me up under my arms. "So you must be Piotr?" she laughed. I was so embarrassed that I'd let myself be caught like that; I felt my cheeks were on fire. All I could do was nod, and she set me down half a step away to get a better look: "I'm Hanka. I'm sure your mama told you. Now run to your room and get dressed and I'll make you breakfast."

What a breakfast! I could barely swallow my roll with the sour cherry preserves, because the young woman whose name was Hanka had sat down on the other side of the table, rested her chin on her clasped hands, and watched me as I ate, her eyes half-closed. And as she watched, everything began to taste completely different. Before I could finish eating and drinking, she was slicing a dark red apple into four pieces. She spooned out the core and the seeds, lay the peeled slices on a plate and arranged them into a star, calling the whole thing a little cookie.

I was astonished and somewhat terrified (after all, she was going to be with us morning, noon, and night!), but I couldn't keep my eyes off her. "Why are you staring at me like that?" she asked, getting up from the table, but I realized right away that she didn't expect an answer. It wasn't because she was pretty, not at all; she was just so different from the other women on Grottger Street—the warm, carefree way she tilted her head, the sheen of her smooth, dark hair, her nimble fingers fixing a strand behind her ear, her metal hairpin...

I ate my breakfast, pretending not to look, while she kneaded some cottage cheese in a bowl with sugar and cream and hummed a song I didn't know. Then she interrupted her humming and asked, "Would you like some?" But if someone had told her that she'd just been humming, I'm sure she would have shrugged her shoulders and said: "Nonsense!" I was fascinated by the way she held the pale gray cup, so gracefully; the way she poured a little cream from the pitcher; the way she puckered her lips gently to blow on the milk simmering in the blue pot; her deft handling of the knife as she chopped the freshly washed vegetables she had laid on the board. And she did all this as if her thoughts were elsewhere. Every time she walked by me she would gently ruffle my hair and say something in her rich voice—which was not too high, and just a little flat—"Well, how do you like it? "Go on and have some more..." "How about a little radish?" All the rustling and hissing sounds tickled my ear and right away put me in an impish mood for fun.

When she laughed, shivers of joy ran down her neck, her shoulders, her back, her stomach... So I knew exactly what Mr. J. meant when I once heard him say to my father, "She has such a laughing body, don't you think?" They were probably talking about somebody else, but I immediately thought of Hanka. Because it was true. Movement, speech, and laughter all came together in her with such harmony that I began to understand why men often speak of women as birds or roses or other beautiful things.

Now everything was done as Hanka saw fit. Mama happily accepted the new state of affairs; only Father grumbled on occasion that something had been moved during cleaning; still, he, too, liked what Hanka did.

Because unlike Mama, Hanka had a very hands-on approach. She enjoyed dipping plates into the hot water, wiping the glasses until they sparkled, arranging the porcelain containers labeled "Zucker," "Salz," and "Pfeffer" on the shelves in the back of the cabinet; she liked taking the chalk to polish the silver spoons with the Gothic *W* monogram, liked arranging them in the bottom of the silver chest with the wine red plush, liked sorting the forks and knives—the small knives went on the left, in the side compartment, while the large blades were sheathed in the slits of the wooden holder that divided the drawer. And the tastes, the textures, the way the food looked, the way it smelled! Everything changed. A braid of garlic and a bouquet of herbs with ash blue leaves showed up on the coat tree next to the chest, and a bucket of brown seeds appeared by the window. A new, deep-blue tablecloth embroidered with little red-stemmed yellow flowers took the place of the old oilcloth. Hanka liked the new color, which made the dish of curd-cheese look like a porcelain boat on a coarsely woven linen sea. And in the morning, when I ran into the kitchen before school, two sliced kaiser rolls were waiting for me, smeared with butter, each with a smiling face made of scraps of radish and dill. Fresh farm cheese with finely chopped chives, in which I could still taste the cool morning garden. Sparrows chirping outside the half-open window, the whisper of birch leaves, someone's footsteps on the sidewalk, warm splashes of sun rippling across the lace curtains. Hanka had already taken her sewing shears outside to snip a bunch of dewy irises, which glistened in the ceramic vase. And beside them was the lidless saltshaker full of coarse salt that we would take on the tip of a knife to sprinkle evenly on the grainy rye bread. Sometimes Hanka would take a teaspoonful of honey and, sitting across from me, stare bemusedly at the amber thread trickling onto a fresh slice of white bread before spreading its sweetness with the back of her spoon. Or she would lick her fingers to test the cream in the enamel pitcher she brought from the Ringeleweskis' by the old mill on Kwietna Street.

Whenever she made sour cherry preserves, I knew that in the middle of the night she would be flitting around the entrance room like a shadow, in a white shirt with stitched-on leaves, and that a moment later I would hear the gentle clinking of her spoon dipping into the brown syrup, first to skim off the foam (or froth, as Hanka called it) and then to fish out first one cherry swimming in the glistening juice, then a second, a third, a fourth... Oh, that soft smacking of lips, those tender bites at midnight, when the house, submerged in quiet slumber, would creak along its floors and the joins of its cabinets.

Through the milk-glass pane in the door I would see the yellow candle, the shadow of her hair, tied back with a red ribbon, drifting along the wall until she disappeared into the kitchen. Then I would slowly crawl out from my blankets, carefully open the door, and glide into the kitchen. As soon as she saw me she would wave me over, motioning for me to walk on tiptoe, so my parents would keep on sleeping like angels. With her left hand, she would hand me a teaspoon (never letting go of her own in her right), then muffling our laughter, we would pick the cherries out of the thick syrup, which tasted best when followed with a smidgen of sour cream dipped on the spoon. The ruddy syrup mixed with the white cream left your lips with a pinkish trace that was so nice to lick off. And in the morning, only a quick glance behind Mama's back betrayed our nighttime secret.

Once Mr. Wierzbołowski told Mama that Hanka had come on a transport from Przemyśl in the east, that she'd lived through terrible things, that someone had done something to her you couldn't speak about, but Father just waved his hand: "What's he saying? If she's a Ukrainian, then my name is Hermann Göring." But Mr. Z. assured us that she had to have come from those parts because she had lived quite a while in Koszalin and was sometimes seen with a tall, dark-haired man who spoke with an Eastern accent. As if there weren't a lot of people who spoke with an Eastern accent. Mama once said she thought Hanka sounded as if she'd come from East Prussia or Mazuria, which made Father laugh—but after a moment's thought he said, "You know, you might be right."

So toward the end of May I gathered enough courage to ask, "Hanka, where are you really from, anyway?" (I wasn't allowed to speak that way; I was supposed to say "Miss Hanka" or, even better, "Aunt Hanka"). "Where am I from?" she repeated, without looking up from the floured board where she was quickly cutting a long roll of dough into dumplings. "The world."

"What do you mean: the world?" I had no intention of giving up.

"From the world, that's all," she said, dabbing my nose with a floury finger. The next day in a fit of anger I tried to open the suitcase she kept under her bed (she had taken over the small room next to the bathroom, with a view of the birch tree in the garden and, farther on, the former Bierenstein house), but it had two latches and even a brass padlock, labeled "Wertheim."

One day, when school was almost over—it was probably the fourteenth or fifteenth of June—I came home a little earlier than usual. Sometimes I liked to sneak inside and surprise Hanka with a shout or a loud laugh, rattling the clasps on my satchel and clattering with my sandals, and then to show how scared she was, she would hold her hands to her breast, raise her eyebrows, and comically roll her eyes. But this time, when I looked inside the kitchen, Hanka scared me, so much that I couldn't say a word. She was standing by the window. I walked over to her, put my hand on her back, and gently ran it along the flowery cretonne, as if stroking the feathers of a startled dove, but she pushed me away with all her might. She had changed beyond recognition, damp shadows under her eyes, swollen eye-lids: she looked so terrible that I started to cry. "Hanka, what happened?" She didn't say anything, only sobbed out loud and, grabbing me by the shoulder, pulled me to her as hard as she could...Later she spent the whole evening pacing back and forth in the kitchen, hardly saying a word to us; she couldn't concentrate on anything; she stood by the window looking out at the garden or possibly farther, at the sky, or the heights be-yond the houses on the other side of Grottger Street.

And then there was that afternoon when I came home at three and they wouldn't let me inside. Mrs. Wierzbołowska was standing by the entrance, and she took my satchel, saying, "Go play at the Korzybskis," and pulled me away from the door.

I slowly walked down the path toward the gate, turning around every few minutes, but Mrs. Wierzbołowska kept wav-ing me to hurry on, as if nothing were the matter. I sensed that something terrible had happened; I walked as if my feet were stuck in clay, but when, a minute later, I heard Andrzej whisper across the fence, "Hanka killed herself," I raced back home.

Mrs. Wierzbołowska held me firmly by the shoulder. "They're taking her to the Academy right this minute." I was hurt to the quick that they were keeping me out, that they didn't want to let me see her, because I had more right than anyone, especially because what Andrzej had said wasn't true, she was alive, only something had happened, they were taking her to the Academy right that minute. But even years later Mama was very reluctant to speak about that afternoon, and I caught only bits and pieces every now and then, by chance, when the grown-ups were talking in the garden.

According to Mr. J., Hanemann had walked right by our door on his way upstairs and hadn't noticed a thing. Keeping his hand on the railing, he'd passed the metal bin on the landing in the stairwell and kept on going until he reached his own apartment. It was then that he sensed an odor in the air. It didn't seem like much, but just to be sure, he went back down to the ground floor and knocked on the door. No one opened, so he knocked a little harder, but once again there was only silence. Now the smell was very distinct. He jerked at the door handle, but there was no movement behind the door, evidently there was nobody home, so he hurried out to the garden, climbed up the wooden trellis overgrown with creeper, and looked through the window into the kitchen. He could see the white ceiling, the lamp with the round shade, the top of the cupboard, but when he climbed higher there was something blocking the upper part of the window—a piece of cloth pressed against the glass. He jumped down off the trellis, ran to the door, lunged at it with his shoulder, but the door didn't budge. Now he had no doubt about the smell . . . He ran back out to the garden, but there was no one around, so he returned to the door, took the iron poker from behind the metal coal bin, shoved it under the lock, pulled it down, and jerked it to the right, then banged and battered on the door until he fell crashing into the dark entry room. As he pushed open the kitchen door, he felt himself getting nauseated, and hurled the bar at the window, shattering the glass.

Next to the sink, lying on the green linoleum, was Hanka. The burner had been flooded with water; gas was hissing under the teapot. Hanka had rested her head on a white towel, her hand under her cheek, her white-stockinged legs curled up to her stomach . . .

| *Corpus Christi* |

HANEMANN WAS SHAKEN by what had happened, but not enough to make him change his life. He was more surprised than anything, particularly when he found himself unexpectedly recalling his youth in Berlin, made blurry by the passage of time; he hadn't imagined it could still produce such strong recollections.

Apart from an occasional twinge of sympathy, he hadn't really thought about Hanka, except when he'd run into her on the stairs or glanced out the window and seen her in the garden with her sewing shears, cutting asters from the bed by the birch tree. And even then he was mostly amused by her resemblance to certain figures from old German paintings—her coloring, her features, the dark hair edged with a thin line of sunlight, her bare shoulders, as he watched her walk back to the house with a handful of flowers. But if his eyes took pleasure in the sight, his heart remained indifferent, harboring no grudges or resentment.

The sight of the stretcher with the motionless body being loaded into the white car brought back scenes from the Althof

Clinic near Moabit, where he had spent several months as an intern with Ansen. The building on Winterstrasse... the high stairway, the dark granite steps, the cast-bronze Atlas bearing the lantern, the brassy shine of the sconces in the auditorium of the Collegium Emmaus, the bust of Medusa on the dais, the purple upholstery of the chairs... And that first trip downstairs... The tiled interior, the Gothic windows, the screens, the ventilation pipes, the lamps with metal shades, the rubber aprons, and the distant murmur of water, as if a huge bathhouse were hidden behind the wall. And then the body laid out on the marble slab table, the childish, naive curiosity, and that same thought he had had so many years before suddenly resurfacing as Ansen slowly ran his scalpel across the naked skin: "Now I'm finally going to see a human soul..."

The fact that he'd wound up in anatomy was hardly an accident; it was rooted in his childhood—so he wanted to believe— or even further back, since a number of Hanemanns had achieved prominence plumbing the secrets of the human body, as army doctors under the king of Prussia. One of them, Heinrich Siegfried Hanemann, from the Second Dresden Horse Artillery, had even received a Prince's Order in 1815 for distinguished service on the field at the Battle of Leipzig, where, in an impressive display of sangfroid, he had saved the life of Colonel Fersen himself. But the biggest influence on Hanemann's choice of a career—or at least the explanation closest to his heart—was his ardent and sinful reading of forbidden books, old anatomical tracts that he found in his father's library. The dark copper etchings taught him that a doctor's work was much more than deft fingers and acquired knowledge. Far from being merely technical, it was shrouded in mysteries forever impenetrable to the human eye—and the prints adorning the great yellowed pages were proof of it.

Often, when his father was away, he would take down *Meyer's Anatomical Atlas,* a heavy volume with marbled edges, and look at the colorful illustrations of naked people, whose skins were covered with letters and whose open bodies were swarming with tiny numbers. But then, sighing with relief, he would reach behind the glass on the highest shelf and take down one of the old books. Because when all was said and done, all those numbers and letters in the Meyer atlas made the human body look like a cross section of plant material! What secret of life could be found in all those lines and numbers? But with the old books it was different; even their Latin titles lent them an air of mystery. These masters portrayed the human essence, not just its shell. Every time he opened the Brussels edition of Van Helden's *Tractatus de Chirurgia,* with the date 1693 beneath the ornamental title, he felt as if he were living in a world whose rulers were Merlin and Melisande. What a book! Just the wood-cut on the title page: a naked young man leaning against a Greek column, untouched by pain, with a wistful smile, although his skin had been hung out next to him on the branches of a thorny bush, like a large, limp overcoat. And all the muscles drawn so beautifully, so meticulously, like threads pulling off a spindle. Hanemann stared at the youth, moved and bemused by his evi-dent melancholy, then turned the yellowed page to discover a beautiful young woman with large, sad eyes, holding a lumi-nous rose in her fingers. Her body was opened like an oyster, so that one could see exactly how the intestines were coiled in the pelvis. Next to her, a naked, bearded man was missing several ribs, so that the readers could examine the secrets of the heart perched among the branching arteries. Not to mention the woodcuts of Ambroise Paré, the etchings from Harvey's trea-tises, the engravings adorning the works of Boerhaave, Mor-gagni, Vesalius, or Falloppio! Gigantic pages showing individuals with the skin removed to reveal the beautiful tangles of muscles and tendons; or pairs of figures holding palm fronds as they strolled across the vast Elysian fields, while a heavenly light rained down on their bodies, so exposed, naked but without shame, and beautiful angels with gentle faces and slender hands floated among the clouds, waving a banner bearing the Latin names of diseases and cures.

Later, however, this idea of the body, resplendent with allegories of Time, Wisdom, and Fortune, which had so moved his childish imagination and set him thinking about divine connections, clashed with his rough experience in the underground rooms of the Althof Clinic. There he saw other bodies, cadavers touched by decay, stripped of the majesty of death, humiliated at the hands of the students and young doctors wielding their knives. "Believe me," August Pfütze told Hanemann one day (Pfütze had already taken one course in anatomy), "whatever you end up finding here, you're going to lose your God. Nothing will be left of your faith; you'll see."

Professor Ansen would have objected strenuously to that. He knew that the bodies that wound up in the underground rooms of Althof came from the lowest strata of the city, the desperate and the damned who had rejected all hope of salvation, but this did not mean—as he stated year after year in his inaugural lecture—that they were deprived of dignity. Any direct confrontation with death, even in its most disgraced form, always brings us closer to understanding the mystery of life. What is it, truly, that keeps us from temptation? And what forces some of us to throw away the gift of life? Professor Ansen had made it his calling to bring these secrets to light, and for years he had served as an expert witness in the Berlin courts. In the large auditorium at Althof, he addressed the first-year students who had come from Munich, Hamburg, Breslau, Danzig, and even

Königsberg. "Bear in mind, gentlemen," he said, "how many regrettable mistakes have been committed either out of ignorance or—and let this be stated clearly—as a result of sloppy police work, and how many faulty opinions have been rendered based on these errors, judgments that are an affront to truth and a disgrace to our profession. But such failures are not only a matter of faulty procedure. Always remember that we must be more than mere doctors: we must look deeper inside the person, until we uncover the corporeal soul teetering on the brink of despair. Therefore let your eyes be keen and patient as diamonds, while you trace the cause. Examine the bodies of these forlorn and rejected souls who have chosen death, but do so to uncover the force in each of us that advances the divine energy of life, the force that is always able to clear the darkness and bring salvation, even in the most difficult moments, when we think we have lost everything. Probe for the medical causes of despair, but never forget that the human being is more than the body alone."

Thinking about Ansen's words, Hanemann smiled. The professor must have read a lot of Nietzsche. But how much remained of the exultation he had felt while listening to Ansen? Because not too long after those inaugural lectures he was wielding his own scalpel with the patient indifference of a mapmaker charting familiar territories. The slow cooling of a human heart. . . . It was the dark side of human life that was revealed to Hanemann in the underground rooms at Althof. At first this inspired dread, but later on? What was left to fear? The looming danger of suicide? Professor Ansen, wearing a white rubberized canvas apron, lifted the burlap off the pallid face of the dead man whom the orderlies had laid out on the marble slab, and his voice was free of the slightest tremble.

"Do not think, gentlemen," he said to the students assisting him, "that death by one's own hand is easy to distinguish from death at the hands of another. Death always hides from us—not only when someone who wants to die mimics a crime. The body invariably lies to us. We must maintain our skepticism, even when we have no doubts. To the untrained eye there is practically no difference between the body of a suicide and that of someone who has been killed. Our mind is all too eager to trust appearances. Look at this young person who was found holding a knife. Commissioner Schinckel believes the man took his own life. But that isn't true. A person who commits suicide by cutting his own neck typically produces a slanted wound that runs from left to right. The incision is deeper by the ear and shallower at the collarbone, because the poor soul's hand weakens with the stroke. In addition, with a suicide we frequently find trial incisions, which are much weaker and generally appear at the initial point of entry, and attest to the victim's extreme anxiety and fear. With a homicide it looks very different: the cut runs straight across the neck and is usually deeper at the end— as here—because the criminal wants to make certain that his victim does not come back to life. And a suicidal gunshot wound?" Professor Ansen crossed to the second table, where the body of an older man had been laid out. "Do not let yourselves be fooled by a revolver in the hand of the deceased. This merchant from Bremen, whose body was delivered yesterday, was found clutching a Mauser. But remember this, gentlemen: a suicide hardly ever shoots through his clothing; he always uncovers the spot he wishes to hit. Never forget that death, however delivered, is always an act of the soul..."

The sun was setting as they headed back to Mrs. Lenz's boardinghouse after another of Ansen's lectures. "You know,"

August said to Hanemann, "he's right. Still, the real question isn't why some people take their own lives, but why most of them don't. It's pretty miraculous, considering how unbearable life can be."

Hanemann recalled another conversation, upstairs in the Althof clinic: "But the body stays silent," August had claimed. "It doesn't reveal a thing. Do you think the bodies of Kleist and Henriette Vogel said anything?"

Back then, Hanemann had shrugged his shoulders: "Come on, August, she had cancer."

"And that explains everything, right?" August gasped, full of sarcasm. "Millions of people have cancer, but there was only one Henriette Vogel."

Knowing that August was spending every evening engrossed in the writings of the Viennese psychiatrist who was attracting more and more attention, Hanemann gave his friend a cue: "Eros and Thanatos?"

"That's exactly right," said August, running his hand through his blond hair. "Every part of our body wants equally to live and to die. Every single cell! And we're always on the edge. Hanging from a bridge by a hair. All it takes is a little breeze."

August's face was flushed. Hanemann gave him a sympathetic look and said, "Don't exaggerate. Because somehow it all keeps going, doesn't it? And right now we're going over to Müller's place and ordering a schnitzel." That wasn't a very smart thing to say: August was offended. But fortunately not for long, and a few minutes later they were running down Winterstrasse toward the pub, flirting with the girls on the way, the girls with their white parasols...

Back then, in Berlin, Hanemann didn't like to go inside Catholic churches. He couldn't stand the sight of the naked Christ. He could tolerate medieval representations of martyrdom, like the visions of Matthias Grünewald. Terrifying as they were—the martyrs were splattered or cloaked with blood— their nakedness was concealed. But the statues in the churches repelled him. Especially the ones he saw set up in the Polish churches at Easter, the plaster figures of Christ in the tomb— they reminded him too much of the bodies on the marble slab table. Everything in him protested: *That's no way to show God!* The Protestant chapels were different. White walls, a simple cross. But there were no longer any Protestant chapels left in Danzig. The big one by the barracks at Hohenfriedberger Weg had been turned into a cinema, as had the smaller one near Jäschkentaler Weg.

From time to time he stopped to look in the Cathedral—not very often, just as he had rarely gone to the chapel on Pelonker Strasse where Pastor Knabbe had delivered his sermons. The first time Hanemann entered the white nave, it seemed to him completely foreign. He happened to go during the worst season possible, advent, when everything was draped in purple, and the sight disgusted him. Inside, in front of the main altar, a line of people were slowly approaching a cross, which was lying on the ground, with the naked figure of God nailed to the wood. The worshipers were touching their lips to the wounds on the knees and hands. It was so hideous that Hanemann walked out of the church. But the image stayed with him, and as he observed his new neighbors on Grottger Street, he felt that they all shared a bond, that they were linked to one another by their common rituals, bowing over the ivory-white body with the nails, touching their lips to the thickly painted red blood.

Although the ritual bothered him, he was far from condemning it. One June morning, as all of Grottger Street, freshly washed and perfumed, headed for the Cathedral, he decided not to stay at home. He went down Wit Stwosz Street, past the streetcar loop and through the park, until he reached Cystersów Street near the chapel of Saint Jacob. Without stopping at make-shift altars along the sidewalks, he strolled around in a leisurely way, and although what he saw was completely alien, he yielded to the beauties of the holy day—the moist, freshly swept street, the little girls in their long batiste dresses, the shiny little purses, the thick yellow candles wrapped in lace, the asparagus fern, mesh gloves, tiny bird whistles made of clay...He passed a small altar decorated with spruce branches, tulips, and narcissus and busily attended by women in cretonne skirts. Several men had taken off their well-pressed jackets, laid them on the grass, and rolled up their white sleeves; they were setting up freshly cut birch saplings among tables with snow-white tablecloths that looked like surplices.

The bells of the Cathedral tolled ten o'clock. Hanemann turned onto Cystersów Street and rested under the horse chest-nut trees. He looked at everything from a distance, even though he was smack in the middle of the well-groomed crowd on its way to the Cathedral. Back then, the first time he'd stepped into the white nave, he had been bothered by the sight of the women with their cheeks pressed to the grate, confessing to an un-known man in a black cassock. He couldn't stand how they bent over to kiss the violet stole that was offered to them in a calm, measured gesture by a white hand coming out of the shadows. When he saw that, he decided the doctor from Wittenberg had been right...The closeness of the faces separated by the grate, that mixing of breaths...And when he saw a man wearing a miter sitting on the cathedra, holding a crook, and the young men dressed in seminarian robes kneeling and kissing the hand with the fat ring—he had had to turn away and walk outside. That had been too much....But now...now, on this warm June day on Cystersów Street, under the chestnuts with their large leaves, startled sparrows darted from one place to another, the puffed faces of the musicians were reflected in their brass horns, the drum slowly beat away as the wavy melody floated into the sky together with the blue smoke of incense. And it wasn't clear whether the ripples of warmth were coming from the pale, cloudless sky or from below the earth, which also is reborn, sending dark shoots up through the turf: lilies with dewy chalices and a light, springtime fragrance. Down the middle of the street, in the shade of the chestnuts, came the Ark, rocking and floating on four staves, covered with a white-and-gold-embroidered baldachin, with the Host like a white eyelid on a radiant metal sun, lifted by hands covered with cloth.

That, too, would have been too much for the doctor from Wittenberg—but now? Now as one sun rose over the roofs along Cystersów Street, another was floating down the middle, a sun there was no need to fear, a sun that neither parched grain nor dried rivers, that did not blind the eye but caressed it with a gentle whiteness. A sun whose center was manifestly alive . . .

Hanemann stared at the golden star radiating under the baldachin, so richly embroidered by a Swedish queen; perhaps the big sun, the glowing white sun already over Wrzeszcz—it was almost eleven—mellowed at the sight of the smaller sun, with its crown of metal rays, sailing over the bowed heads. The luminous June morning was suffused with tranquillity. It warmed the heart and melted the icy joints. Hanemann squinted, trying to maintain his ironic detachment, struggling not to give in to the warm breath that was caressing him the way his mother had stroked his hair. It's just the spring air, he told himself, but he got up and little by little joined the crowd as it moved through its own warm haze beneath the chestnut trees. He walked along the cobblestones sprinkled with fresh water and strewn with flowers from gardens and fields, coloring the streets like a host of fallen butterflies, cast by little girls wearing dresses of rustling gauze. Now he lost all desire to argue with the papists, now everything he saw around him merged into some kind of whole that contained more than the voices from the courtyard at 17 Grottger Street, more than the swish on the stone floor as people knelt to kiss the cross, more than the strangely sibilant nursery rhymes, the leisurely twilight hours by the window, the lackadaisically tended flower beds. Even the way Mr. Wierzbołowski and Mr. D. staggered home at night, wavering along the hedges and sailing into the dark porch at Number 14, their arms locked around each other's shoulders—even that now seemed to Hanemann not only the most natural thing in the world, but also absolutely right and proper.

He smiled to himself. What would the Wittenberg doctor think of this! The women's shoulders, draped with batiste and tinged with a tiny spray of perspiration as they walked alongside the baldachin, were so beautiful that even the crush of children crowned with wreaths of daisies, the glistening foreheads wiped with handkerchiefs, the shaved necks already tanned by the June sun, the rumble of steps, the push of the crowd, the exhaustion—none of it could diminish the light he felt filling his soul.

Even so, once he was back at 17 Grottger Street, sitting in the armchair to catch his breath, his eyes were relieved to find the familiar picture hanging on the wall in its brown frame: a color lithograph based on Caspar David Friedrich's *Cross in the Mountains,* showing a dark hilltop, a stand of spruce trees, the black symbol of the Lord, and not a single living soul.

| *Return* |

MAMA LED HER carefully, by the elbow, but at the gate Hanka freed herself from Mama's grasp. I watched from behind the curtain as she walked quickly through the garden, her head held high. She probably sensed that everyone was watching her from behind curtains, just like me.

There was no reprimand, neither then nor later. Maybe if it had been someone else . . . but with Hanka? Everyone seemed to have silently agreed not to show that they knew. But could they possibly keep it hidden? As the two women passed between the rows of arborvitae, Mr. Wierzbołowski interrupted his pruning: "Hello, ladies."

Hanka looked down, her eyes half closed: "Hello." But she said it just a little too strongly, with unnecessary emphasis, as if she meant to insult Mr. Wierzbołowski. For his part, Mr. Wierzbołowski, in whose voice I detected nothing out of the ordinary, looked at her a little longer than he normally would have before he resumed trimming the hedge at Number 14.

"She kept up appearances," he said later. But I was watching from behind the curtain, and I saw how Hanka took larger steps than usual to escape more quickly from view.

The noise of the door being opened. She sighed deeply, like a diver emerging from the water. She stepped into her room without closing the door. Quickly, impatiently, she pulled the wicker suitcase out from under the bed, reached for the towels that Mama had washed and hung on the nickel-plated bed rail— including the one they had found in the kitchen, white with a red border. She jerked that particular towel off the rail and placed it, a little uneasily, on the bottom of her suitcase, beneath the dresses and blouses.

Mama was standing in the doorway. "Stay here, you still have to get your bearings."

But Hanka didn't even look up: "No."

"At least take off your coat. And eat something."

She mechanically tossed her coat on the bed and went to the kitchen.

We ate in silence. Only Father laughed lightly as he told how Mr. Wierzbołowski went out yesterday and bought the Mierze-jewskis' old Warszawa, and today the car already needed to be repaired. Hanka said nothing as she sliced the bread, chopped garlic on the cutting board, and filled the porcelain boat with sour cherry preserves. At first Mama sat her down at the table and began making the sandwiches herself, but when Hanka saw Mama's timid way of wielding the knife, and sensed that Mama's extreme carefulness was on account of her, she just moaned and took the knife away from Mama, then proceeded to cut the bread with quick, strong strokes.

"Everybody's talking, I'm sure of it. . . ." She paused for a second.

"No, not at all," Mama said quickly.

"They're talking all right, I know. . . ." She didn't look up. But then she adjusted her blouse and stood up straight and added: "Anyway, who cares. Let them talk. And you"—she looked at me—"what are you staring at? As if you'd never laid eyes on me before?" Then she ruffled my hair gently, a little more slowly than usual. I tried to smile, but nothing came of it. The dishes clanged.

"Come on and join us," Mama said, waving her over to the table.

But Hanka just shook her head. "I'm not hungry." And she went back to cutting the bread, though it wasn't necessary, because when she placed the slices in the basket, nobody took a single one.

Later she washed the dishes and set them in the wire drainer to dry. "Well, that's that," she said, wiping her hands.

"Wait," Mama said, without moving, "where are you planning to go?"

Hanka hung the towel on the hook: "Is the world so small a place?"

"Come on, where are you planning to live?"

But Hanka just turned around. I grabbed her hand. "Hanka, don't go anywhere. Stay with us."

"No."

"Why not?"

She shrugged her shoulders, then went inside her room, opened the wardrobe, threw the hangers onto the bed, and started packing. She held the dresses up to the light for a moment, one by one, as if checking to see if they were intact, then folded them and laid them in the suitcase. Father paced around the kitchen. Mama sat at the table and stared out the window.

From the vestibule I saw Hanka in her cretonne skirt, her back bending over the suitcase, and the bed covered with colored blouses. The birch tree rustled outside the window.

Father stepped closer. "Really, Hanka, this doesn't make sense. Nobody here has the slightest thing against you. At least stay till tomorrow. You won't find anything at this hour. Believe me, they don't have anything against you at all."

Hanka stopped packing for a moment. "You mean they pity me?"

Father groaned. "Oh, come on. You think they don't have enough problems of their own to worry about?"

She looked at him carefully. "The last thing I want is pity."

Father put his hands in his pockets. "So what are you planning to do now?"

She flicked some bangs off her forehead. "Nothing."

The suitcase was already full. Hanka pressed down the wicker cover, put on the brass padlock, and turned the key. She thought for a moment, then reached for the pillow and removed the pillowcase. Mama went over to her. "Don't worry about that; I'll take care of it." But Hanka just ignored her, turned the case inside out, and folded it. Then she did the same with the duvet cover with the metal buttons. When she shook that out, some feathers went flying in the air; one landed on her hair. She pulled the sheet off the mattress. She placed the pillow and the duvet at the foot of the bed. The mattress lay bare on the springs, gray cloth fabric with blue stripes.

"This doesn't make sense"—Father wasn't giving up. "You'll see," he said, his voice sounding impatient, "a little time will pass and nobody will remember a thing."

She looked around the room to see if she had forgotten anything, checked the wardrobe, reached for her suitcase. She put on her coat and went to Mama. "I'm sorry that everything..."

Mama hugged her, rubbing her on the back, but Hanka stiffened and removed Mama's hand. Then she went to Father. "And now I've caused you so much trouble..."

"What trouble?" said Father, holding out his hand. "Remember that if something doesn't work out you're always welcome here with us."

She pretended not to hear him. Then she came over to me. She ruffled my hair. "And you promise me that you're going to eat well, all right?"

I nodded. I felt a cold wave seeping into my heart. "Where are you going to live now?" She didn't answer. She buttoned her coat and lifted the suitcase. Then Father remembered something:

"You ought to say good-bye to Hanemann."

She stopped in midstep. "You're right. Of course, I forgot..." But instead of going straight upstairs, she went to her room and closed the door.

We sat in the kitchen in silence. Father took out his tobacco and tried to roll a cigarette, but the brown shag just crumbled in his fingers, so he crushed the paper and tossed it on the table. I stared at the green linoleum. Mama adjusted her hair. Not a sound came from Hanka's room. From outside we could hear the sparrows chirping in the branches of the birch. A breeze lifted the curtain.

The door creaked and Hanka came out. She had taken off her coat and was still wearing the dark cretonne skirt with yellow and red flowers. But when she stood in the light, I saw her face: her lips were red, thick with lipstick, her eyebrows and lashes blackened, her eyes lengthened with black liner, and her cheeks powdered and rouged. I had never seen her like that before. She seemed taller than usual, too; she was wearing platform shoes with cork soles. A tight necklace of red beads divided her neck in half like a very thin, deep cut.

At the sight of Hanka, Mama started from the table, but Hanka quickly passed through the vestibule, and a minute later we heard her steps moving slowly up the stairs. Then the clatter of her shoes stopped, and we heard her knock on Hanemann's door.

No one answered. Hanka knocked once more, impatiently, as if to signal that she didn't have time to stand there waiting, and then the lock squealed, the door opened, and I heard Hanemann's voice but couldn't make out the words. Then he was cut off. Hanka was speaking quickly, I heard snatches of sentences but still couldn't understand a thing. Next there was a shout, Mama and Father looked at each other, Father sprang out of his chair and ran upstairs, there was a commotion and another shout...

When he reached the second floor, he grabbed Hanka by the hand and pulled her away from Hanemann's door. Her hair was disheveled, the rouge on her cheeks smeared with mascara and tears. Father grabbed hold of her shoulders and shook her firmly, but she kept shouting: "You...you kraut...who asked you...why did you have to stick your nose...I hope you..." Then she started to gasp for air and cough. "I don't want to live...leave me alone...I don't want to live...I wish all of you would..." Father held her arms, but she kept shaking her head, with her eyes pressed shut, her lips transformed into a painfully ragged purple stain...

Hanemann was standing in the doorway, holding his cheek. Next to his lips was a thin streak of blackish blue.

BUT HANKA STAYED with us. After she "said good-bye" to Hanemann, it was clear that my parents weren't going to let her out
of their sight for the next few days at least; beyond that we
would have to see. When Father brought her downstairs, she
threw herself onto her bare mattress, convulsing with sobs. It
was so bad that I ran to my room and stopped my ears. Then
Mama made Hanka's bed, with freshly starched linens still
smelling of dried wild-rose petals, and forced her to lie down.

She slept that entire day and night and through the next
morning. Mama looked in a few times to make sure she was all
right, because Hanka's head was buried in the pillow, flushed,
with swollen lips; her breathing was labored; she seemed to be
struggling to break through layers of smothering dreams. Her
hair was matted, the pillow stained with lipstick, and her cheek
was smeared with purple streaks, as if she'd been scratched by
thorns. She woke up and asked for something to drink, so
Mama, thinking she might have a fever, gave her some linden

blossom tea. Mama wanted Father to get Doctor Badowski, but what was really happening, Hanka later said, was that her body was getting rid of the Evil One. All the evil was coming out of her skin. Her nightgown was dark with sweat; she had to change it twice.

At around noon the following day she got up, went straight to the mirror, and said, "My God, just look at me." She tried unsuccessfully to smooth out her hair, but the damp curls just slipped through her fingers. Mama filled the tub, I saw the two women walk slowly to the bathroom, and then Hanka sat in the hot water for almost an hour, her eyes closed, her head arched back, breathing carefully, as if she were afraid her beating heart could be heard throughout the house. Afterward she rubbed herself vigorously with a rough towel, tied her hair up with a ribbon, and put on a bathrobe. When I went to the bathroom I saw that the water in the tub was completely gray. I heard her door bang shut; she stayed locked in her room for almost half an hour, completely quiet; we were uneasy. Then I heard that phrase, pronounced while she was combing the tangles out of her hair: "I'll show you!"

Whenever I think about our old apartment, I hear Hanka speaking after a long silence. Because when Father brought her downstairs, both Hanka and I were feeling pretty abysmal. I watched her sob and felt that everything was falling apart, and now things were popping up again like grass after the rain. I couldn't understand why.

The next day she went out to the Puskarczyks' grocery, at a time when it was full of people. The women talked to her about trivial matters—their households, the neighbors—without letting on in any way that they knew the whole story. In their own homes they probably said something else, but there in the store. . . . Hanka bought a package of yeast, a dozen eggs, cream, a bag of powdered sugar, and some vanilla extract, and as soon as she came back she scrubbed the large pastry board with a cloth. The cooking tins rattled as she smeared them with a thick coat of butter, flames shot out from under the stove, the smell of flour and hot butter filled the room, egg yolks splashed into the faience bowl one after the other, the whites foamed under the quick beating of a fork, and I sat at the table holding a piece of warm bread and doing nothing but watch. She still wasn't humming as she used to, still wasn't tossing her hair out of her face as she had before, but in every movement I could sense that phrase, those wonderful words that were to help me many times later on. "I'll show you!" And though it wasn't clear whom Hanka was addressing, I felt that with every twist of her body, every turn of her shoulders, she was paying someone (or something) back, blow for blow, as if here, in the kitchen, she were surrounded by some unseen evil figures that she constantly had to reckon with. They were the ones she was hitting with her elbow as she kneaded the ball of yellow dough on the pastry board; they were the ones she was punching in the mouth as she cut the sugar into the yolks inside the ceramic mixing bowl. But who were they? All of us from Grottger Street?

Afterward, even Father had to taste a little of the crumb cake (though he preferred the glazed poppy seed roll Hanka sometimes made on Saturdays). Then, when Hanka asked Mama and me to come to the table, she brought out a steaming apple tart fresh from the oven, though Christmas was a long way off, and she normally served that on Christmas Eve. And while we were all happy to see the change, Mama suspected that there was still something lurking beneath the yeasty sugar-glazed joy, some evil thing hiding behind the flour-white hands, the flashing cake tins, and that this something was liable to explode again at any moment.

Little by little, however, Hanka returned to herself. On Saturday, when Mama and Father went out to the Falkiewiczes' on Kwietna Street, where they stayed till nearly midnight, Bożena and Janina came over from Number 14 across the street. As I drifted asleep, I could hear their warm voices murmuring in the kitchen, as they sat gossiping about everybody on the street, house by house, from distant acquaintances to close friends! And I caught every word, every laugh, as if shiny coins were being tossed into my room. Hanka's voice, which was still a little muted, occasionally regained its old sharpness, and her laughter vibrated almost exactly the way it had before—clean, lively, and a little sassy. She sounded somewhat like a clever child recovering from a bout of crying, trying very hard to enjoy some new activity, no matter how pointless. My eyes barely open, my cheek snug against my pillow, I let myself drift into that rising and falling fog of women's voices, as they hungrily and mercilessly devoured Grottger Street—because no one was spared, everyone had to be discussed and transformed into some amusing anecdote, and I was happy that everything was working out fine.

Nevertheless, ever since that day when Mrs. W. hadn't let me inside the door marked 17, and had waved me away with half-scolding, half-hurrying gestures, I couldn't look at Hanka the way I had before. And even if she went on ruffling my hair the way she used to, which I had always liked, now my pulse jumped whenever she reached to touch my head. Had she changed, or had I? Even though my heart wanted so badly for everything to be the way it had been, my eyes discerned the slightest difference in the way she shook her head, the way she gestured while talking... Was there a shadow deep inside her pupils? Was the glow inside beginning to fade? A tightness around the mouth? A new tic—touching her temples? Did she still have a laughing body? After all that?

What about Hanemann? We didn't speak of him at home, just as we never spoke about that day. When Hanka passed him on the path or on the stairs, she would return his greeting, to all appearances the way she always had, but it wasn't the same. Earlier she had been amused by the man who lived above us, the overly serious man who taught German to the neighborhood boys. Now and then she would see him making his way to the garden, where he would very meticulously snip a few irises under the arborvitae: she had always had to stifle a laugh when she returned his greeting. "Hello, Dr. Hanemann," she would say, casually, with a hint of irony, a tiny bit sassy, a touch too loudly. Now she picked up her pace whenever she passed him.

Sometimes, in the evenings, if my parents weren't home, Hanka, Bożena, and Janina would join their pretty voices in the kitchen, with Hanka conducting, like a triumphant chorus. At first a quiet whisper: "Ha! Ne! Mann! Ha! Ne! Mann!" Then a little faster: "Ha! Ne! Mann!" And then faster and faster and louder and louder until finally they burst out laughing. Bożena would stand in the middle of the kitchen and, sticking her hands in the pockets of her apron, would imitate Hanemann's gait. Her cork soles would bang on the floorboards like a drum playing a happy dance: Boom! Boom! It was so wickedly funny I would hide my head under the duvet cover, choking with laughter.

| *Shades of Skin* |

LOOKING INTO THE mirror, Hanemann touched his cheek. The thin blackish blue line along his lip. How odd: that aggression, her hands slashing at him like that. He couldn't figure it out. What was she after? He tipped the flask and dabbed the ball of cotton on the scratch. That violence, her raised hand, her eyes. Was she in pain? Had he seen tears? He looked in the mirror. What was he supposed to do now? Go downstairs? What for? He didn't understand. Maybe he had inadvertently hurt her sometime in the past, and it was just now coming out? But when? How? Everything had seemed normal. They would pass each other on the stairs, on the path in the garden, on the street. She would say, "Hello." Or sometimes, "Hello, Dr. Hanemann." But apart from that they floated by each other like fish in an aquarium. He had his life; she had hers. They kept out of each other's way. Indifferent politeness. Neighbors just by chance. Was she afraid?

But now something had changed. A tear in a veil. Hanemann shrugged his shoulders. She'd undoubtedly been through a lot. But that aggression? The speed with which she'd reached for his face. Her splayed fingers. And that scream. What had she been screaming? What hadn't she wanted? Should he have reacted differently back then? Should he not have broken down the door? Just stood there and waited? Nonsense.

But there was something else. Her breath. Her perfume. The flowery dress while they were struggling. Shoulders, hips. Contact. She had pushed him so hard he had almost fallen. Then Mr. C. had come running up from downstairs and pulled her away. She was screaming. But why the lipstick? Why the eyeliner, the mascara? Why the earrings? He'd never seen her like that before. Had she suspected that he might have feelings for her?

In any event, now, whenever he saw her walking down the path to the gate, he hid behind the curtain and didn't leave the window. Quick, firm steps. A bright dress, a wicker basket— green lettuce leaves, a long loaf of bread, something wrapped in paper. Was she pretending not to see him? Cork heels on the flagstones. Was their clatter different? He hoped it was. He hoped she would show some trace of what had happened. But there didn't seem to be any. Not the slightest hint, as if he didn't exist…He quickly jumped to a rationalization: What does it matter, anyway? She hurried out the gate, nodding to someone, and disappeared behind the arborvitae. Hate? The idea was ridiculous. After all, he hadn't been thinking of her in the least, back then. He'd simply sensed that odor on the stairs. That was the only reason he'd broken in like that…

He tried remembering what she really looked like—her complexion, shoulders, hair. But everything was obscured by that face in the door, covered with powder and rouge. He couldn't remember anything else, and now he didn't see her except in passing, fleeting glimpses of her hand, her hair. Or else he heard her steps on the stairs. Her strong, rich voice calling to the boy from the window. But what was the exact shade of her skin? How suntanned? Was it golden brown? A flash of bare elbows, rolled-up sleeves. What about her lips? She'd never used lipstick before, had she?

On his way downstairs, he noticed that she retreated into the ground-floor apartment at the sound of his steps. Was she ashamed? He walked by slowly, sensing that she was right behind the door. Should he knock? Better not. He went outside. Was she watching him, from behind her own curtain in the kitchen window?

One day he met me on the path. "What's up, Piotr?"

I nodded a greeting. "Hello, Dr. Hanemann. Hanka was saying very bad things about you."

He smiled. "That's because she's all worked up. You shouldn't pay attention to that."

I looked at him: "I know. But she wants to leave us."

Hanemann arched his eyebrows. "Is it that bad? Maybe I should stop in?"

"No, I don't think so." I looked down at the ground. "It's probably better if you don't. She's very angry. But she'll get over it."

"You think so?"

"Then she'll be exactly the way she was before. She's pretty smart, you know."

Hanemann felt himself getting restless. He felt his body waking up, or rather—stirred by the painful scratch—shaking off its paralysis. But it was a change he didn't welcome. At night he dreamed about women he'd never seen before, wandering through an unfamiliar room, losing a lipstick or powder box, grazing his face with a fan, and it was all so real that when he woke up he would search the carpet for whatever had fallen out of their white hands. Something purple? Something pink? An entire world of women's things he had thought no longer existed for him suddenly sailed out of the shadows and became painfully visible. Meanwhile, outside, Hanka, wearing a bright blouse with rolled-up sleeves, was hanging the freshly washed laundry on the line. Linen nightgowns, a bra, cotton stockings, a kerchief—swaying in the wind, all irritatingly intimate and unseemly, since each piece belonged to her. When she lifted her arms to pin the white sheet with the Walmann monogram, the straps of her stiff bra showed through her batiste blouse. And Hanemann, book in hand, would break off the German lesson, hypnotized by the fluttering sheets, bras, and nightgowns, until Andrzej Ch. looked up at him, puzzled.

"If we're done for the day, sir, then maybe I should go?" asked Andrzej.

Hanemann came to as if he'd been startled from his sleep. He shrugged, feeling thoroughly ridiculous. "No, why don't you stay. We still have a little time. Go ahead and read." Andrzej went back to his conjugations, but Hanemann seemed not to hear his voice.

Once again the cork heels clattered on the sidewalk, but this time he resolved not to go to the window, and held up the book to read. But no sooner had he begun than a cretonne skirt came flashing across the rows of letters, and in the rustle of the turning page he heard the warm swish of the flowery red and yellow fabric. He tried to keep focused on the words and sentences, but she wouldn't stop, she skipped on without a care in the world, up and down the lines between the Gothic letters, knocking down heavy black majuscules, leaping over paragraphs, jumping from one page to the next, and laughing out loud. Hanemann squinted at the letters, and the quick steps faded away, down the path between the arborvitae, and now she was calling out to Mr. Wierzbołowski. More loudly than usual? This was ludicrous. He got up and shut the window. Her voice set him on edge, so care-free, without a hint of shame or anxiousness. He grimaced: How could she be so unfeeling, so—he searched for the right word—so plantlike? Evidently the incident hadn't left the slightest mark on her, as if—he thought with a spite that instantly amused him—as if she didn't even have a soul. Soul? He realized that he was angry with her without reason. Soul? What did he want from her soul? He must be going crazy. She'd obviously been through a lot; that laugh of hers, which he found so annoying, was probably just a way of protecting herself. Why hold anything against her; what could he possibly want from her? And besides—he looked out the window with unconcealed spite—she didn't come close to ... He returned to Kleist writing to Henriette, struggling against the distraction for several moments, but then the cork heels once again intruded—this time more muffled, distant—and instead of the book, Hanemann saw in front of him the flagstone walkway between the arbor-vitae. And her hand, deftly tucking a strand of hair behind her ear ...

Something from long ago, something he had struggled against with all his might, something very, very painful, slowly slipped back into his heart. The memory of a different face, crowned with light hair ... Nonetheless the dark-haired one kept racing up and down the page in a flowery cretonne dress. Pink fingernails. Eyelids. Not mere recollections but light, living breaths. The Gothic letters glinted black on the pages, he forced his eyes from one paragraph to the next, but his thoughts! He laughed out loud in an attempt to shake off the distraction. And he wasn't even thinking of her as a whole person so much as a number of separate parts: the indentation over her collarbone, her temple speckled with light, a bare elbow, a knee, her fingers. Amusing thoughts, perilously close to passion.

He remembered what Anna had told him that beautiful afternoon, could still picture her white hat. She had taken him by the arm: "You can't go on living like this." So what was it he was feeling now—hate? Anger? Regret that something was pushing him back into the current of life? After all, and it was hard to admit, he could see with his own eyes that while he was deeply moved by the whole incident, she didn't seem affected in the least. He wanted her to feel the same light humiliation, the same bitterness. He had the right to hurt her. It wouldn't be too difficult, either, he thought.

He snapped out of his brooding. After all, back then, on the stairs—her trembling lips, that scream, those hands . . . what was cold about that? She'd obviously been carrying some hurt inside her for a long time; it wasn't about him at all. What made him think she disliked him? His heart pirouetted like a ballerina. He found whole levels of tenderness inside himself that he had never suspected existed. He was ready to go downstairs and explain everything. He could see her features softening: "No, it was nothing. Just nerves. Why don't you come in and stay a moment?" But then he remembered Mama's request to stay away for the time being, because every conversation would only rub salt in the wound. So once again he reached for the German text and checked Andrzej's notebook, underlining the mistakes with red pencil, hoping to bury himself in some mechanical task.

In vain. Because she reappeared. He watched her pass through the beam of sunlight into his room. And now the azure shimmer of the sea slowly opens up right before his eyes, and she is walking along the beach at Glettkau, heading toward the landing, wearing her flowery dress and carrying her shiny purse. Hanemann can see her fixing her hair. The fear rises in his heart as he watches her step onto the tarred planks of the empty pier, where that same white boat is waiting. He tries to grab her arm, to pull her back onto the beach, but she doesn't see him, just keeps on walking straight toward the white boat with the tall slanted funnel, the sun's so bright her hair looks golden as she tosses it behind her. The boat is empty, just a few steps more to the gangplank, he hears the even clatter of cork heels hitting the dock, harder and harder, his heart is pounding in his chest, he wants to break through to her, through the layers of air, he grasps at her sleeve, but Hanka's hand unravels like a strand of fog, his fingers are left clutching the air, the white ship is growing larger, it's starting to tilt, and Hanemann shields his head, because the black hull of the *Bernhoff* is looming over him like a skyscraper on the verge of collapse, he shields his head because high overhead, Mrs. Walmann's daughters are jumping off the burning deck, plunging heavily into the black water, the fire spills overboard in a growing stain of smoke and flames, someone's hand is reaching up, someone's eyes, someone calling, sobbing, and he is adrift on a tiny raft with room enough for only one...

| *The Empty Bed* |

"WHERE SHE FOUND HIM? Let me think a moment." Mr. J. paused. "I had to piece it together from what little I heard—you know how people are when they're talking about things they would just as soon forget..."

In those days there weren't many people who dared go poking around the hills behind the train station, up in the old Prussian fortifications—deep trenches with the brick chambers overgrown with blackthorn, wormwood, and wheatgrass. Rumor had it the whole place was mined, that there were even Germans hiding underground; some people swore they'd actually seen one or two. In November, someone had reported seeing a light among the trees; evidently he had seen firelight flickering through a crack in the wall, so officers S. and W. went from the police station on Kartuska Street to investigate. Weapons at the ready, they climbed down the steep slope, trampling the branches as they went, all the way to the brick wall. Stepping over piles of broken glass, they climbed down a small opening into a barrel-like vault, but the little fire vanished in the darkness. The place was dank and smelled of wet paper and tar; they were struck by the silence that seemed to come from deep inside. They were beginning to think that the strange flickering might have been nothing more than the reflection of the city lights in a broken pane, and they considered going back. They stopped for two or three minutes at the wrought-iron gateway and stood there without moving, their rifles pointed at the darkness. They were on the verge of leaving when they heard a noise, followed by quick, startled footsteps. A tin can clanged in the darkness, something rolled across the brick flooring, the policemen shouted "Stop!" but the steps faded away. S. and W. went back inside. Shining a light along the slanted wall, they wound their way through the tunnel, passing old tin cans, a spent artillery shell, a few webbed belts, and a helmet gleaming in a black puddle. They heard something clang against the bricks farther on. "Come out!" they shouted, but their words died without an echo in the corridor. Then they moved cautiously ahead. In a large chamber they found soot and other traces of fire on the walls, so they raised their weapons and ran their flashlight over stacks of crates, illuminating the dead bulbs that hung by wires from the ceiling...

They found him in a jumbled pile of old army coats, canvas capes, gas-mask cans. Seeing the oddly shaped lump, S. tore off the topmost coat.

The boy was curled up with his knees against his chin. "Why did you run away?" asked S. Then, since the boy was shivering with cold, S. draped the coat back over the boy; he could smell the dampness, the odor of a long-unwashed body. "You can't stay here. The place might be mined."

But the boy didn't move, so S. shook him: "Get up."

"Let's leave him alone for a while," mumbled W. They sat down on a crate and smoked a cigarette. A few minutes later the boy took his hands away from his face: his features were dark, and in the flashlight beam, they thought, he looked a little like a Gypsy. His cheeks were covered with coal dust, his hair tangled and knotted. "All right, let's get up," said S., stepping on the cigarette butt. Once again the boy covered his face with his hands; he crawled out from the pile of coats and took off running toward the entrance. But W. was quicker; he grabbed the boy by his jacket and held on tight. Together the two officers hauled him, kicking and screaming, out of the trenches and into the snow. Then they wrapped him in a long Wehrmacht coat that dragged on the ground, and headed through the blackthorn along the icy path toward town.

It was already getting late and they didn't know what they should do with the boy. S. wanted to take the boy home, to Wschodnia Street in Orunia, but on the way to the station the boy broke away, ran off, and disappeared among the ruined houses. Footsteps racing through the rubble, a distant echo. All in a single moment. They searched for him until midnight.

It's impossible to say for certain if that was the same boy Hanka saw a few days later, on her way to the train. On the little square by the station, between the small cashier's booth and the train crew's quarters, she saw a group of people standing around a brazier, keeping warm. One man was wearing a beige fur cap, a long coat, felt boots, and woolen gloves cut so that his fingers could run up and down the keyboard of his Russian accordion. He squeezed the bellows back and forth, coaxing a melody from the reeds, sometimes plaintive and high, sometimes soft and low, like a gentle, soothing wind. "On the banks of a stream in the forest, grew a snow-white wayfaring tree..." People tapped their feet, less to keep time with the music than to keep warm (an early freeze had left the sidewalk icy), but the man didn't seem to notice and only stared straight into the fire as if no one else were there. After a moment he raised his head and rocked the bellows to make a loud chord that sounded like a fanfare. He nodded to someone behind him, and that's when Hanka first saw the boy, wearing a black jacket and a gray scarf.

Slowly, as if he were dragging himself ahead, the boy stepped up to the fire and stood in the warm pool of light. The fanfare stopped. Hanka watched the boy closely, studying every movement, and began to sense that there was more to him than met the eye. At first glance everything seemed normal, but then she noticed that the boy's gestures were overly distinct, as if he were sketching objects in the air, with sharp, invisible lines, whimsical figures that quickly dissipated in the darkness. She moved closer to get a better look.

The boy took an old hat with a few crumpled banknotes lying on the bottom and made a show of setting it on the ground next to his leg—as if he were afraid someone might filch the dirty blue money. Then he went on sketching, some-times with his right hand, sometimes with his left, casually, un-hurriedly, tracing curves and angles. His fingers pulled invisible objects out of thin air, one after the other, while the people around him guessed what they were. Then he stiffened up and jutted out his jaw. He bowed and lit an invisible cigar, waving his hand to put out the invisible match. Invisible bills rained down from heaven, which he collected, leaning on his cane with gentlemanly nonchalance . . . Everything fit the character, except his eyes and a hint of tension in his face. It was all funny, even a little offensive, a shade indecent—but when the women giggled, he broke off and shot the spectators a reproachful glance, then put his hands on his face as if to express his shock,

held them there a few seconds, and quickly took them away . . .
It was all very funny, but his slightly evil smile, that sharp look
in his eyes, also revealed a deep-seated pain, which made the
woman standing closest to him recoil. Even Hanka felt a little
uneasy. A moment later the accordion woke up, the bellows
groaned, and the man in the fur cap played a song about a star
shining for the sailors at sea, as the boy slowly picked up his hat,
bowed to the left, then to the right, danced around the fire, tapping his heels, and suddenly relaxed into an angelic smile. The
woman in front sighed with relief, a man muttered something
about a damn fine performance, and one woman reached for
her purse.

The Tczew local was running late again. More and more
people came up to the fire; the cold wind off the shipyards fluttered the wet banners above the station tower; people pushed
and shoved, peering over shoulders to get a better look; a few
coins clinked together in the hat.

But Hanka had stopped laughing. She stayed another moment before heading onto the platform, a strange feeling in her
heart. On the train she heard someone say how bad it was to
have children earning money that way; it ought to be against the
law. Somebody else grumbled, "What do you want, what should
they do with them? They steal, they run away, you think there
aren't a lot like that these days?" Hanka looked out the window
and saw two railroad guards slowly walking toward the brazier.
But the boy and the man with the accordion were no longer
there.

A few days later, on her way back from Mrs. K.'s on Szeroka
Street, she went in the station lobby and saw the boy a second
time. He was lying on a bench in the corner, by the radiator,
asleep; his hands were tucked under his jacket; his face was
flushed. Oversize ski boots with dangling laces. Once again she

had that same feeling that something was amiss. She touched his shoulder. He woke up and immediately shielded himself. She shook her head at him. "Are you hungry?" He didn't answer. She went to the cafeteria, looking over her shoulder to make sure he didn't escape, and bought a roll with some cheese and a glass of tea. She brought him to a table, and when they sat down he took his hands out of his jacket. His fingernails were black. She studied him carefully and asked, "Where do you live?" He just shrugged his shoulders. "Do you want to stay here?" He made a face.

Mama was a little surprised when they both showed up at our door, but there wasn't any question what she would do: she agreed to take the boy in "for the moment," and said that he could sleep in the extra bed by the window in my room. The light wooden bed was always made, even though no one ever used it. Mama called it our guest bed. Every night, as I was falling asleep, I would turn over on my right side and face the window; even in the dark I could easily make out the bed. Then I would feel a kind of anxious waiting, since the guest bed seemed a lot like the place at the table Mama set on Christmas Eve, following tradition, for any unexpected guest. The unexpected guest who never came.

But the boy was definitely here, unwashed, dressed in a mended black jacket that seemed part military, part railroad uniform. He stood in the middle of the kitchen, and Mama immediately started pulling off his jacket: "What's your name?"

Hanka quickly, gently touched her arm: "He doesn't speak..."

Mama was a little taken aback, but immediately recovered. "So what's his name?" Hanka just shrugged as she pulled the shirt off the boy's head.

Then they filled the tub with warm water, and through the crack in the barely open door I saw them scrubbing him with a sponge. He let everything happen, patiently, now and then squinting at the light over the mirror.

He doesn't speak...I was surprised to find someone who doesn't speak so close. Of course, I'd seen them before, but always from a distance; now I felt both curious and afraid. Afraid of the moment I would have to say something to him, and all he could do would be to watch my dumbly moving lips.

| *Fingers* |

NEVERTHELESS, the boy could understand us (he probably read our lips), even though he couldn't express everything with gestures. Mama learned from Mrs. Stein that Hanemann might be able to help out, so she advised Hanka to pay him a visit.

Mrs. Stein was right. During his residency with Ansen, partly at the urging of August Pfütze, Hanemann would occasionally spend a free afternoon visiting the Collegium Emmaus, which was housed in the Academy. There, on the fourth floor of the building at Winterstrasse 14, in a small auditorium adorned with statues of pagan gods, Professor Petersen from Freiburg taught a seminar on the theory and practice of sign language to a group of young doctors. Hanemann was fascinated. After so many days spent in the underground rooms of the Althof clinic, he had acquired an odd contempt for the spoken word. The papers, too, seemed saturated with lies; he hadn't bothered to read the dailies for some time. Words? He trusted only his eyes and fingers. August shared his attitude. In the evening, in a small room on the first floor at Mrs. Rosen's boardinghouse, they would talk about the faces of the suicides whose bodies wound up on the marble slab table in the clinic; in a burst of enthusiasm August proposed a whole new field, "thanatopsychology," which was the somewhat overblown term he suggested for the difficult and highly risky art of reading the physiognomy of the dead. And even though the idea was close to Hanemann, in the bottom of his heart he doubted whether such a science was possible.

Still, he had to concede that August was right about one thing. Because although Professor Ansen analyzed the position of the body, the arrangement of the hands, and the form of the wound to determine the cause of death, August could never forgive him for overlooking what he himself considered the most important clue: the face. If only we could read the eyes of the dead, shut behind their lids, if only we could decipher what the lips would tell us if they were free of deceptive lividity, if only we could decode the wrinkles and furrows, frozen at the very moment when life ceased! Shouldn't we turn there to discover why we sometimes give in to that strange temptation and squander the gift of life?

One evening, on their way back from the Collegium, Hanemann and August stopped in at the Café Elephant, on Wilhelmstrasse, which had a large sign in the window advertising a mime from London known as "Mr. Outline." August was in a good mood, and the prospect of what he called carnival entertainment made him feel even better, so they went laughing down the stairs and found themselves in a round room buried in a dim reddish light. They took their seats right in front of a stage that was lined with mirrors. Just then a tall man dressed in tails came out, and Hanemann gave a start, because the man's powdered face looked uncannily like the ones they had seen on the marble slab table at Althof. As if sensing Hanemann's unease,

Mr. Outline came right up to them and laid a white-gloved palm on Hanemann's shoulder. As the music went quiet, the powdered face bent over; Hanemann could smell the whiteface and moved his head back, but Mr. Outline didn't budge; his two black pupils bored right into Hanemann's eyes. The man had large, fleshy lips, like jellyfish; his eyelids were lined in black above his whitened cheeks. Hanemann thought of the mimes he had seen as a child; they had danced around the stage grimacing and sketching webs of invisible lines, hoping to snare the souls of the audience. But this was different; lurking under Mr. Outline's thick whiteface was something motionless, something still. Hanemann sensed that the whole room was watching them, and he felt his own face going red, particularly when it dawned on him that this strange man in whiteface and tails knew—he could feel it—this Mr. Outline knew exactly what he, Hanemann, did in the underground rooms at Althof.

After that Mr. Outline went onstage. In perfect German he asked the audience to call out their requests, and the performance began. From the right of the house, a beautiful woman with a silver-fox stole shouted the name of Neville Chamberlain; a moment later the British politician appeared on the mirrored stage. An officer in the company of a slender brunette asked to see the Russian leader, and a mustached man walked on, smoking a pipe. The likenesses were striking, and the audience applauded enthusiastically. But what most affected Hanemann was the finale, when Mr. Outline sat on a chair in the center of the stage, peered around the hall, and began imitating every member of the audience. Each new presentation brought warm bursts of laughter: no one felt hurt, because it was obvious that it was all in fun, and highly amusing. The last face to appear on stage was Hanemann's.

After the performance, Hanemann and August walked back along the Spree to Mrs. Rosen's. Lively, carefree music floated out of the cafés and cabarets along Siegfriedstrasse and mixed with the fragrance of mignonette from the gardens; swallows streaked across the sky, which by the time they reached the Siegfried bridge had turned from white to a grayish blue. The water itself looked purple in the twilight, as if bruised by the setting sun. "Did you ever notice," Hanemann asked August, "how much we tend to imitate the dead? Whenever we want to say something, we insist on using nothing but words: it's pounded in from childhood—use your words and not your body. Mothers are always telling their children not to wave their hands around, not to point! And the rest of you is supposed to keep absolutely stiff and still." August was a little taken aback, since he was rather talkative himself. For him it was a sign that he was bubbling over with life.

In the morning Hanemann went to the dimly lit auditorium with the Greek and Roman gods to hear Professor Petersen lecture on old and new sign languages, but he went as much for the presentation as for the subject matter. During the spoken lecture the professor barely moved—except for his left hand, which rose to punctuate certain words or phrases—but everything changed when he started to sign. And what a transformation! Hanemann had heard of the American dancer who performed barefoot, wrapped in diaphanous scarves—as audiences at the Palladium had been able to see for themselves—and he wasn't in the least surprised to hear one student whisper maliciously, "Who does he think he is, Isadora Duncan?"

Petersen really was quite a performer, which probably explained why so many came to hear his lectures. He would raise his arms until the hall was absolutely quiet, and then his face would light up and his white hands would flutter over the lectern like a pair of doves. And what hands! Professor Petersen, a member of the Berlin Academy, twice decorated by the kaiser for philanthropy and service in the field of science, would wave the signs in the air, visibly pleased at his own supple movements—as if his arm had just been freed from a plaster cast. While the sun's rays warmed the oak figure of Cronus standing behind the podium, Hanemann learned about dactylology and finger-spellings, about ideograms representing whole phrases and sentences, and about Petersen's own alphabet of "chiro-grams"—a language of syllables formed by touching one's fingers to one's chin, cheeks, nose, temple, chest, and shoulders. Petersen believed the whole body should speak, laugh, and cry. And on the podium next to the lectern with the carved head of Medusa, he showed how it could be done, fluidly, fluently, with delicate strokes, balled fists, and gentle clasps. Fingers opening like flowers. Trembling. Touching his lips. Bowing. Squinting. How different from Professor Ansen, his face so tense, with a gravitas anchored by his solemn black bowtie.

One day Hanemann went with August to the Amers Theater, a neoclassical building on Goethestrasse, to see a Japanese troupe, and he had the impression that they had found the other extreme, as he put it. The actors floated across the stage in black and white kimonos, their faces like alabaster masks, all silk and silence, interrupted only by flutes and the twanging of a koto—but the bodies! An entire story told with gestures, light steps, bendings of the waist! A medley of living shoulders, hips, hands, and feet! After that, Hanemann couldn't bear the sight of dancers doing the one-step or the Charleston, swaying in the golden lamplight behind the windows of the cafés. What puppets! Mannequins! Wind-up figures from a wax museum, jerkily set into motion! The dance of the Japanese actors, on the other hand, had pulsed with life. Their bodies, fused with the black and white silk, expressed fear, hope, love; they bent in the gusts of an unseen wind, straightened like grass after rain. What need had there been for words? In the bright light of the stage, their powdered hands spelled out every sign with marvelous clarity. Long fingers, undulating like the tentacles of a sea anemone, effortlessly weaving a web of light and shadow. Japanese actors! Who else could speak so eloquently with their bodies?

It was then, walking back along Friedrichstrasse to the metro station, that Hanemann had first thought about deaf people. It dawned on him that every time he'd seen a girl or boy gesturing silently, in a café, at the station, in the train, he'd always admired those hands, so expressive, so precise. He could watch them for hours, though like everyone else he pretended he wasn't looking, since that wasn't proper. He thought about the inherent contradiction: Clearly the world they lived in was impoverished and incomplete; still, he couldn't help but think that God had given them something he was lacking, some peculiar freedom, as if to compensate for their obvious constraints. Amazing agility and clarity of expression, to balance their helplessness and vulnerability. At times they seemed wretched; at other times they appeared to stand above the noisy crowd, silent and yet full of inaudible language. So Hanemann went to Petersen's lectures, eager to master all the signs, twisting and turning his fingers so that he could see into "their" world.

And then there was that September evening, still fresh in his memory, when he stepped off the subway at Bellevue Station on his way home from the Collegium. Those two girls on the platform. He went up to them and, for the first time in his life, actually "said" something with his hands—and they answered with lighting-fast movements of their own. That had been fun, even beautiful: saying something, understanding the answer, and watching the passersby cast furtive, embarrassed glances over their papers, under their hats, pretending not to look. They probably considered him one of "them," he boasted the next day to August, with joking pride. That's great!

When Hanka took the boy, whom we now called Adam, upstairs, he bowed—a little unwillingly, as if holding back some inappropriate gesture—but she was visibly delighted. Hanemann smiled: they even resembled each other a little. Hanemann seated Adam at his desk, opened a large chart with hand patterns for every letter (Mama had borrowed it from Dr. Michejda at the Academy), set up a small mirror, and sat down next to him. Then both began arranging their fingers in the positions shown on the chart. Hanka sat by the window and didn't take her eyes off Adam and Hanemann. The boy re-created each sign with an ironic, slightly impertinent smile, and within a few minutes he was amusing himself by choosing random letters and tracing their signs in the air. Hanemann started his spelling lesson with *Adam*. It went so quickly that he asked, "Did you learn that before?"

Adam only made a face. If he stumbled over a certain letter and had to consult the chart, he grew impatient, and started telling a whole story with gestures of his own, shrugging his shoulders, puffing out his lips, squinting his eyes, his face dancing and his hands singing. It was so spontaneous and contagious that both Hanka and I joined in despite ourselves. When Hanemann stepped out of the room for a minute, Adam rose from the desk, extended his neck, lowered his head, raised his eyebrows, and with those few gestures gave an accurate portrait of his new teacher. Hanka jumped up from the divan: "Stop it, Adam! Don't make fun of people!"

But his imitation was so amusing and so well executed that her indignation quickly gave way to laughter. Every move was crystal clear: the way he showed Hanemann thinking—holding his forehead, crossing his legs, running his fingers through his hair. Hanka tapped Adam on the back, as if to scold him, but he wriggled away from her grasp and ran behind the armchair to the hat rack, took down Hanemann's hat, put it on his own head at a slant, and threw himself on the seat, where he froze in the position of a thinker. Hanemann was standing in the doorway and called out, "Mr. Hanemann, we take our hats off at the table!" Adam handed him the hat, bowing low, and Hanemann ruffled his hair lightly, casually, as if joining in the mischief.

It took me a moment to realize it was the exact same gesture Hanka used on our hair. She probably noticed it too, since her eyes knitted up into a mocking smile. She was beginning to enjoy seeing that tall man with the long, light-skinned hands, as he bent over the boy, carefully and tenderly helping him set his fingers for more difficult letters. He seemed so different from the serious man she had passed so often on the path. She even felt ashamed that she had shouted at him and attacked him as she had, back then on the stairs.

Hanemann invited her to join them—"so you can see better." She sat down next to Adam and started making the same signs they did, although she did feel a little embarrassed twisting her fingers like that in front of a mirror. Looking at her own reflection, she said, "I have no idea how to move my fingers like that."

Hanemann took her hand and shaped it into the sign for *R*, bending her ring finger and her little finger and following with her thumb, but her little finger kept popping up, so they patiently started all over. "There. Now look in the mirror," he told her. "It should look exactly like that, you see?"

Of course she saw, but what of it? Her finger wouldn't stay where it was supposed to. Biting her lip, she pressed it onto her palm. "Like that?"

Hanemann glanced at the mirror. "Just don't let go of your thumb." Adam and I were both about to choke with laughter—those silly grown-ups!

Later the mirror was no longer needed. Hanemann sat across from Adam, and they "talked" to each other with rapid finger movements. Adam could easily read lips, but not Hanka, so Hanemann sat her in front of him and slowly whispered, "Please don't get up," his lips overenunciating every syllable.

Hanka answered with finger signs, slowly, carefully tracing each letter: f-i-n-e. Then she burst out laughing, and just for a moment, their knees bumped. Adam watched the scene and reenacted it, with a perfect imitation of Hanka's slowly formed reply to Hanemann.

But at times Adam's stunts went too far, such as the time he ran outside in the pouring rain and strutted up and down the path with an invisible umbrella—while getting soaked to the skin—shaking his hips exactly like Mrs. W. Next he showed Mr. Boruń marching off to church on Sunday, and then Mr. Orze-chowski taking a nail out of his mouth and hammering it into an invisible wall composed of pattering drops, light and trans-parent, which sprang up in the middle of the garden, sparkling with color in the late-afternoon sun. Some of the renditions were carefully construed; others Adam just tossed off, noncha-lantly, but they were all perfect imitations of our neighbors.

Who hasn't wanted to be somebody else, at least once or twice? I ran outside to join in that mean but very entertaining game. I looked up and yelled, felt the warm drops of August rain running down my cheeks, and we took each others' arms and danced in the puddles, spraying the brownish water, faster and faster, over and over—until Hanka opened the kitchen window and, threatening with her fist, called out, "Won't you two stop? What's got into you? You'll have the whole neighborhood feeling offended and we'll be to blame!" Then, out of breath and exhausted, leaving damp sandal tracks on the green linoleum, we ran into the kitchen, where she dried our heads with a towel and said to Adam: "You're soaked to the bone. Running around in the rain like that. What on earth possessed you?" But Adam turned away and didn't even wave a finger in response.

And then there was the time, toward the end of August, when he came back with a bloody lip. Hanka was aghast, "Who did that to you? Tell me!" She pulled him close to her, like a mother hen protecting her chick, and some drops fell on her dress and dotted it with red. "Tell me who did it—I'll scratch their eyes out!"

I had an idea who it might be. Adam liked imitating the Stremski brothers, who lived a few houses down; it had to have come to that sooner or later. Hanka ran outside, but what could she do? She came back full of tears. Meanwhile Mama was holding a wad of cotton to Adam's mouth. "You'll be fine," she told him. "But you'd better keep an eye out for those boys."

That evening we lay in our beds—his next to the window, mine by the radiator—energized from playing in the rain; my legs were still shaking from our dancing and splashing in the warm, yellow-brown water, and I was eager to pry open every secret. Mama was moving around the front hall, keeping quiet; I lowered my voice so she wouldn't hear: "Adam, are you asleep? Are you from Gdańsk, or did you come here from somewhere else?"

But Adam just stuck out his tongue.

I wasn't going to give up yet: "Don't you have anybody? Are your parents alive?"

But he just turned toward the wall and covered his head with the duvet. I looked at the pile of bedding, which was shaking, either from sobs or laughter. My heart froze up. "Adam, what's the matter? Come on, I didn't mean to..."

I lay on my back and stared at the ceiling where the shadows from the birch tree were drifting back and forth, and the white heap of bedding slowly stopped moving. Headlights flashed in the windowpanes: Mr. Wierzbołowski was coming back from the Anglas chocolate factory. I heard him close the door of his Warszawa and then come through the gate.

The shade of the street lamp rocked in the wind.

I couldn't sleep.

| *The Painter's Razor* |

NOW AND THEN Mr. J. returned to the subject of the painter who had killed himself in the eastern marshes. Hanemann wasn't terribly interested, but he tried not to let it show.

However, one afternoon, as they were sitting over a glass of red wine, Mr. J. told a story that shook Hanemann out of his pleasant, somewhat melancholy indifference. The story concerned Andrzej Ch., Mr. J's student from the lyceum whom Hanemann had tutored some time before, and who had always made a good impression. Evidently the boy had recently been rummaging through his father's books and found an old copy of a novel published in 1930, written by the same painter they had spoken of so often. The novel described a "yellow peril" that had invaded Europe. Mr. J. asked what Andrzej thought of the book, but the boy answered in such a way that it seemed he was intentionally trying to challenge or even offend his teacher: "You know, the man was right. Just look around. Do you think this system makes any sense?"

The conversation had upset Mr. J. He had thought the novel would give the boy a necessary distance from everything that was going on around him. But Andrzej, whose father had served as a cavalry officer with the Jazłowiec Uhlans and later had been imprisoned by the new regime following a brief trial, had misread the book as an accusation against his own passivity.

Mr. J. explained to the boy that the painter had made a mistake, that he had cut his wrists because he was running away from life, and that you can't just run away, that life is always a struggle and escaping is the easy way out. The painter was simply scared, afraid of prisons and camps, but one should bear in mind how many people had survived them.

"So you're saying he was a coward?" the boy asked, sarcastically.

Mr. J. paused a moment. "No, I'm not saying he was a coward. He just expected too much from life."

"So we shouldn't expect much from life? We should expect just enough, and nothing more?"

Mr. J. was unable to hide his impatience. "That's not the point."

"So what is the point?"

"I mean," Mr. J. said to Hanemann a few days later, "haven't we moved on? Isn't that chapter finished? Aren't we living in the very world the painter was escaping from? Things might not be the way we want them to be, but we're here, aren't we? He chose to cut his wrists, but there are millions of people who didn't. Millions. So?"

"So what?" the boy had asked. "You're saying he should have put away his razor and gone on living the way we do? Here, in this new Poland? Would that make you happy?"

Hanemann felt his interest growing. He suspected that his friend was no longer talking about the painter as if it were just the story of an aging man who had decided to cut his wrists during the first days of the war. Now Mr. J. made it sound as if this were a matter of national importance. His friend's sympathy for the painter, Hanemann felt, was really sympathy for himself and his "poor fatherland."

But Hanemann's own interest lay elsewhere. Mr. J. had recently returned from Warsaw, where he had attended the funeral of a friend (the one who had known Czechowicz). The man had left his belongings to Mr. J., who had brought what little there was to Gdańsk, to his apartment near the old Protestant chapel: a few sketches by the painter, a painting by Waliszewski, a small sculpture by Pronaszko, some photograph albums bound in black leather, newspaper clippings, a handful of oddly printed futuristic poems . . . Mr. J. had intended to donate it all to the museum at the Church of the Holy Trinity, but Mrs. Lehr, the custodian, whom he had met once at the Steins' home on Klonowa Street, suggested that he hold off for the moment. "Different times and different tastes," was how she put it.

Mr. J. had been both amazed and amused by some of the photographs he found in one of the albums, and he took them to Hanemann so his friend could have a look.

At first Hanemann thought it was a joke, and he was about to ask Mr. J. what it all meant, but Mr. J. just smiled and said, "Exactly! That's the painter I was telling you about!" Hanemann picked up the photos. Each one showed a different face. But there was something . . . yes, the eyes! The eyes were the same— calm and cold. The faces, though, were different, as if some cruel being had simply pasted them together without any stable features. For a moment Hanemann wanted to ask Mr. J. to show him a normal picture, so he could get at least some idea what the famous painter had looked like, but he soon realized that there was no sense in even asking, since such a picture un-doubtedly did not exist.

So that's him . . . A slightly round face peered up from a pho-tograph, a light-skinned country boy with his mouth half-open and his cap turned backward. But in the next picture the coun-try boy became an aristocratic officer of the Czarist guards. After that came an artist, slender and fragile and vulnerable, fol-lowed by an iron commissar in a leather jacket, a jovial arms dealer, a plump priest . . . Features constantly in flux: mouth, eye-brows, cheeks. It was unsettling. Because wasn't it the people who couldn't escape their own faces who were always the first to die? The ones who couldn't hide their accent, their gestures? They were the ones with the pistols aimed at their heads. What religion? Nationality! Place of birth! Political inclination! Who are your friends? Your enemies! Where are you escaping? Show your hands! Look straight at me! Your accent gives you away! The shape of your nose! The slant of your eye! But nothing seemed impossible for the face in these photographs. Anyone with features so elastic could choose his own fate. So why the suicide?

Hanemann felt a tremor of laughter: the photos really were very funny. Then he grew tired of the constantly turning kalei-doscope of grins and scowls and grimaces . . . He flipped through the remaining pictures indifferently, politely asking what they represented. "Are these portraits of women?" Mr. J. squinted and nodded meaningfully: "If you only knew—the man had a whole harem."

But the paper was so dark it was hard to tell if they really were women who were peering through the smoky chiaroscuro . . .

What was it his Polish friend had said about Kleist? A boy in the uniform of a Prussian officer, eyes glowing with madness? Without a doubt—still, Kleist had had a madness of a different hue, full of gravity and power, even though death was there, too, lurking in the depths. But the photographs spread out on the table showed a man grimacing at the world because he was getting older and life had slipped through his fingers. Maybe if he had been younger he could have borne it all? The idea upset Hanemann, but he was convinced that the painter had crossed some invisible threshold beyond which there is nothing but decay. Kleist never did that. He realized that the fault lay with time itself, that once you cross the threshold, you have already lost everything.

Hanemann flipped through the faces dancing on the photographs and thought that old age was a horrible thing and that there was nothing to be done about it, although the man he was looking at wasn't really that old at all. Then again, at what moment did it really begin?

"An amazing man. Unbelievably talented, even though a lot of people claimed he was a little crazed, that something was always driving him to the bizarre. But show me one of them who could do even a fraction of what he accomplished . . ."

As he listened to Mr. J.'s tribute, Hanemann thought about the woman somewhere in the eastern marshes, scratching out a shallow grave. He pictured a small, blond girl boarding a train headed east, walking with the painter across a meadow to a huge tree, and swallowing the tablets—struggling to get them down— even though she had no real desire to die. Was he responsible for her being there? Had he entranced her with his ever-changing features, his pliable face of living wax? What had he looked like when he handed her the cup with the luminal, when he removed his razor from its leather case? "Don't fall asleep before me, don't leave me alone." Were those his words?

Mr. J. went on telling about his visit to the apartment on Bracka Street, but Hanemann cut him off: "What was her name?"

At first Mr. J. didn't understand. "Who? Oh, her..." Because in his mind, at a time when Poland was overrun by foreign armies the important thing was what happened to the painter, not the woman.

Even so, Hanemann repeated his question. He wanted to know exactly what had become of her, what she was doing now, how she lived with what had happened. Because—and this was an unexpected realization—while they were sitting in the sunny room at 17 Grottger Street talking about the painter who died in the eastern marshes, and looking at the old yellowed photos, she was still alive, somewhere, walking down the street, having a conversation.

Mr. J. didn't know much. He'd heard this and that from various people in Warsaw and had seen a few things with his own eyes, but who was to say how much of it was true?

They found her under the huge tree, where she lay unconscious for several days. People came running from all over the village—shouting and hollering in their eastern dialect: "A man has killed himself, a Polish gentleman." They were kind, brought her eggs and cheese; someone even gave her a small pillow embroidered with green leaves. She was seventeen years younger than the painter. People whispered: "What kind of father would want to kill his own daughter?" She went back to Warsaw, where friends of the painter took care of her, while she kept herself busy organizing some of his papers. After the Warsaw uprising, she was sent to a camp in Germany, where her sister found her. One day she was sitting on her bunk trying to cut her wrists with a piece of glass; her sister came in and tore the glass out of her hand. The girl struggled and shouted—how could he have left her behind like that; after all, he knew all about poisons. She claimed he had let her survive on purpose, it was his fault, he loved her, he gave her just enough so she would fall asleep while he finished with himself, so she wouldn't interfere. He had left her alone. She'd never forgive him for that. She cursed. They had to tie her down so she wouldn't hurt herself. She lay on the bunk with closed eyes. She didn't cry, but only kept her lips shut tight.

She survived the camp but had no place to return. Everything in Warsaw had been burned down. She wandered from one apartment to the next, then moved to a small town in the mountains where a few people remembered him. She was still young, but she couldn't bear the sight of men. Then she started feeling pain. A detached retina. Headaches. She worked in a sanatorium, silent, distant, never opening up to anyone. No one realized she had been the painter's girlfriend. Only now and then she would say something about waiting "until everything is fulfilled." She wandered for hours in the mountains, to the limit of her endurance. "I'm not alive," she whispered to herself. "Always looking for death, she never could see life," was how an acquaintance described her. She couldn't stand being around people. She burst into a rage at the slightest provocation, was bothered by the gentlest breeze, as if she were an open wound and the air were salt. And all the time she considered herself his wife, because back then, under the huge tree, they had married each other, and priests recognize that kind of vow. She called her small apartment her tomb. Even when she was sick, she never went to bed during the day, just covered herself with a sheepskin coat and waited in the armchair. She couldn't forgive herself for having agreed to do it, for not having stopped him. She never ceased thinking about that moment when she woke up and collapsed on his dead and bloody body. She signed letters with his name—capitalized and underlined. People made fun of her, but she wanted everyone to know exactly who she was. Everywhere she went she introduced herself as his wife, even though she was well aware that his real wife was still alive. She worked in an office, but she began dressing like the women he had surrounded himself with. Outlandish, flowing gowns, necklaces, a large black beret, just like his, broad silver bracelets and armbands. "Cuffs," people whispered, claiming she wore them to cover the numbers tattooed from the camp and the scars from the razor... Whenever she spoke with someone she said "we," meaning he and I, my husband, the man who died in the marshes...

Mr. J. was reluctant to speak about the girl. Of course it was all very sad and depressingly painful, but it was hardly a unique case—the painter, on the other hand, was truly important. The girl had got mixed up in something bigger than she was, and she should stay in the background. As far as Mr. J. was concerned, she was nothing more than a source of information about the painter's death. Naturally he sympathized with her, but she had annoyed him with her constantly raw nerves, her anxiety, her sudden outbursts. Was it any wonder he felt so relieved when he left that tiny apartment, filled with cardboard portraits of a blond girl with big eyes and a pageboy haircut?

Hanemann, however, couldn't focus on anything else. He remembered the painter's last words, but now he couldn't erase from his mind the picture of the girl sitting on a bunk, cutting her wrists with a piece of glass, cursing the painter for tricking her and departing without her. And then the "cuffs," the snickering, the mocking sneers.

Something in her story touched him, and he felt afraid.

Kind fortune, unkind fate. By comparison, the story of Kleist and Henriette, their shared death on the Wannsee, seemed to Hanemann a gift, one that had evaded the couple in the marshes. A gift that comes on its own, unfairly, undeservedly. What sense was there in the fact that this girl had survived? That she was still alive today? Was there any punishment more cruel? Upset and embittered, he sought comfort in those other images, so clear, so bright: the deep-blue water of the lake, red maples, a white tablecloth gleaming on the grass, two pistols beside the wine-glasses, and a narrow, golden path leading up to the clouds... As if painted by Caspar David Friedrich.

But that was so long ago, and today his heart was following a different road: he was enjoying the visits of that deaf boy and that young, dark-haired woman who had also tried to do violence to herself, although fortunately she had not succeeded. He enjoyed practicing the hand signs with them, their fluttering fingers, the funny birdlike gestures they used to convey trivial words and schoolbook phrases, the way each sign seemed a distant echo of his years in Berlin—Petersen's seminar, his debates with August, Mrs. Lenz's boardinghouse, the strange meeting with Mr. Outline, and his deep satisfaction the first time he actually "said" something to those two girls at the Bellevue station and had understood every word in their reply. What was he doing? Trying to quarantine Hanka? Erase his own guilt? Shouldn't he do everything possible to make sure she didn't suffer the same fate as that girl the villagers had saved in the eastern marshes? Why did he feel guilty, anyway? For having pushed her back into life?

Was it really guilt?

Hanemann put down the pictures.

Meanwhile, Mr. J. was heading back to his home along Jaśkowa Dolina Street, brooding over the words of his neighbor Mr. B., who had stopped him a few days earlier by the gate: "What do you go there for, anyway? Don't kid yourself. He looks down on us, like every kraut. Right now they hate the Russians and the Russians hate them, but as soon as they get friendly again, Russia is going to give Gdańsk back to them. And let them do whatever they want with us. You think I'm joking? You think it's impossible? You're from the Free City, you didn't see anything. But I did. Trains. They'll pack us in the trains. It's just a matter of time. One or the other will do it. And here you go on visiting that man. What on earth for?"

"That's odd," thought Mr. J. "Why all the talk about trains? He should have said that when the time comes, the only way out will be the painter's way. Why didn't he say anything about razors?"

| *Whiteface and Purple* |

AT THE END OF September, when the creeper on the facade of the parish hall turned a dark red and the huge pumpkins in the burdock ripened into yellow, Father Roman stood in the sunlight facing us and, squinting his eyes, spoke of divine wrath and the unworthy moneylenders in the temple.

As he lectured in front of the blackboard, Father Roman's hands flew up in the air like doves and then came crashing down, raising columns of sunlit dust; still, despite my efforts I was unable to focus on what he was saying. Now and then, when his voice began to thunder with threats and warnings, I wondered how the image of the Lord's wrath—so well illustrated by Father Roman—could be reconciled with the story about turning the other cheek, which we had heard the week before. But mostly all I could think about were the boys who I knew were determined to take revenge on "that cripple," and although I had no idea what he had done to them, the thought that they might hurt Adam made my blood boil. Impatiently counting the minutes, I glanced back and forth between Adam and my own sweaty hands: If only the bell tower would ring three o'clock!

The doors opened with a bang, and we ran outside, and there, just around the corner, standing by the hedge on the path to the church, I saw them. But Adam didn't; he blithely went on walking toward the hedge, so I hurried as fast as I could to warn him.

How exalted I felt—full of righteous power, the kind that guided Him when he chased the moneylenders from the temple, the kind that guided my father when he chased the men out of Hanemann's apartment (I knew by heart the story that my mother told about our first day at 17 Grottger Street). Propelled by the same holy impetus, the same noble force, I balled my hand into a fist and charged ahead, my face flushed with indignation. But then a sudden whistle, a sting, something hit the back of my neck, I felt myself being pulled backward, and a voice I didn't recognize in the confusion roared in my right ear: "What's this? Picking on people smaller than you? And not two minutes after religion class!"

Father Roman's voice was burning with the rage of the Old Testament prophets. I trembled. Everything was spinning. Familiar and unfamiliar faces, squinting eyes, girls' braids, colorful shirts. They were pushing in for a better look: at last something interesting had happened, and they craned their necks, hissing, snickering, singeing my cheeks with their hypocritical condemnation. Father Roman shook me again and again, and for just a moment I saw the deceitfully humble faces of the boys I had wanted to chase out of the temple now shrouded in perfect innocence. Should I defend myself? Explain? Right then and there? I could cry out, "But it wasn't me, they were the ones threatening, I was just defending!"—except I knew for a fact that it would only be more fuel for Father Roman's fire. Behold the un-

repentant sinner, cowardly blaming others for his own mis-
deeds! It was enough to break my heart...

Meanwhile Adam was in a panic, contorting his face to explain what had really happened. He pointed at the Stremski
brothers, then at Menten and Butry, he threatened with his fist,
lifted his eyes toward heaven. Father Roman stopped shaking
me; his eyes narrowed, and he began to brim over with rage.
"And a deaf-mute on top of that? A crip—an invalid!" he said,
correcting himself. "Aren't you ashamed?"

The earth was sinking beneath my feet. I tried to break out
of his painful grasp, but Father Roman...

All of a sudden he stopped thundering; and I was certain
that at that moment he was possessed by the image of Christ in
a beautiful Gothic temple, raising his hand to drive out the Isra-
elite merchants who had profaned the House of God. The thundering stopped, and his voice darkened into a whisper, which
always meant the worst. "Have your mother and father come to
the parish hall tomorrow after mass at six o'clock." Then the
priest's cold fingers twisted my ear into a burning shell: "And
now you will sit in the hall to think about what you have done."

Pain, humiliation, shame. In a silence heightened by the
swishing of his cassock, Father Roman led me back to the parish
hall. As I followed him I caught one more glimpse of the faces
of my "victims"—hidden in the crowd, a little scared and still
jeering.

The parish hall that now belonged to the Cistercian church
was formerly a Protestant chapel. Here there was no baroque
gilt, no stuccowork clouds, sun rays, palms, rococo hangings, no
putti—none of the wondrous, boudoirlike atmosphere of the
Cathedral, where we went each Sunday to commune with God.
Father Roman took me to an empty rectangular room with
walls as white as chalk and black benches marked with Gothic

numerals, then, pointing at the dark wooden crucifix over the blackboard, he closed the double doors and turned the heavy key in the lock.

I sat among the shadows—nameless, thoughtful, and transparent—of those who had once come to hear Pastor Knabbe and who never left the bare, white room except during Father Roman's papist homilies. A chasm opened up before me, one I had never known existed. I was prepared to understand and forget the whole incident, but I could not find any precedent to help explain what had happened between Father Roman and me, neither in the New Covenant nor the Old, neither in the words of the prophets nor of the apostles. I could understand, or at least my trembling heart intuited, the martyrdom of Saint Stephen, Saint Paul, Saint Cecilia—those beautiful deaths by stoning, crucifixion, and torture that caused angels to trumpet, suns to appear over the heads of the martyrs, and their blood-bedewed temples to be crowned with palm branches lowered from the clouds—but what was the purpose of *this* pain? The Book we consulted every Sunday, the Book in which I placed my trust, gently turning the pages marked with a red ribbon, had forsaken me, leaving no suggestion as to how the soul should behave in the face of such misunderstanding, where sobs mixed with stinging giggles and evil looks. I was all alone, abandoned, humiliated, wounded; I knelt at the Protestant prayer desk and silently moved my lips: "Why?" I didn't understand. Hatred? Perhaps a little, at first, but I really didn't hate Father Roman—after all, weren't we both victims of the same joke, which took advantage of my lack of power and his lack of knowledge? We were both innocent, and yet we were both facing punishment, since, I knew, the minute he learned the truth, he would feel embarrassed for having treated me the way he had.

A wave of bitter pity unleashed a fog of tears that for a moment veiled the stern outline of the cross with the tiny tablet INRI, and then I pounded the desk and summoned my tried-and-true curse: "I'll show you!" I wasn't thinking of so much of revenge (on whom?); I was just stunned by the course of events; it didn't make any sense, especially according to the distinct logic of guilt, punishment, and reward (for a moment I entertained the wrong question: "And what if your holy exaltation had actually come from the fact that they really were weaker?"—but then I dismissed that idea as misleading). I couldn't figure it out. Staring at the black cross, I looked for some precedent, some context in which I might place the incident, some connection to the understanding world of adults, the intelligent world of Saint Stephen, the healing at Gennesaret, the flight into Egypt, the razing of Sodom...

At that moment I felt something open up inside me, slowly, reluctantly. A tender, painful feeling that was still indistinct, challenging me to view the world in a different light. It made me think of Hanemann, the peculiar care he took to arrange his shells from faraway Japan, the tender way he polished his silver, the careful manner in which he held his pen to the paper or cleaned the leaves of a geranium with a rag dipped in water. Previously I had looked on all those gestures as a little absurd, embarrassing and unmanly, but now they seemed to be tinged with a seriousness I found disquieting, or even daunting.

Something banged against the window, and I looked up— Adam? What was he doing here? Had he lost his mind? What about Father Roman? But no, there was his suntanned face, his crinkled eyes, his lips curved in an innocent smile. He climbed onto the sill using the trellis Pastor Knabbe's wife had placed against the wall, now overgrown with creeper, pressed his face against the windowpane, and started making signs to me.

I waited until he was gone, then opened the window and,

after a moment's hesitation, followed Adam down, careful not to damage the creeper, which I always enjoyed looking at on Sundays when we walked home from the Cistercians.

Choking with laughter, we ran through the gooseberry and currant bushes toward the huge pumpkins by the wire fence. One jump, the wire rattled, and we were racing down the meadow by the Lyceum, past the Cistercian church whose steeple cast a long, pointy shadow, then across the courtyard to Number 7, through the flowerbeds, and up the sandy slope recently washed by the rain. We ran into the woods, among the beeches. Out of breath, arm in arm, happy it was all over, we tumbled on the ground, half in play-fight and half just to roll across the dry leaves.

Afterward we shook the leaves off our shoes and made our way up to the first of the old estate buildings, then turned left and went uphill, through the forest, between the tall beeches and pine trees, to avoid pursuers from the parish hall. I was certain that Menten and Butry weren't going to let us get away with anything. Adam lowered his head and looked at me with the stormy face of Father Roman, puckering his cheeks until they turned a beautiful purple color and then letting his lips burst out in voiceless indignation: "Picking on an invalid! An in-va-lid!" All my fear dissipated, I laughed until I was out of breath, it was all so wild and painfully funny. When we calmed down a little and our pace evened out, Adam started tracing in the air, his hands and fingers light as Japanese quills. He recapitulated what had happened an hour earlier, by the hedge: Father Roman hauling me off to the parish hall, his cold, talonlike hand stinging my ear, then seating me on the oak bench with the Gothic numerals. Then he showed me facing the crucifix, kneeling...and holding my hands in prayer! Hot with shame, my ears burning, I threw myself on him, hitting with my fists. Because back in the empty parish hall I had done more than defiantly shout: "I'll show you!" At one point I had lowered my head, and begun to whisper: "who art in Heaven, hallowed be Thy name, give us this day our daily bread...and lead us not into temptation...and forgive us our trespasses...now and at the hour of our death..." So Adam had sensed what I was doing? While he was spying on me through the window? His face, dark from the sun, delicately twitching and conjuring images of my pain, fear, and joy, telling the story of a boy piously praying before a black wooden cross. What torture!

How good it was that the story was over. Out of breath and heated by our fighting, with fresh scratches on our shoulders and our knees scuffed and stinging—we had tumbled into some junipers—I felt a light emptiness growing inside me, fortifying me, a healing, refreshing breath. This new sensation might not have been good, but it was better than what I'd just been through. Adam, meanwhile, stopped on the path covered with needles and began to trace—possibly to postpone our return to Grottger Street, whose house we could already see flashing through the trees. He sketched friends, acquaintances, and neighbors, one by one, enjoying his own dexterity. First Mr. Wierzbołowski, trimming the hedge at Number 14, then Mrs. Wardoń beating her down quilt, Mr. J. walking upstairs to visit Hanemann...Adam waved his dark hands, bent his neck, and I saw Mr. S's sons hurling an iron crowbar across the cobblestones, sending up bluish sparks...He pulled his chin back, raised his eyebrows, stooped his shoulders, and Mr. C. came out of Number 11 and slowly headed for work at the Daol paint factory, carefully closing the gate behind him. It was incredible, and I wanted to join in, to be able to sketch other people like that, with silent, nonchalant precision. I tried to repeat each of his gestures, to re-create the single most important one that captured the essence of similarity. If only it were possible to speak like that, in a hundred languages, to have a hundred souls, a hundred voices—birdlike, human, young, old, ancient, new, male, and female! And so we rambled through the trees, immersed in our game, engrossed in our imitations of the defenseless adults, unbridled, beyond punishment, happy to have escaped the trap we'd fallen into an hour earlier, taking a dark, wicked pleasure in the game of transformations, free, craning our necks to the sky as if we were becoming someone different. We looked up and felt the Lord's chastising gaze falling on the beech woods in back of the Cathedral, on the streets of Oliwa, on the beach and on the sea. And as we followed the path beneath the swaying, swishing branches of the beeches and pines, the shadows of people we knew went with us—fragile, summoned from the wind, helpless, making exaggerated bows, doffing hats, shaking hands, wagging fingers, dozens of shadows from Grottger Street went walking with us over the dry beech leaves, as if they wanted to be alive, more alive than our own bodies. How nimbly they danced on the path, just out of reach. At moments I couldn't tell who was more real: the two of us, flesh and blood, climbing up and down the hills, or the others, conjured from the sunlight with a wave of the hand, reduced to a single gesture, a single grimace that brought them temporarily to life before they dissolved into nothingness a moment later, with a light, carefree joy. Because it's possible that back then, high in the forest, it was already clear, already decided, that that was how they would be preserved in memory (if there is any memory left of Grottger Street), just as I saw them there, on the path, sprinkled with warm reddish needles, dappled by the sunlight filtering through the branches, silent against the constant murmur of the beeches and pines. Fascinated and indignant, I gave in to Adam's game, tinged though it was with vengeance or perhaps the intent to hurt, and was happy and scared, while Adam painted every face he summoned with a soft cruelty, whitening the cheeks and purpling the lips, blackening the eyebrows. And each face was signed with a teardrop underneath an eye, and a mouth wrenched in painful laughter, which fixed our wicked mood for all posterity, our greedy, prying, mistrustful curiosity.

But in all this play that made us soar so high above the woods, dispelling our fear and warming our hearts, in all the parade of shadows from Grottger Street, never once did Adam touch Hanka or Hanemann.

| *The Slope* |

VOICES WERE coming from the vestibule, muffled, hurried, and too indistinct for me to make out the words. Who was it? What were they saying? Why so late? Harsh whispers trailing off. I could see faces through the cloudy pane in the door, but couldn't tell whose they were. Startled from my sleep, I sat there shivering, rubbing my eyes, listening to the strange commotion in the apartment in the middle of the night. No, it was still light out. Maybe I'd just dozed off and it was only later in the evening. My eyes could barely stay open, I fought off the drowsiness—I must have been deep asleep. So it couldn't have been evening. Was it already morning? The sky in the window was just turning gray, the dim light made the curtain look like fog. But there were still no birds out, as I teetered between my sleep and the new day. Adam was slumbering on in his bed by the window, his head buried in his pillow. Rosy cheeks, disheveled hair. His ears, his suntanned neck. Who was that talking? Why were they in the kitchen and not in the living room?

I decided to see what was going on, and step by step headed for the kitchen. The door opened. "My God, we've woken up the children," said Mama. She ran over, took me by the hand, and led me to the bathroom. I peed into the bowl, a yellow stream, foam. Then back to the room. She tucked me into the down bedding. But my heart was still pounding, my eyes open, fixed on the door. Who was that man in the coat sitting in the kitchen? Mr. J.? At this hour? I went to the door and pushed down on the handle; it opened easily, without a squeak. The dark vestibule. My cheek against the cold plaster wall. What was going on? My heart refused to calm down. I could see that Mother and Father were in the kitchen—already dressed? No, they'd just thrown their coats on over their shoulders. No sign of Hanka; she was probably in her room. Another voice—whose? Snatches of words. The water in the teapot boiled and hissed. The clink of glasses. "Please, have a seat," I heard my mother saying. Then something about hurrying, "to wake up Hane-mann," and the words "Right now?" The front door opened, and I heard quiet steps on the stairs. Then coming back, slowly. Hanemann stepped inside, followed by Father. "Good morn-ing." A chair was moved inside the kitchen.

"Good morning, Dr. Hanemann. Please, have a seat."

"What's happened?"

I heard someone whispering—Mr. J.? Quiet words. Tea-spoons stirring against glasses.

"Did you see the *People's Tribune*?"

"Yesterday's?"

"Yes."

"I did. What about it, what's happened?"

Mama walked to the door and checked the hall to make sure no one was listening. Then she came back into the kitchen.

"Dr. Hanemann, please don't be so naive. You're in trouble."

"Are you sure?" It was my father, by the window.

"Of course I can't be certain," Mr. J. went on, "but I heard that..." More whispers.

Then Hanemann, very calm, "They're exaggerating. Please, don't worry about me, it doesn't mean a thing."

"Come on, you can't go sticking your head in the sand. There's going to be another trial. Contacts with Operation Werewolf and the Western Zone. Among the ones who stayed."

My father by the window: "Where did you find out about it?"

"I happened to be in Chrząstowski's office when some man in civilian clothes came in and asked about you. Chrząstowski said he was thinking of hiring you when I retired, to which the man said: 'Hanemann? You better drop that idea. It looks bad. All the clues point to the West. Don't even touch that one, take my word, as one party man to another.'"

"That doesn't mean a thing. Why me?" Hanemann's voice sounded impatient, raw.

Mr. J. sighed. Now he addressed my father, "Could you please explain it all to him? Because I can't seem to get anywhere."

I heard my father's voice: "Dr. Hanemann, I saw a whole city deported overnight; believe me, this is no laughing matter."

Hanemann: "So what am I supposed to do? Run away? Where to?"

Mr. J.: "You saw what happened with Bishop Kaczmarek."

"I'm not running away anywhere."

Silence. My heart was pounding. What did Hanemann have to do with the clergy, and Operation Werewolf? The voices were scary, the undertones even more so. The silence continued. They were sitting at the table, drinking their tea, looking at each other without saying a word. Then Mr. J. looked up.

"There's one more thing. They want to take the boy away from Hanka."

I felt a cold needle stab my heart. I looked back at our bedroom; Adam was still asleep. Had he heard? I wanted to close the door. But what if he were standing there? I didn't move. Silence in the kitchen.

Hanemann's voice, quiet: "What do you mean, take him away? Who?"

"Please don't ask stupid questions. They've already been here once."

"But why?"

"I think they have something on her. From back when she was in Tarnów. Or even earlier. Maybe something with the partisans..."

Mama put her hand to her mouth. "My God..."

I heard Father shift uneasily. "How do you know?"

"My wife heard it at the office, at the Juvenile Board. The papers are all drawn up. They're putting him in a home in Szczecinek. Breach of duty as guardian and inadequate material resources. Have you signed anything?"

"Nothing."

"Then they'll be showing up here with a paper for you to sign saying you have difficult living circumstances."

"But that's nonsense!" Mama was practically shouting.

"Don't shout," Father whispered, "you'll wake the boys."

My eyes went dark; I felt my throat growing taut. It couldn't be. How could they take Adam away from us? Where to? What about that afternoon when he first showed up, his sooty old jacket, the lessons in signing, the escape from the parish hall, rolling on the ground in the woods? It all came back, every single moment. Where could they take him? What had we done? And Hanka loving him so much. He likes it here with us. What did she do? They have something on her? What does that mean?

The door creaked open, and a beam of light fell on the floor, just a few steps away from my feet. I pressed against the wall and didn't breathe. Hanka passed through the room, barefoot, swaying slightly, holding her robe to her breast. Her eyes were sleepy, her hair tied up with a red ribbon. She went into the kitchen: "What's going on?" She drew back at the sight of Hanemann and Mr. J. "Oh, I'm sorry . . . I didn't realize . . ."

Mama pulled out a chair. "Sit down." More tea, a spoon set on a saucer, the lid coming off the sugar bowl.

Hanka mumbled something about the tea being too hot. Father leaned over her and whispered, then Mama, even faster. The sound of a chair moving. Steps. Hanka ran across the vestibule, crying out, "No!" She burst into the room, Adam jumped up, startled. Hanka hugged him, and he hugged her back; he didn't understand a thing. I joined them; they were shivering. Hanka was crying. Mama appeared in the door, then Father. In the kitchen, Mr. J. looked out through the window. Hanemann waited in the vestibule.

Mr. J. got up: "I'll go out through the garden. It's better that way."

Hanemann nodded and shook his hand. "Thank you."

Mr. J. turned around. "Don't say anything. It's better if I don't know."

Hanemann nodded again. Mr. J. walked out and a moment later vanished behind the arborvitae.

Hanka is stroking Adam's hair. She kisses his forehead, his eyes, his cheeks. She whispers, "I'm not giving you to anybody, you understand?" Adam looks at her, he still doesn't know what's going on. "You'll be with me forever." Adam gently touches her face and traces a small cross on her cheek. He's beginning to catch on. Hanka presses him to her as hard as she can. "They're not doing anything to us, you understand?" Adam only blinks in response. Then he signs to her, "I love you." Hanka takes him by the hands; he looks at her with dry eyes. I can't stand to look, and turn away.

Were there tears? Hanka tucked Adam back into bed.

"What are you going to do?" asked Mama.

"I don't know."

"Is there anybody you could go to?"

"There might have been, once. But now..."

"Come into the kitchen, let's think things over."

Hanka smiled at Adam and kissed him again on the forehead. "I'll be right back."

They went to the kitchen. Whispers, a cut-off cry of protest, more whispers. Hissing through teeth. All I could make out were the words "Wrocław" and "maybe Zofia." But Aunt Zofia lives in Cieplice, far away, by the Czech border. "Dr. Hanemann, please, try to persuade her. It's just for a while."

I went over to Adam, who raised his hand to sign: "I'm not going anywhere."

"You have to."

"I'll hide in the woods."

"What about Hanka?"

"She'll hide with me."

My God, he must be crazy. He raked his hair and scratched all over. I was barefoot; the wooden floor felt cold. More voices from the kitchen—Hanka's: "Dr. Hanemann, please think it over. That doesn't make any sense. They won't do anything to us."

More whispers, indistinct words. Adam watching closely. He gets up, puts on a shirt, and buttons it.

"What are you going to do?"

He doesn't say anything, puts on his socks, tosses his hair off his forehead. Hanka comes in. "Why are you getting up? It's still early."

I nod at Adam: "He wants to hide in the woods."

"My God!" Hanka tries to hug him, but he wriggles out of her embrace. "Hey, where do you think you're going?" She grabs him by the arm, and he tries to get away, but she is stronger. "What's all this about? What kind of behavior is that?"

Adam gives her a snarling look. She calms down. "Now, you want to tell me what you're after? We can't go doing anything stupid. We'll probably leave for a little while."

In the kitchen, my father pulls a train schedule out of a drawer and spreads it on the table so he and Hanemann can look it over. "Arrival Tczew at twelve-six, change for Bydgoszcz, then at three o'clock..." The voices fade.

I'm standing in the middle of the room. My legs are shaking, as if I were ready to take off running at any minute. Mama comes in. "Don't stand here in the cold. Get dressed. You'll have to help Adam." I pull my shirt over my head. Then pants. I reach for my leather sandals. The buckle flashes. I close my eyes. It's impossible. It must all be a dream.

WE WERE READY by nine o'clock. Mama went out and paused a minute in front of the house, then headed for the grocer's, where she bought bread, cheese, and milk. At the gate she looked up and down the street to make sure there was no one around. Inside, Hanka was packing Adam's things. They tied the bundle together with a leather belt and rough, shaggy twine. Strong knots. Adam tightened the fuzzy ends. In the kitchen, Mama sliced some bread; the knife hit against the oak cutting board. Pink wafers of ham and sausage. Tomatoes. Fresh cucumbers. Yellow cheese on white bread. A sprinkle of parsley. The wax paper crackled; she placed the round little packages in a cloth bag and added a small bottle of tea, wrapped in a towel.

They left at half past nine—first Hanka, then, a few minutes later, Hanemann. Without any bags. She went out through the front; he through the garden. The rusty gate creaked open, a screech of iron, then steps on the stone stairs. Hanemann passed the patch of iris, stopping for a moment beside the arborvitae, but no, he didn't turn around. I was standing at the window. He put his hand in his pocket and looked at the trees. I saw his head bob away behind the iron pickets of the fence....

They were supposed to wait for us by the viaduct on Piastowska Street; there would be few people at that hour. They went separately, slowly—no need to attract attention by hurrying—first along Kaprów Street, then Grunwaldzka, then Poczta Polska, and then, just past the intersection of Hołd Pruski, they turned right and stepped onto the entry ramp, just minutes away from the train station. The train was scheduled to arrive shortly after eleven. The 11:07 from Gdynia.

We carried the bags out to the vestibule. Father went down to the basement and brought up the old iron stroller Frau Walmann had used to push little Marie, before they bought a new one at Julius Mehler's shop on Ahornweg, with a tin shade and little oval windows. The new one had burned that night in front of Schneider's warehouse at Neufahrwasser, while they were waiting for the *Bernhoff,* leaving only a few pieces of twisted tin lying in the wet snow by the loading dock. The old, well-rusted veteran of so many passages between Lessingstrasse and the park had stayed in the basement. As long as I could remember, it had stood by the wall next to the water meter, prey to cobwebs and dust.

Spring suspension, a long bentwood handle. Father squeezed Hanemann's and Hanka's suitcases onto the metal frame, added Adam's backpack and the cloth bag with the food, wrapped everything in a sheet, and tied it with string. Why let people see what was inside? I'd often used the Walmanns' old stroller to carry similar white packages to the laundry at 11 Derdowski Street, so nobody should be surprised to see me this time, creaking and rolling my way up Grottger Street toward the Cistercian church.

On the surface everything looked normal, but what I felt inside...Adam was walking next to me, keeping the load from toppling over, as the large bundle, tied tightly to the metal frame, swayed slightly. He walked unevenly, his gaze fixed straight ahead. His shirt was buttoned all the way up for the first time ever. The stroller's springs squeaked. In my pocket I was carrying a little paper, folded into quarters, on which at the last minute I had written a few words in green ink....We walked past the homes and gardens, the crooked fence posts and closed gates with tin boxes marked *Briefe*, making our way to Derdowski Street; Adam looked at me with his sweet, mischievous eyes, cocked his elbow, closed his fingers into a fist, and tapped them against his wrist.

It was the sign that he was beginning—even though everything was ending. The sign that it would all start right away, that the shadows would soon be dancing in front of us once again, captured by a pair of dark-skinned hands, thin traces in the air, tiny finger movements, shaking heads, birdlike gestures—light, tender, and carefree. And the curiosity: What's he going to show now—whose laughing, whose crying? The stroller creaked, the white package rocked from side to side as if it were a wave of snow, bright flashes in the branches—for a second it seemed to me that doves had sprinkled the whole street with floating flakes of downy white—but no, it was only the sun, breaking through the clouds over the hills behind the church, shining on the dusty cobblestones. The rim of the stroller banged, the wheels groaned, and we crossed to the other side of Derdowski Street, where the shadows of the linden trees—fluttering like moths—ran across our shirts, and Adam was already beginning, had already lifted his hands, was already running alongside the stroller, making me shout "Watch out!" because he was about to make me lose my footing. But he simply laughed voicelessly and quickly started signing to me. I couldn't make out what he was saying, so sassy, so impatient, just like back then in the sloping woods behind the church, as if he wanted to repeat that moment.... Was it to amuse me? Provoke me? He started to trace portraits, first of Mr. J., then of Mrs. S. And if Adam went away, where would they go, those light figures he snatched so easily from the air—where would he take them? He could summon them at any moment; he had them in his eyelids and the tips of his fingers, in the raising of a brow. How I envied him! He had all of us. Including me. And Mama. And Father. He could be anybody he wanted...

We rolled the stroller onto Wit Stwosz Street, the tram bell rang, the red wagons rattled toward the terminal in Oliwa, the windows flashed, the stroller hopped onto the tracks, one left turn and we were already on Kaprów Street, the sidewalk under the well-trimmed lindens, climbing roses in the gardens, tall foxgloves and dahlias, little ponds with green water, and Adam—weaving and unweaving his hands, recounting the short history of our meeting and parting. Was that irony in his hands and in his face? A light sarcasm he used to defend himself against us? Did the warm gestures he was now using to re-create our own bodies mean that he was forgiving us? Me, too? And even the ones who had beaten him until he was bleeding? That he didn't regret having stayed with us? Despite everything? In every sign I felt his promise never to forget us.

But why such a big farewell! It was just for a few days, a month at the most. So why such heart-wrenching tenderness? Did I want him to be the way he always was? Ironic and alert? Furtive? Slightly cruel? Because that cold dance of gestures that had amused him so much up there in the woods had softened a pain and resentment hidden inside me—against whom? Adam tapped me on the back, I turned around, and all bad thoughts vanished at the sight of those two squinting eyes brimming with so much hurt, and so much joy. The linden leaves rustled overhead, the bell of the Cistercians sounded close by, clear and resonant, pigeons picked at straw lying in the cobblestones and carried it back onto the red roof—a world full of outdoor ceremony, just as on Corpus Christi. Our steps evened out, the stroller beat in rhythm, and even if I did say, with an artificially casual tone, "Take care of yourself, don't give up. I won't forget. I'll be waiting for you," it wasn't at all necessary, because it was understood, just as it was understood that the day would grow sunnier and sunnier, that there would be nothing but singing and dancing, that the clouds over the cathedral would stay clean and light and fluffy like that great white dove now cradled in the sky over the morainal hills behind the ravines named Valley of Joy and Valley of Clear Water.

We took off running. A cream-colored Warszawa drove past us down Grunwaldzka Street, and in the window over the Biały Zdrój bar a beautiful woman wearing curlers was fluffing up a pink down pillow. We waited to cross the street until three trucks from the barracks on Słowacki had passed, the soldiers singing under the flapping canvas: "Here the River Oka flows / wide as the Vistula at home . . ." The song faded in the rumble of the motors, the wheels rang out against the cobblestones, sparrows fluttered in the blackthorn, and we ran beneath the chestnuts down Poczta Polska Street, turned at Hołd Pruski, then passed the brick homes of the railroad personnel to the corner, and, flushed and out of breath, climbed higher and higher up the sloping ramp, following the handrail across the small Icelandic paving stones, pushing the wobbly load ahead of us.

"They're here!" Adam was so happy he clapped his hands. In the middle of the bushes, under the iron trusses of the power-line tower, near the path that led to the train station, beside a bench that someone had taken from the park and shoved beneath a branch of lilac, I saw Hanemann and Hanka. They waved to us: "It's about time!" I untied the sheet. They took their bags. Adam shouldered his canvas rucksack.

From where we are standing, under the lilacs, I could see the viaduct at Piastowska, the railroad ballast stretching toward Sopot, and the clump of trees by the overpass at Pomorska Street, where the local train would come from Gdynia. But we still had a few minutes left. Hanemann wanted to wait until the last minute and board while the crowd was getting on and off, so we still had those few moments. Adam looked up at the tracks and beyond, at the flocks of starlings and sparrows flying in from the garden plots, at the white clouds slowly drifting out to sea and on toward Sweden, at the huge trees where the smoke would appear as soon as the locomotive reached the bridge. Hanka held out her hand to me. "Well, Piotr, thank your mother and father for everything they've done." Hanemann ruffled my hair, using the same gesture as always. "And don't forget us."

Forget Hanka? And Adam? And that tall man who lived above us? How could I? In one single instant Grottger Street had become deserted. How did it happen? Why? How could we go on without them? "Hanka"—I tried to smile—"don't you forget about us."

She waved her hand. "Keep hold of yourself. We won't let them get us, will we? Right? We'll show them!"

"Hanka, write to us now and then."

Hanemann put his arm around her. "No, no letters for the moment. Maybe later on." But he said it without conviction, glancing all around, at me, the sky, the tracks, as if he were hesitating. We stood in silence. I didn't know what to do with my hands, so I fixed the sheet that was lying in the stroller. I took out a handkerchief, wiped the bits of rust off my fingers. Hanemann looked at his watch. "It should be here in three minutes." Adam turned around and pointed at the clump of trees beyond the bridge.

Here it comes! Clouds of smoke coming through the lindens on Pomorska Street. We still couldn't hear the clatter of the wheels, but the black locomotive with the tin plates on either side of the boiler rolled out from all the green and onto the bridge. "Adam!" I shouted. He ran to me, squeezed my hand, and then folded his own in a warm sign like a crouching sparrow, trembling in the breeze. It was very funny.

They set off for the station building: first Hanemann, then, a few steps behind, Hanka with Adam. As if they didn't know one another. I watched them through the leaves. For a moment Adam turned around, but Hanka gave him an impatient tug. They walked into the tunnel and disappeared behind the milk-glass windows. I knew I shouldn't show myself on the platform or around the station, that I shouldn't wave or shout words of farewell; still, I didn't leave that place beneath the lilacs. The train stood on the platform a little longer than usual, or so I felt, and for a moment I thought of a hundred reasons that might keep it from going, but then the smoke rose from behind the station building, the couplings creaked between the cars, and seconds later the tall caboose disappeared behind the white wall of the station.

My eyes were looking at the glassed entrance to the tunnel, the white station wall, the kiosk where they sold cigarettes and candy, but whenever I return to that moment, what I see is something else: the beech woods in the hills, and three people walking down a slope toward an open clearing—a woman, a man, and a child—leaving behind Oliwa and the Cathedral, the park, the Valley of Joy and the Valley of Clean Water, passing through the woods on to the bright fields beyond, while ahead of them, far on the horizon, a giant sun glows a gentle, muted red, a sun you can look at without fear because it could never singe or burn your eyes, or scorch the earth.

| *Frost* |

CLOUDS WERE moving in from the west. The earth turned slowly, carefully counting off minutes and hours. A wet fog gathered over the North Sea and was carried off by a wind that skimmed the surface of the water, toward the sun rising over the plains of Lower Saxony and Mecklenburg. Restless gusts lifted the fog over the Straits of Denmark, and by dusk, when the wind died down, its cool wave had reached the pine forests of Rügen and drifted on to the sandy beaches of Łeba and Rozewia. As dawn opened over the Hel Peninsula, the fog—now thin and barely visible—landed on the shores of the Gulf of Danzig and finally dissolved over the beech woods in the hills behind the Cathedral and over the houses on Grottger Street. In the morning, we went outside to find the birch leaves coated with a glassy dew; we had to duck, so as not to bump against a branch, when every jolt or breeze would shower us with drops of cold.

The sky above the park grew darker, so Mama lit a large candle and set it in the window, even though a radiant turquoise light was glowing from the picture that hung in the living room next to the mirror, where a beautiful angel was leading a boy and girl across a narrow footbridge. Mama wasn't superstitious; she dismissed the notion of avoiding hotel rooms marked *13*, as her acquaintance Mr. K. jokingly advised—after all, she'd made it through the Warsaw Uprising without so much as a scrape. Still, there were some things, like lighting candles during storms...and she absolutely refused to shake hands over a threshold.

Mrs. W. was no longer to be found in the Bierenstein house, watching through the second-story window, and the embroidered cushion she had liked so much had been tossed out among the dried-up mallows in the garden at Number 14, where the sparrows pecked little bits of seaweed from beneath the faded velvet. A streetcar came rattling down Wit Stwosz Street, and the sun flashed off the windows and bounced up the wall of the house, igniting the mirror, the crystal vase with the bouquet of irises, the windows of the cabinet and the glasses inside, filling the entire room with a yellow glare so strong we had to squint. In the evening, as the air cooled off after the warmth of the day, the tree in the garden dropped its rusty apples, and swarms of wild bees darkened the grass as they sipped the nectar from the open fruits. A few nasturtiums and asters were flowering in the sun-browned patch of herbs beneath the birch tree, while the creeper on the southern wall of the veranda had turned yellow, its leaves ringed with dry black: a trembling cobweb of shadows. It was all so beautiful, so saturated with color and light and fragrance—who could imagine that within weeks nothing would be left of the flowers, the leaves, the grass except a curl of smoke from a fire smoldering in the garden...

Under the lindens along the former Delbrück-Allee, the air was quivering with summerlike heat. Workers with rolled-up sleeves were taking away any wooden crosses that were missing the brass nameplates, pulling them out of the earth, knocking them against the trunk of a birch tree, and setting them aside, a growing pile of decaying stakes between the hedges. They patiently pried up the granite slabs with pickaxes, carefully removed them from their stone houses, and carried them away like great stacks of ancient books, out to the heavy Merzbach and Star trucks waiting across the street from the Anatomy Building.

The freshly opened graves lay drying in the sun like upturned cabinets, full of dust, cobwebs, and pinkish groundbeetles. Startled moths darted high overhead among the beams of light that cut through the pines. At noon or a little later, someone came and stood beside a pile of yellowing wet earth, bending over the pit to read a tablet covered with ivy; the workers took the opportunity to lean on shovels stuck in the ground and silently smoke a cigarette. Slabs of gray and black marble lined the path like dominoes, the worn names fading in the dust: "Friedrich," "Johann," "Aron." Slowly, unobtrusively, the cemetery was dying, in the quiet rustle of sprinkled earth, like a sun going out unnoticed in the ash gray fog of an evening rain.

On Sunday, in the bright October morning, while the fog was still covering the Rathaus and the Mottlau was gleaming with the cool transparency of dawn, we walked down to the landing at Zielona Brama, then along Długie Porbrzeże past the burned-out homes on Mariacka and Szeroka Streets, near the booksellers' stalls set up at the fish market, past the bomb-twisted gates and shattered terraces, up to the bend in the channel, where the stone banks flattened close to the water. There we planned to travel even farther, on to the Island of Holm.

The ferry came in slowly. I looked on in admiration as two men in black caps with shiny visors prepared for the landing. With cigarettes stuck to their mouths, they picked up the wooden handles and with sure, smooth movements hauled in the oiled steel cable, which slowly rose out of the water alongside the hull, throbbing as it was cranked through the winches, and then disappeared, still dripping wet, back into the lazy waters. The black planks of the ferry deck smelled of diesel fuel and tar. Dark green water with rainbow streaks of gasoline drummed against the hull. Maybe that was the reason we always fell quiet as soon as we were under the canvas awning. Some taller men ducked to avoid hitting the taut canvas. Once on board, they quietly smoothed out their hair and shook the sawdust out of their pant cuffs, as if they were embarking on a long voyage from which return was never certain. The only noisy passengers were the women, who banged their cork heels against the wooden deck as they hurried to claim the best seats.

We sailed by the grain elevators, and the iron frame of a small dock came into view, beyond which we could see the cranes of the Old Port, like huge birds looking for food. A pair of rails ran from the warehouse to the mooring, where an old excursion boat with a tall, slanted stack was tied up. Although the newly welded hull had recently been painted, the shadows of a few Gothic letters could still be seen beneath the topcoat of white, right next to the words "Zielona Brama—Westerplatte—Sopot." But none of us could make out the former name.

In the garden on Grottger Street, the leaves turned yellow. Every morning the sun rose over the spit, climbing above the beech woods in the afternoon and disappearing at dusk behind the Cathedral. As they had every day and every year, as they had always, the clouds came drifting in from the German plateau, the Saxon lakes, the Mecklenburg woods, and the Pomeranian beaches. The day began in a fire of infinite hues, proudly looming over the gulf, drowning the fishing boats in color as they set out to sea. Water shimmered around the remnants of the pier that had been hit that night by the howitzers on Ziganken-berg—two rows of charred pilings, a double file of toppled columns. In the evening, when the air was clear and cooling and darkness filled the sky above the city with peace, the North Star glowed with a cold November spark. The days were getting shorter and shorter.

I waited for a sign. After all, there was that page I had torn out of a lined notebook, where I had written the name of Grottger Street using my absolute-best handwriting, underlining the number 17 and adding a 1 for our apartment. I had folded it into quarters, and then, by the viaduct, I had stuck it into Adam's pocket, so that he would never forget. So there was no way he could have forgotten.

Whenever I took the mail out of the brass box labeled "Briefe," after I had removed all the letters, I would run my hand inside the dark box, where a little rust had crumbled onto the bottom, checking to make sure no envelope had caught on the lid.

But the letter never came.

The arborvitae rustled in the garden. The wind swept over the roofs of Grottger Street, high into the hills, where it rocked the beeches and pines. My mother picked up her shears and cut some asters beneath the birch.

And on the tiny boxwood leaves you could see the first white glimmer of frost.

| Note on the Translation |

STEFAN CHWIN'S NOVEL is strewn with German words and names—bits of past life trapped in amber—that carry a unique charge in the Polish original, as the world that was Danzig is summoned and then shown ceding to the world that became Gdańsk. To preserve some of the complex resonance, I have generally used German names (Brösen, Langfuhr) for places in Danzig and environs when the prewar city is described, and Polish names (Brzeźno, Wrzeszcz) for post-1945 locations. Occasionally both versions are given, particularly during the period of transition—"Langfuhr (or as we would know it, Wrzeszcz)." While most Polish street names have been anglicized (17 Grottger Street), most German street names have not (Lessingstrasse 17). This is partly to reflect the foreignness of German in the Polish original and partly because the German is often transparent to Anglophone readers ("Strasse" for "Street"). However, the literal meanings of these names themselves have not been translated (Obrońców Westerplatte Street, not Defenders of Westerplatte Street). Places outside Danzig may appear in either German or

Polish (Königsberg, Poznań) or, where commonly used, English (Krakow, Warsaw).

A bilingual index is appended to help readers map and retro-map their way through the city.

The unnamed man referred to in the novel who committed suicide in the eastern marshes is the Polish writer and painter Stanislaw Ignacy Witkiewicz, known as Witkacy—the novel referred to is his *Insatiability*.

—P.B.

| *Index of Place Names* |

GERMAN	POLISH*
Adlershorst	Orlowo
Adolf-Hitler-Strasse	Grunwaldzka Street
Ahornweg	Klonowa Street
Allenstein	Olsztyn
Ander Reitbahn	Bogusławski Street
Artushof	Dwór Artusa
Bahnstrasse (Oliva)	Poczta Polska
Bischofsberg	Biskupia Górka
Brabank	Stara Stocznia
Breslau	Wrocław
Breitgasse	Szeroka Street
Bromberg	Bydgoszcz

*With some names in English

Brösen	Brzeźno
Brösener Weg	Bolesław Chrobry Street
Danzig	Gdańsk
Delbrück-Allee	Skłodowska-Curie Avenue
Dirschau	Tczew
Eichenallee	Dębinki
Elbing	Elbląg
Elsass	Alsace
Emmaus	Emaus
Espenkrug	Osowa
Falkweg	Topolowa Street
Frauengasse	Mariacka Street
Freudenthal	Valley of Joy (Dolina Radości)
Friedrich-Allee	Wojska Polskiego
Frische Nehrung	Mierzeja Wiślana
Frischwasser	Valley of Fresh Water (Dolina Świeżej Wody)
Georgstrasse	Obrońców Westerplatte
Glettkau	Jelitkowo
Goethestrasse	Tetmajer Street
Goldenes Tor	Złota Brama
Gneisenaustrasse	Kaprów Street
Grosse Allee	Aleja Zwycięstwa
Gotenhafen (Gdingen)	Gdynia
Grünes Tor	Zielona Brama
Hakelwerk	Osiek
Hochstriess	Słowacki Street
Hohenfriedberger Weg	Szymanowski Street

Hohes Tor	High Gate
Hundegasse	Ogarna Street
Holm	Island of Holm
Jagowstrasse	Derdowski Street
Jäschkentaler Weg	Jaśkowa Dolina
Johannisberg Strasse	Sobótki
(am Johannisberg)	
Johannisthal	Matejki Street
Jopengasse	Piwna Street
Kaisersteg	Piastowska Street
Karlsberg	Pachołek
Karrenwall	Okopowa Street
Karthäuserstrasse	Kartuska Street
Katharinenkirche	Kosciół Św. Katarzyny
	(St. Catherine's)
Klostergasse	Cystersów Street
Kokoschken	Kokoszki
Kohlenmarkt	Targ Węglowy
Königsberg	Królewiec
Köslin	Koszalin
Krantor	Old Crane (Żuraw)
Kronprinzenallee	Aleja Sprzymierzonych
	(Avenue of the Allies)—
	later: Wit Stwosz Street
Lange Brücke	Długie Pobrzeże
Langer Markt	Długi Targ
Langfuhr	Wrzeszcz
Langgasse	Długa Street
Langgasser Tor	Złota Brama

Lessingstrasse	Grottger Street
Lindenstrasse	Tuwim Street
Lothringen	Lorraine
Magdeburger Strasse	Kościuszko Street
Marienburg	Malbork
Marienkirche	Kosciół Mariacki (St. Mary's)
Marienstrasse	Wajdeloty
Marienwerder	Kwidzyn
Max-Halbe-Platz	Komorowski Square
Memel	Klajpeda (Lithuanian: Klaipėda)
Mirchauer Weg	Partzyantów Street
Müggau	Migowo
Neu Schottland	Nowe Szkoty
Neufarhwasser	Nowy Port
Ohra	Orunia
Oliva	Oliwa
Ostseestrasse	President Roosevelt Avenue— Later: Karl Marx Avenue— Then: General Haller Avenue
Oxhöft	Oksywie
Pelonker Strasse	Polanki Street
Pietzkendorf	Piecki
Posen	Poznań
Rathaus (big)	Ratusz Głównego Miasta
Rathaus (little)	Ratusz Staromiejski
Rosengasse	Kwietna Street
Schäflerstrasse	Hołd Pruski Street
Schidlitz	Siedlce

Schwabenthal	Dolina Radości
Schwarzer Weg	Czarna Street—
	Later: Montwiłło-Mirecki
	Street
Seestrasse	Pomorska Street
Speicherinsel	Wyspa Spichrzów
St. Michaelsweg	Traugutt Street
Stadtgraben	Podwale Grodzkie
Steffensweg	Stefan Batory Street
Stettin	Szczecin
Thorn	Toruń
Trinitatiskirche	Church of the Holy Trinity
	(św. Trójcy)
Warnow	Warnowo
Weidengasse	Łąkowa Street
Weichselmünde	Wisłoujście
Zigankenberg	Cyganki, Cygańska Góra
Zoppot	Sopot
Zuckau	Żukowo

POLISH (or English)	GERMAN
Aleja Sprzymierzonych	Kronprinzenallee
Aleja Zwyciestwa	Grosse Allee
Alsace	Elsass
Biskupia Górka	Bischofsberg
Bogusławski Street	Ander Reitbahn
Bolesław Chrobry Street	Brösener Weg
Brzeźno	Brösen
Bydgoszcz	Bromberg
Cystersów Street	Klostergasse
Church of the Holy Trinity (św. Trójcy)	Trinitatiskirche
Cyganki (Cygańska Góra)	Zigankenberg
Czarna Street	Schwarzer Weg

Derdowski Street	Jagowstrasse
Dębinki	Eichenallee
Długa Street	Langgasse
Długie Pobrzeże	Lange Brücke
Długi Targ	Langer Markt
Dolina Radości	Freudenthal
	(also Schwabenthal)
Dwór Artusa	Artushof
Elbląg	Elbing
Emaus	Emmaus
Dolina Świeżej Wody	Frischwasser
Gdańsk	Danzig
Gdynia	Gotenhafen (Gdingen)
General Haller Avenue	Ostseestrasse
Grottger Street	Lessingstrasse
Grunwaldzka Street	Adolf-Hitler-Strasse
High Gate	Hohes Tor
Hołd Pruski Street	Schäflerstrasse
Island of Holm	Holm
Jaśkowa Dolina	Jäschkentaler Weg
Jelitkowo	Glettkau
Karl Marx Avenue	Ostseestrasse
Kartuska Street	Karthäuserstrasse
Kaprów Street	Gneisenaustrasse
Klajpeda (Lithuanian: Klaipėda)	Memel
Klonowa Street	Ahornweg
Kokoszki	Kokoschken
Komorowski Square	Max-Halbe-Platz

Kosciół Mariacki (St. Mary's)	Marienkirche
Kosciół Św. Katarzyny	Katharinenkirche (St. Catherine's)
Koszalin	Köslin
Kościuszko Street	Magdeburger Strasse
Królewiec	Königsberg
Kwidzyn	Marienwerder
Kwietna Street	Rosengasse
Lorraine	Lothringen
Łąkowa Street	Weidengasse
Malbork	Marienburg
Mariacka Street	Frauengasse
Matejki Street	Johannisthal
Mierzeja Wiślana	Frische Nehrung
Migowo	Müggau
Montwiłło-Mirecki Street	Schwarzer Weg
Obrońców Westerplatte	Georgstrasse
Ogarna Street	Hundegasse
Okopowa Street	Karrenwall
Oksywie	Oxhöft
Olsztyn	Allenstein
Old Crane (Żuraw)	Krantor
Oliwa	Oliva
Orlowo	Adlershorst
Orunia	Ohra
Osiek	Hakelwerk
Osowa	Espenkrug
Nowy Port	Neufarhwasser
Nowe Szkoty	Neu Schottland

Pachołek	Karlsberg
Partzyantów Street	Mirchauer Weg
Piastowska Street	Kaiersteg
Piecki	Pietzkendorf
Piwna Street	Jopengasse
Poczta Polska (Oliwa)	Bahnstrasse
Podwale Grodzkie	Stadtgraben
Polanki Street	Pelonker Strasse
Pomorska Street	Seestrasse
Poznań	Posen
President Roosevelt Avenue	Ostseestrasse
Ratusz Głównego Miasta	Rathaus (big)
Ratusz Staromiejski	Rathaus (little)
Siedlce	Schidlitz
Skłodowska-Curie Avenue	Delbrück-Allee
Słowacki Street	Hochstriess
Sobótki	Johannisberg Strasse (am Johannisberg)
Sopot	Zoppot
Stara Stocznia	Brabank
Stefan Batory Street	Steffensweg
Szczecin	Stettin
Szeroka Street	Breitgasse
Szymanowski Street	Hohenfriedberger Weg
Targ Węglowy	Kohlenmarkt
Tetmajer Street	Goethestrasse
Topolowa Street	Falkweg
Tczew	Dirschau
Toruń	Thorn

Valley of Joy	see Dolina Radości
Valley of Fresh Water	see Dolina Świeżej Wody
Traugutt Street	St. Michaelsweg
Tuwim Street	Lindenstrasse
Wajdeloty	Marienstrasse
Warnowo	Warnow
Wisłoujście	Weichselmünde
Wit Stwosz Street	Kronprinzenallee
Wojska Polskiego	Friedrich-Allee
Wrocław	Breslau
Wrzeszcz	Langfuhr
Wyspa Spichrzów	Speicherinsel
Zielona Brama	Grünes Tor
Złota Brama	Goldenes Tor (Langgasser Tor)
Żukowo	Zuckau